chaletgirls

Balancing Acts

EMILY FRANKLIN

nal
JaM
books

NAL Jam
Published by New American Library, a division of
Penguin Group (USA) Inc., 375 Hudson Street,
New York, New York 10014, USA
Penguin Group (Canada), 90 Eglinton Avenue East, Suite 700, Toronto,
Ontario M4P 2Y3, Canada (a division of Pearson Penguin Canada Inc.)
Penguin Books Ltd., 80 Strand, London WC2R 0RL, England
Penguin Ireland, 25 St. Stephen's Green, Dublin 2,
Ireland (a division of Penguin Books Ltd.)
Penguin Group (Australia), 250 Camberwell Road, Camberwell, Victoria 3124,
Australia (a division of Pearson Australia Group Pty. Ltd.)
Penguin Books India Pvt. Ltd., 11 Community Centre, Panchsheel Park,
New Delhi – 110 017, India
Penguin Group (NZ), 67 Apollo Drive, Rosedale, North Shore 0632,
New Zealand (a division of Pearson New Zealand Ltd.)
Penguin Books (South Africa) (Pty.) Ltd., 24 Sturdee Avenue,
Rosebank, Johannesburg 2196, South Africa

Penguin Books Ltd., Registered Offices:
80 Strand, London WC2R 0RL, England

First published by NAL Jam, an imprint of New American Library,
a division of Penguin Group (USA) Inc.

First Printing, October 2007
1   3   5   7   9   10   8   6   4   2

NAL JAM and logo are trademarks of Penguin Group (USA) Inc.

LIBRARY OF CONGRESS CATALOGING-IN-PUBLICATION DATA
Franklin, Emily.
Balancing acts : chalet girls / Emily Franklin.
p. cm.
Summary: Three teenaged girls try to prevent their secrets from interfering with their love lives and their
goals as they work at Les Trois, an exclusive Alpine ski resort, over the winter.
ISBN: 978-0-451-22219-0
[1. Resorts—Fiction. 2. Dating (Social customs)—Fiction. 3. Skis and skiing—Fiction. 4. Secrets—
Fiction. 5. Switzerland—Fiction.] I. Title.

PZ7.F8583Bal 2007
[Fic]—dc22   2007010791

Set in Granjon   •   Designed by Elke Sigal

Printed in the United States of America

For Heather S., Heather W., and Liz H.

Balancing Acts

UNOFFICIAL CHALET GIRL RULES

#1 Don't believe what you see in the brochures.

#2 Attitude takes up space.

#3 When in doubt, smile.

#4 Get rest when you can.

#5 Look everyone in the eye—even if you make a mistake.

#6 Flirting is not a crime, but it's not going to get the job done, either.

#7 Be yourself—but not too much.

#8 Days are long, nights are longer.

#9 There is nowhere to hide.

#10 Want tips? Put your head down and do the work.

#11 Beware of tangles as you decorate.

#12 Once borrowed, forever owed.

#13 Don't let your dirty laundry pile up.

#14 Check the weather every day.

#15 Check the weather every day—twice.

#16 When you chop enough onions, crying is inevitable.

#17 Keep plenty of sweets on hand.

#18 Seriously, there's nowhere to hide.

#19 Sharing is important.

#20 Even on your day off, you're still on.

#21 Changeover Day is more complicated than you think.

1

Don't believe what you see in the brochures.

"Bright blue skies, gleaming mounds of snow, days spent on the slopes, and nights spent enjoying the social atmosphere are just some of the reasons young people choose to find seasonal work at ski resorts," the blond, bubbly twentysomething tour administrator says. "By now you have your jobs assigned—cook, cleaner, ski guide, host, or—as the locals like to say as a general term—chalet girl. Don't go into this thinking it's all one long party—the job's tough. But it's worth it. After a season at Les Trois, your life will never be the same."

Melissa Forsythe looks out the tinted bus window and wonders if this is true—if her life will change. Before she zips up her bright red ski coat, she listens to the last words the administrator offers before she leaves the bus, clipboard in hand. "There's an old saying: Even if you don't have one when you arrive, you will leave here with a secret. Everyone does."

Melissa tucks this saying away, hoping her own secrets haven't followed her here, and gets ready for her first steps into the resort area of Les Trois—the Three Alps. She checks she has both of her gloves, and tumbles off the oversized tour bus. Outside, the air is frosty but sun-filled—and Melissa has a good feeling; the view is already better than last year at Courchevel—then again, she could never go back there.

Sliding her hands into her navy blue wool gloves, Melissa sucks in the chilly air and takes in her surroundings. To the left is the small village complete with restaurants, a world-renowned spa, bars, and clubs so elite they have no signs or names, and a luxury hotel. *The Mountain Inn—winter home away from home for Olympic hopefuls and hot Europeans alike,* Melissa thinks, remembering all the travel guides she read on the long-haul flight from Perth, Australia, to Paris, then the excruciating bus ride to Les Trois Alpes. Tucked into her backpack Melissa has the *Global Guide to Ski Resorts* in which Les Trois is described as the premier winter destination for those in the know. There are tons of mountain resorts—Montvale, aka "Las Vegas with snow," Mullee—nickname Bootee—Courchevel where Melissa worked last winter break and still blushes when she thinks of it, and so on. According to the guidebooks Melissa devoured at the travel agent's office, other places might have slightly better powder or access to more shopping, but Les Trois Alpes reigned supreme for class, calm, and cool refinement.

Turning to the right, Melissa holds her dark curls back from her face so she can check out the rest of the sights: A log structure too large to be called a cabin is set back from the roadway. Outside, various people—some whom Melissa recognizes from the bus ride—mill around in front near a sign marked REGISTRATION. In back of the log building is a parking lot with vans marked with

Les Trois Alpes' signature fleur-de-lis; rumor has it that some girls finished the season with a tattoo of that design. Melissa cannot imagine having a working holiday go so well that she'd want to engrave herself with memories of it—but then again, she's the first to admit that you never know what can happen. Stick a bunch of hot holiday people in a remote area with nothing to do but ski and socialize, and anything's possible.

Towering over everything are the three alps themselves—enormous mountains covered in snaking ski trails and snow, ski lifts, and the skiers themselves who seem bug-tiny. Even though Christmas and New Year's are only three weeks away, the buildings are unadorned. No decked holly, no twinkling lights, no red bows or New Year's horns. No mistletoe. *Maybe just as well,* thinks Melissa, flashing back to her only past brush with mistletoe. Having survived a season, Melissa figures that a crew of her fellow workers will be put to the task of decorating tomorrow once they've settled in.

"It's so peaceful here," Melissa mutters, not totally aware she's said it out loud until she hears a small snort of laughter from behind. Normally bouncy and brimming with enthusiasm, Melissa takes a second to steady the image of Les Trois in her mind. She wants to remember it now, as it is, before her job starts, before the holiday season kicks into high gear, before all those secrets threaten to come loose.

"If you think it's peaceful, clearly you haven't been here long." The voice and the laugh-snort belong to Lily De Rothschild, all of five feet two inches with a mane of silver blond hair so thick and lustrous Melissa figures it must be fake; she stares at the length of it long enough to make Lily tuck it protectively under a knitted ski hat. Melissa takes her for a vacationer, not a worker—the girl's too pretty, too refined—too something.

Melissa slides her backpack from her shoulder, unzips the top, and grabs for the guidebook. "It says here." She points and reads aloud. "Wait—yeah, right here. 'Peaceful.' "

"So you're an Aussie," Lily says. "And an avid follower of the dreaded travel guide."

"Obviously," Melissa says, overdoing her accent on purpose. "And you're a Brit." Lily nods. "Anyway—listen: 'Set in an idyllic village with three glorious mountains as backdrop, Les Trois Alpes is a vision of serenity and simple chic.' " Melissa raises her eyebrows at the pixie blonde before her and closes the guide as though she's proved her point. "What's wrong with reading guides? They tell you a lot."

"Hasn't anyone ever told you not to believe everything you read?" Lily shivers slightly in the brisk wind and puts her small hands inside the pockets of her quilted black coat.

Melissa wonders what, exactly, this girl means. Of course she doesn't believe absolutely everything—but don't the photos that accompany the travel verbiage tell the truth? Online and in the books everyone at Les Trois is all smiles, kicking back around a roaring fire, hot chocolate in hand, or clinking champagne glasses on a balcony, or—Melissa's personal favorite—walking as a couple, hand-in-hand in the newly fallen snow.

"Well, everything looks great—just like in the books."

"I wouldn't be so sure," Lily says. "I have to run. See you around?"

Melissa nods. "Sure. I'm Melissa Forsythe, by the way." Lily nods at her but doesn't offer up a return introduction. "And you are . . . ?"

"Lily de—" She halts herself and stammers just slightly. "My real name's Lily, but most people just call me Dove."

Melissa looks at Lily's pale skin, the shape of her small face, her petite frame, and decides Dove is the perfect nickname for this girl. "I have to go register, anyway," Melissa says just in case Lily—Dove—is giving her the brush-off. "I'm here for the season."

"Oh, yeah? For what position?" Dove perks up and takes a step back toward Melissa. Melissa thinks that Dove is just being nice, inquiring after the help or something.

Melissa pauses for a second and Dove wonders if she'll have to consult her guidebook to have an answer. "I was hoping for Hostess . . . ," Melissa says but then remembers why she didn't get that role—at least not this year. "But they gave me Cook instead."

Dove's face stays completely neutral. Melissa gets the feeling that it would take a lot to break Dove's façade. More than just announcing a job placement, anyway. "Cook's not bad. . . ."

"Yeah, if you actually know your way around a kitchen. Which I semi-do." Melissa hopes she hasn't made herself sound like a gourmet chef—she's anything but that. Sure she knows how to throw together a salad or make chili, but nothing gourmet. Not that she didn't stretch the truth just a tad on her application. The weight of her bags makes Melissa's shoulders ache and she starts to walk toward the registration building, hoping Dove will come, too. It would be nice to have someone to talk to. "But it's not like I'd qualify for Pack Leader. . . ." Melissa looks up at the slopes and nods. She's not a novice, but not nearly as advanced as she'd have to be to get Pack Leader. Typically, that job went to the older girls, the ones in college or who'd been wintering at places like this their entire lives.

"Well, it could be worse," Dove says, her English accent clipping each word.

Oh, Melissa thinks, *so maybe Dove is working here—maybe she's an ace skier and works as a private trail guide. Or maybe she's a cook, too.* A few more steps and they'll reach the steps of the log building. They walk on the cleared pathway, the sunlight glinting off the snow-topped roof, their breath coming out in puffs of white. Melissa kicks the dirt and snow mixture from one of her boots with her opposite heel. She pictures being in the giant restaurant-style kitchen of the brochures with a white hat serving intricate dishes. "Cook might be one of the most demanding positions—that's what I hear, anyway—but it's a hell of a lot better than being the cleaner. That I just totally couldn't deal with . . ."

All of a sudden, Dove stops walking forward and takes a step to the side. "Nice to meet you."

Melissa pauses just long enough that her bag topples off her shoulder and drops into a mound of snow. All around her she can hear a mixture of French and English, some German and Italian, too. "I wish I spoke more French. I only know a little. . . ."

Dove doesn't feel that now's the time to say she's fluent, so she smiles without showing her teeth and takes another step away.

"Where're you going?" Melissa asks. "I thought you were registering, too?"

Dove shakes her head. As if they've just had tea, Dove politely sticks out her hand. "Nice to meet you, Melissa. I must go. Best wishes for settling in." Her voice sounds almost snooty to Melissa, who tries not to feel personally offended but has a habit of taking things the wrong way. True to her name, Dove flits off in a half run half walk. Melissa thinks she'll at least turn around to say good-bye, but she doesn't.

The front door of the log building is double wide and built to look hundreds of years old, or maybe it really is—it's hard to tell what's real and what's made-up here. Melissa watches two girls who chat and laugh and go inside, then a couple of nondescript guys in dark jackets, and then, right when she's about to go inside herself and register, she's pushed aside by a sharp elbow to the ribs.

"Ouch!" she says, flinching. When she looks up, a way-too-familiar face is smiling meanly back. "Celia Sinclair!" Melissa starts and then realizes she probably sounds like an idiot, a drooling fan. In her backpack near the travel guides are magazines in which Celia Sinclair is featured modeling everything from clothing to scented body balm—often without much more covering her than the balm itself.

"Aren't you clever," Celia says. "I've never been greeted with my own name before." Celia stares at Melissa again, and Melissa stares back with more gawk than she'd like—Celia, famous or not, just elbowed her out of the way, after all. But maybe it was an accidental bump. "Um, are you going to move?"

Fine, so she did it on purpose, Melissa thinks in disbelief. She feels dumb now and looks at her feet while she moves aside so Celia Sinclair, a child star who was actually successful in her transition from cute television kid to art house actress, can grace the log building's interior with her presence. Celia opens the heavy door, realizes the building is being used for staffing registration, shakes her head and leaves as though she's smelled something putrid. The door bangs closed, leaving Melissa, her bags, her hurt ribs, and dented ego outside in the cold. She'd read on the plane about celebrities vacationing at ski resorts, but she didn't think she'd bump into one. *Hopefully, she's not in my chalet,* Melissa thinks. *Then again, it would provide an opportunity to serve her spoiled milk or something—if you were that kind of vindictive person—which I'm not.* Melissa wonders if all the guests will be as rude as Celia Sinclair. The travel literature made it sound as if the staff and the guests were a team, working and playing together. Melissa sighs.

"If you're going to let every famous face here get the best of you, you're in for a long season." Leaning back onto the side of the log building is a guy in an orange and black ski jacket. If she had her glasses on, Melissa would be able to see his face better, but her glasses are in her bag and after the long flight she didn't want to put in her contacts. Because of the lack of visual clarity, Melissa looks at this guy—but registers the black and orange jacket more than his face.

"I'm not a total pushover, if that's what you're implying," Melissa says and moves her shoulders back so she doesn't appear to be slumping, even though she feels sluggish. It's been only ten minutes since the bus brakes squealed to a stop and she's already been cast off by a blond Brit named Dove and dissed by tabloid royalty. *Maybe coming here was a mistake,* she thinks, *but at least I'm starting fresh.* No one knows what went down last year—it was miles, mountains, and a year in the past. She's almost so distracted by her thoughts that she's surprised to hear the ski guy still talking to her.

"I would never imply anything—I don't even know you." He stands up from his leaning position and saunters over to Melissa. When he's close enough that she can make out his stunning features, she sees he's the kind of guy she'd read about in a magazine, not talk to up close. She instantly has to busy herself with a brochure in her bag to keep from staring at him too much. His face is slope-tanned, a different kind of color than beach-tanned, a bit ruddy with caramel-colored cheeks, and his smile makes Melissa feel as though she's missed a step. "Hey—I'm . . ."

Shouts from near the parking lot interrupt his introduction. "JMB—come on! We're heading out!" Guys in matching orange and black coats wave to him.

Melissa sticks out her hand, determined not to miss this opportunity with the random hot tiger-coat guy. "JMB? Good to meet you."

"We didn't," he says, his voice serious. But then he gives her a grin that makes her fingers shake. "A meeting would mean exchanging names. . . ."

"Oh, right." Melissa wishes there were a guidebook for handling talking to hot ski instructors. Or a guide to dealing with guys in general—it certainly would have helped last year. Then she figures there probably is a guide like that, but reading it—studying it even—wouldn't help her. She's just naturally tongue-tied—and not in the way so many of the girls got last season.

"See you?" JMB stares at her. His eyes are standard-issue blue at first, but when she looks more closely, Melissa sees flecks of green, a few dots of yellow in each. JMB, she thinks, is the kind of guy whom she could sum up with the word *breathtaking* if she wrote a guidebook describing him. And . . . leaving, she realizes. JMB takes long strides toward the parking lot, no doubt to join his ski buddies in town.

"I'm Mesilla!" she shouts. As soon as the word is out of her mouth, she starts to crack up at herself.

"Fine. Now we've been properly introduced. Nice to meet you, Mesilla!" JMB shouts into a cupped hand. "I'll make sure to remember that."

Melissa can't believe her own verbal clumsiness. *Mesilla? He thinks my name's Mesilla?* But then, before she can dwell on that mistake too long, she's amazed at everything—the azure skies, the crisp air, the fact that this gorgeous random guy just talked to her out of the blue. Already Melissa can tell everything is changing—or about to.

From the nearby chimneys, smoke filters out in wispy lines,

and the mountains above are majestic rather than ominous. She looks down at the brochure in her hands—the one sent by Les Trois staffing—"Whether you're at Les Trois Alpes for one season or many—you'll never forget it!" *Maybe Dove was wrong,* Melissa thinks, *maybe you can believe what you read.*

2

Attitude takes up space.

"Next!" The woman behind the registration desk points to the boy in front of Melissa and he takes his sweet time going to her. "Move that slowly on the job and you won't last a regular day, let alone the holiday rush."

The scene in the log cabin building—which Melissa now knows is called the Main House even though apparently no one lives in it—is a mess of suitcases and staff, some standing, some sprawled on their luggage. Some are leaving—and others, like Melissa, are just arriving and waiting for their placements. One couple is lip-locked to oblivion; another girl is in tears saying good-bye to her boyfriend.

"I'm just going to miss you so much!" the girl cries as her boyfriend hugs her. Melissa feels sorry for them, that they're parting, and yet also wishes she had someone to miss like that. She knows how intense the chalet scene is, how fast friendships and relationships move—it's part of the allure. Melissa sees the person standing next to her, a girl her age—seventeen or so, with a perma-scowl—make a face at the teary couple.

"Get over the drama already. He'll forget you by the time your shift is over." With her arms crossed over her brown leather jacket–clad chest and her true chestnut-colored hair back in a ponytail, the girl shakes her head.

Melissa corrects her without thinking much about it. "Changeover. When your guests leave and new ones come in, it's called changeover." The leather-jacket girl stares blankly ahead. Melissa knows that terms are important here—like any job, the ski season life comes with its own language: *Chalet staff* serve the *guests, burn-out* happens if you partake in too much of the nightlife and slopes, *midseason blues* are a given (as amazing as it is to wake up surrounded by mountains, snow, and a routine that's different than homeroom and classes, it's still a routine), and *bunking in* describes the rooming situation. *Singles*—as in the room—almost never happen, and the dreaded *mezzanine rooms*—where a bed opens from the center of the living room— are the most feared (you can't go to bed until everyone else is asleep, and what little privacy you have is taken away). Melissa thinks about a certain term—*humble pie*—when the inevitable embarrassing incident involving a friend, fling, or flame ends in an uproar.

"Next!" shouts the check-in woman to all the people standing in line. "Get over here or lose your place. Even if we're here all night, you still have to work tomorrow. And for most of you— that means up, dressed, and socially presentable at seven A.M."

"Are you going or what?" brown leather-jacket girl asks Melissa.

"You go ahead," Melissa says, figuring she'll be nice.

"Suit yourself." Her worn-in boots and straight-legged jeans make her seem even taller than she is.

Then Melissa remembers what JMB said—she shouldn't start the season being trampled on. So she takes her passport and other identification papers and tags along with the leather-jacket girl to the registration desk. Conversation and flirting are already thick in the air around them, with all the staff trying to figure out who lives where and with what job; cliques abound with the hosts at the top rung of the social ladder, cooks in the middle with the nannies, and the maids the lowest. The ski aces, the ones trained for the elite guide positions, formed their own, impenetrable pack, giving ski tours and exploring unplowed trails. Melissa remembers the same kind of check-in last season, how it took so long some people fell asleep on their bags, others played cards, a few couples went to the bathroom—together.

"What do we have here?" asks the check-in lady. She has a thick accent and a sour face. "You two twins or something?" she laughs.

"No," Melissa says. There's no way she'd ever be mistaken for this girl's twin. Everything about Melissa is round—her great tight ringlets, her cheeks, pink as lemonade, and her full mouth. Her hips have a little padding, and her chest is full enough that she's never once thought of a push-up bra. More the push down kind. She feels like an apple shoved into her ski gear—the ski pants add weight but were too puffy to fit in her bag. *I'm an apple,* Melissa thinks, *and she—the leather-jacket girl—would be celery. If celery were really sexy.*

"I'm Harlan Iverly. Harley." She leans forward onto the desk, causing her jacket to make a crinkling noise. Melissa watches her check in. Harlan. Harley—even her name is cool. Leather jacket, killer legs. The jacket rustles again. The sound makes Melissa think about someone else she knows—or knew—with a jacket like that. Harley remembers the brochure she read about being a Chalet Girl. Back in Breckenridge, Colorado, the cozy accommodations, candid photos of smiling girls and cute guys setting up for the holidays seemed the perfect escape. Then again, she'd have given pretty much anything to get away. The rooms in the brochures looked spacious and sunny, and the people in the photos—teenagers on break looking to make some money, or college kids taking a year off to earn some funds and have fun—all seemed caught up in the fun. *Who cares about work and what's expected,* Harley thinks while she waits for the woman to assign her a place to live; anything's better than her world back home.

"And you?" The counterwoman looks at Melissa and waits.

"I'm Melissa Forsythe." Melissa wonders how many times in her seventeen years she's already said her name. Too many times without enough happening. She sneaks a look at Harley next to her—probably when that girl says her name explosions occur. *And the one time I said it and something could happen, I managed to call myself Mesilla. Nice.*

The woman checks her papers, prints out some documents, and hands both Harley and Melissa folders. "This is your binder. In it is all the information you'll need for a successful season. Matron will come and check on you this evening once everyone here is registered and set up." Matron is the mountain equivalent of a school principal, and just as officious. The folders are heavy and navy blue with the signature red fleur-de-lis in the center. Melissa grips hers tightly. Harley shoves hers under an arm and sighs. All around them impatient people tap their feet, waiting to be assigned their jobs and cabins.

"Are we done here?" Harley asks.

The counterwoman furrows her brow. "Why, do you have

better places to be?" The woman pauses while she consults her clipboard. Harley considers saying yes, she does—she could be walking around, anonymous in the village streets, or better yet, up on the mountains, free. "Do you know where you're going?"

"Don't trouble yourself," Harley says and shakes her head. She swipes a canvas bag from the ground, flings it over her shoulder, and heads for the door. "I'm sure I can find it on my own."

"Good luck!" the registrar snickers. To Melissa she adds, "There are twenty-seven chalets, six private houses, three yurts, two big cottages, and one castle. It'll take her all night to find hers." Melissa looks back at the door and then to the window where she can see Harley trekking up one of the pathways to a random cottage. "Don't tell me you feel sorry for her. . . ."

Melissa nods, causing her ringlets to bob. "It is cold out there. . . ."

"Never you mind, dear," the check-in lady says and points to her clipboarded list. "No need to be the mother hen. That's what Matron's for. By the way, you're in number fourteen."

"Number fourteen," Melissa says and nods again.

"Up the hill, round the back of the skating pond. And your friend—the one who is sure she can find it on her own—she's in there, too."

"Thanks," Melissa says. She backs up from the desk and goes outside to her duffel bag, glad she brought only one big one and her backpack. She looks for the brown-leather-jacket girl—for Harley—to say they can walk to number fourteen together, but she's nowhere to be seen. Up the hill and behind the skating pond. Melissa is about to start off when she can't wait any longer before opening up the binder. It's like reading travel guides—Melissa loves that, finding out what might be in store. Reading about places or events, what to expect.

She opens it up carefully and starts to read.

"Anything good?" Melissa looks up from the binder to see Harley sitting on top of the railing near her. "I figured I'd come back to make sure you were okay."

"Oh, like I need the help?" Melissa rolls her eyes but is glad for the company. "We're in fourteen, you know. Together."

"I know—I saw her list—your name was next to mine," Harley says. She has a habit of looking past people, off into the distance, and it makes Melissa annoyed.

Melissa shakes her head. "Fine. You know everything. Better?"

Harley bows and leaps off the railing. "I've just got this." She points to her small bag. Melissa can't imagine that the bag could hold all of the required clothing. "I figure I'll just get things as I need them."

"Looks like you left in a hurry," Melissa says to Harley, still eyeing the small bag. Melissa remembers leaving last season as fast as possible—at night—how quickly she shoved everything into one suitcase and booked it out of there, never to go back.

Harley nods. "I'm a light packer, what can I say?" She looks around and then back at Melissa. "Ready?"

"Sure," Melissa says, determined to carry her duffel with grace and without asking for help.

"Here," Harley says. "You take a handle and I'll take one."

"Thanks," Melissa says. It's the first nice thing anyone's said or done for her. Second, if you count JMB and his words of wisdom—which Melissa does. She and Harley walk like that with the heavy bag swinging between them, past the parking lot. Melissa can't help but look at the vans and cars to see if JMB is there, standing out in his orange and black jacket against the white snowy background—any background. But he's not.

Harley looks at her boots as they tap the pavement. *They look worn-out,* she thinks, and her jacket does, too. Her face is plain, not a trace of makeup, and it feels great to her to be free of any foundation, gloss, or hair spray. To be free of everything she left behind.

"So," Melissa says. "Did you look in your binder yet?"

Harley shoots her a look like she's crazy. "Um, no? I've been in possession of it for all of three minutes."

"Well, it has lots of useful info—tips and rules and social things. . . ."

Harley stops in her tracks, jerking the duffel bag and Melissa to a full stop. With wisps of her hair blowing into her rich, dark eyes, she flips open the top of her mail-carrier bag. She pulls out her binder and comments as she reads, "Blah blah blah—meet here, go there . . . don't fraternize with the guests . . . whatever." She goes to shove it back in without tidying the papers inside, which makes Melissa cringe—she isn't the queen of organization, but maybe the next in line.

"Wait," Melissa says. "You'll ruin it." Carefully, she takes the binder from Harley's hands and slides the papers inside in order. "See? Here's the welcome letter."

Harley gives an exaggerated sigh. "Fantastic news—thanks. What's it say? Wait, let me guess . . . welcome?"

Melissa smirks at the sarcasm but reads aloud in her best voice. " 'Hello! We'd like to take a moment to welcome you after a long journey to Les Trois Alpes, your home away from home for a week, a season, or a lifetime.' " She looks up to see if Harley will say which one she's here for, but she keeps quiet. " 'After you find your housing situation, please read through this manual in its entirety. I expect by our first meeting tonight that you will have memorized the rules, regulations, and duties for your specific job. Signed, Matron'. . . . I wonder what she's like?" Melissa has visions of Matron being like Julie Andrews in *The Sound of Music*—fun but firm—someone everyone can confide in who will bake cookies and make the girls hot cider on their day off.

Harley twists her mouth to the side and gives her head a shake. "Let me guess, you're actually going to this welcome meeting. Sad."

Melissa looks at Harley and figures that this girl has never been anything but cool, so of course required meetings seem dull to her. "Anything else worth noting in there?" Harley thumbs to the binder. "This is probably the only exposure I'll have to the contents, so you might as well read."

Melissa pages through various colored sheets of paper, documents, and then closes it. She can read it later, when she's settled in. "We should get going, don't you think? Find our housing?"

"All I know is we're in . . . The Tops, whatever that means." Harley scans the houses in the distance as if one might announce itself as theirs.

"Yeah—I don't know what that means, either. The Tops. It sounds luxurious," Melissa says. "I mean, it's not my first season or anything . . . but it's my first *here*." Melissa waits to see if Harley will tell her seasonal ranking and status, but she doesn't. Instead, Harley looks over her shoulder. Melissa tries to crack a joke. "What, you think someone's following you?"

Harley's face falls to a frown. "No. I mean, why—did you see something? Did anyone say something?"

Melissa shakes her head. From where she stands, the Main House looks smaller, the mountains still enormous, and the streets and chalets filled with possibilities. Harley takes another look over her shoulder, and Melissa licks her lips in the cold wind as she wonders if the tour bus guide was right—maybe everyone here does have a secret—or will before the season is up.

3

When in doubt, smile.

Leaving the nearby town, ski lifts, and Main House behind, Harley and Melissa trek up the steep path and finally find a small rectangular sign marked #14—THE TOPS.

"If you weren't looking for it, you might miss it," Melissa says, pointing to the brown and white script on the sign.

"But you wouldn't miss that," Harley says. "Check it out." She tries to hide her awe, but the chalet in front of her is so amazing she can't quite contain her cool. "Is that a hot tub?"

Melissa nods and sucks in the cold air. "Oh my god—this is incredible! Even better than the photos." She remembers what Dove said, that you shouldn't believe what you read, but smirks thinking Dove was obviously wrong. The Tops is better than in the books.

"It's huge," Harley says and takes the last two steps in one big stride so she's in front of the door. She turns the wrought-iron handle without ringing the bell. "Why is it locked?" She pounds her fist on the thick wood. Melissa notices that Harley's thumbnail has just a little bit of red nail polish on the side, as if the rest had been picked away, and thinks it's weird—with her boots, rugged good looks, and so far free-roaming spirit, Harley doesn't seem the type to paint her nails. "Damn it—I can't get it to open and no one's answering."

"Well, maybe we should look for another way in." Melissa leaves her stuff and begins to look for a side door, a back door, any way into the palatial building she's going to call home for the next few months. "Come on."

Melissa ducks behind the carefully clipped hedge, and all the way at the back, covered by vines, finds a regular door. "Here. Let's try this!" she shouts to Harley, who stands with her arms crossed over her chest like she's bored or suspicious or both. Melissa knocks politely on the door, half expecting no one to answer.

"Maybe we're at the wrong place," Harley says. Over her shoulder she stares off at the mountains, the dots of skiers. There aren't many yet—it's the same thing back home in Breckenridge. If you live in a vacation town, you get used to the seasonal swings. Harley knows in a week's time the crowds will come, wealthy couples, families, singles—then the slopes will fill up. And with any luck she'll be on them.

Just as Melissa's about to give up hope that she'll ever see the inside of The Tops, ever roam around the luxurious accommodations depicted in her guides, the door opens with a loud squeak. Harley's first thought is that she'd better acquire some WD-40 to make that sound go away—loud doors are the first giveaway when you sneak in at night.

As Dove stands in the doorway with a toilet brush in one hand

and a green bucket in the other, her face reveals nothing of what she feels. "I take it you're both attempting to get in here?" She puts her hand on her hip, then realizes the toilet brush might touch her and holds her hands in front of her.

"Hey—Dove, right?" Melissa points to herself. "I'm Melissa? We met before? And she's . . ." She goes to point to Harley.

"I don't need you to be cruise director. I'm Harley." Harley breezes by Melissa and goes past Dove in the doorway.

"Charming girl," Dove says as she watches Harley stomp her dirty boots onto the rugs. "Hey—I just vacuumed there!"

Melissa steps inside the small mudroom and looks around. This must be the staff entrance. In front of her is a narrow corridor. "I thought you were a guest," Melissa says to Dove. "I'm sorry. . . ." Out of respect, Melissa takes off her shoes. She notes that each cubby in the mudroom has a name tag—only no first names are used, just job titles: Cook, Cleaner, Nanny, Guide. "Depending on your guests and their needs, staff may change per holiday week," she remembers reading. Suddenly it occurs to her just how much her identity will be wrapped up in her job. She also notices there's no cubby marked *Host*—so she assumes someone forgot to allot a space.

"Don't feel bad for me." Dove breathes deeply and stands up straight. Bits of her thick bright blond hair fall from her messy bun, making her look stunning even though she's wearing a ratty T-shirt and stained work pants.

"I'm not trying to . . ." Melissa bites her lip. "I'm not trying to offend you—it's just . . . everyone knows cleaner is the worst position . . . and you don't seem the type. . . ."

Dove puts the toilet brush into the bucket, sending bleach fumes into the air. She laughs under her breath. "Listen—I know what being a cleaner entails. Believe me. . . . I have no delusions.

Picking up people's wet towels, making their beds, scrubbing their bathrooms—especially after they've been drinking . . ."

"Gross." Harley comes back into the mudroom, kicking off her boots too late. "Hey, what's the deal? Don't I get a locker or cubby?" She makes the rounds, looking for her job title. "Hey—someone forgot to make a place for little old me."

"Wait—don't tell me you're . . ." Melissa looks at Harley. Melissa wishes that she hadn't assumed anything about Harley, or anyone for that matter, but being completely open and unbiased is difficult, something she's working on. *I'll try harder next time,* she thinks. *I won't assume Dove is anything other than what she is— pretty, soft-spoken, and a maid.*

Harley shoots Melissa a look. "Right—you thought I was another maid, I bet? What is it about me that's so . . ." She hesitates, not wanting to associate her name with words she'll regret.

"Nothing," Melissa says. And really, what was it about Harley that suggested the lowest rung on the Chalet ladder? *Nothing superficial, looks can't tell you much,* Melissa thinks and blushes.

It's not her looks, Dove thinks. *It's her attitude.* Dove eyes Harley, thinking that her street-cool clothing can't hide what's underneath. Then Dove tries to switch tacks, worried that if Harley's icy exterior is semitransparent, her own veiled attempt at anonymity might be, too.

"Wrong." Harley unzips her leather jacket and points to her chest. "Not a maid."

"You're a guide? How long have you been skiing?" Dove asks. Even with her scrub brush she looks dignified. She even looks like she knows what she's doing, although this is the first time in her life she's ever cleaned anything, let alone a toilet. And she still has no idea how to clean the windows without leaving streaks.

Harley stands statuelike in front of Melissa and Dove. "Welcome to The Tops; I'm your host." She likes the way that sounds, *host*. "And by the way, I've been skiing since I could walk." She looks again for a cubby. "So if you could please tell me where I can stash my stuff . . ." Harley scowls.

"I guess you haven't read your guide, have you?" Dove puts her cleaning supplies down and points down the long corridor. "Your area—the host's place—is with the guests. Not with us. You keep your jacket and boots and things upstairs, near the front door. The one *we're* not allowed to use." Dove groups Melissa with her, standing closer so when they look at Harley it's clear there's a dividing line. "Don't you get it? You're one of them."

"We can't use the front door?" Melissa asks.

Dove turns to her. "No." She recites in a monotone British voice as though reading from the Chalet information packet. " 'Aside from Host, all staff must enter and exit via alternative doors.' "

"What'd you do, memorize the rules?" Harley shakes her head.

Dove nods. "Basically, yes. I can't afford to get in trouble. . . ." She stops short of saying why or what it would mean.

"Well, I'm taking off," Harley says. "Gotta check out the slopes."

Melissa holds out her hands in protest. "Don't you want to unpack? And we have our meeting. . . ." But Harley's in her boots and out the back door before the sentence is completed.

"She's doomed," Melissa says. Then she remembers she hasn't even seen her room, not to mention the gourmet kitchen she'll be creating fabulous meals in. "Can I have a tour?"

"I'm the cleaner, not a guide," Dove says, suddenly feeling sorry for herself. Harley's off exploring the town, where Dove ought to be. And Melissa doesn't smell like bleach. "I have to get back to work. When Matron comes, she inspects everything—and I mean everything. Feel free to look around—it's your place as much as it is mine. More actually, if you go by the pecking order, which everyone does."

"You know a lot about this place," Melissa says, wrinkling her brow. "Have you worked here before?"

Dove blushes and coughs. "Um, no. No. I just . . ." She looks at the ground, thinking about what to say, how to explain. "Haven't you ever heard that the maids always know the most?"

Melissa nods. "Yeah—I guess. . . ." She can't take the waiting any longer—patience is not one of her strengths—and feels a big need to see the interior of the place she'll call home for a while. "I can't take the suspense—I'm not very good at waiting. I'm going to check this place out."

Dove shrugs as though she's seen it all before—which she has in a way, but not from this perspective. She sighs. "Obviously, I've had the privilege of seeing this place top to toes, but I'll come with you—I have to mop the kitchen anyway."

At the front door, Melissa pulls her bags inside and starts the tour. "So this is what it looks like from the guests' point of view. Wow!"

"And the host's . . . ," Dove says, wondering how a girl like Harley, with no manners, no sense of rules, a full-time scowl, landed the cushy job of Host.

The front door leads to a paneled boot room made of wood with heated slate floors. "So their feet don't get cold after skiing all day," Dove explains. "And of course here's the immediate relief stock." She shows Melissa the shelves with bottles of water, rolled up towels, individual disposable hand-warmers, and a silver bowl of fruit.

"So you just come in off the slopes and help yourself?" Melissa asks. "Nice life." She looks at an empty space on the shelves. "What goes there?"

"The Melissa special," she says. "Or whatever you'd like to call it. Each chalet has its own treat—apricot rolls, spiced apple muffins, cookies—and you need to bake them fresh every morning so the guests can take them on their way out the door."

Melissa's face shows her sudden nerves. "And just when am I meant to know how to make these? Where are the recipes?"

Dove looks truly surprised. "Recipes?" She studies Melissa and her dark curls, her friendly, smiling exterior, and realizes the girl has no clue. "Have you been a cook before?" Melissa shrugs and wrinkles her nose. "So you don't know anything?" The jobs were assigned seemingly at random, causing some mixed reactions.

"I know what other people our age know," Melissa says. "Eggs, toasted cheese sandwiches, chili, a couple of basics . . ."

"Oh, dear . . . ," Dove says and leads Melissa to the next room, the tri-level living room. "I guess you have a lot to learn."

"Oh my god!" Melissa can't contain herself in the cavernous room. "This is unreal!" The living room's thirty foot ceilings are highlighted by the wall of windows at the front. "That's why they call it The Tops, I guess." She goes to the window-wall and looks out. "You can see everything from here!"

"Didn't you say you worked a season before?"

Melissa immediately blushes, wishing for a rewind button that would work on her life. "I did . . . but I was a nanny, not a cook."

"And?" Dove waits for more details.

"And that's all—nothing big. Just a job. Now I'm here—or there. . . ." She points in the direction of the kitchen that she's yet to see.

"Well, we do have an awesome view from here." Dove looks out the window to the far-off mountains. The three peaks form a jagged cursive *m,* with the first one slightly smaller than the second two. Then Dove looks at the L-shaped chaise with the pillows she's plumped, the polished furniture that gleams because she dusted it with a chamois. "And don't forget there's a view from there." Dove points to the interior balconies. "Each of the guest rooms has an outdoor viewing deck and an inside one."

Melissa shakes her head, the curls swaying back and forth. "What's the point of having a balcony overlooking the living room?"

Dove raises her eyebrows. "Think about it . . . fireplace, rugs, wine. . . . There's a lot to see here." She smiles and then it fades as she adds, "You never know when you're being watched here. You can get caught at any time."

Melissa wants to ask Dove if she's speaking from personal experience, but Dove takes this moment to continue the tour. "So you've got your living room, and wraparound hot tub out there. Which, by the way, I have the luxury of cleaning," Dove says, sweeping her arm out toward the feather-plump couches, the ten-foot-high fireplace, the curved bar. "You have your bar . . . which I need to clean." She checks her watch. "Think you can manage on your own?" She rechecks her watch. "I actually have to go make a phone call."

Melissa nods, "Sure—I'll be fine," and watches Dove leave. Standing alone in the high-ceilinged room she feels small. Upstairs she checks out the crisp beige guest rooms and suites since she won't see them after the guests arrive—only Dove will when she cleans them—and then the dining room with its long rectangular table. Made of light wood, the table has space for fourteen guests and Harley. *Fifteen dinners I have to make,* Melissa mumbles, and sets off to find the amazing kitchen she read so much about.

When she sees the cooking space, she's so shocked she has to talk aloud. "Holy crap!"

Rather than the stainless-steel restaurant-quality room she was expecting, the kitchen is maybe ten feet wide, with a small fridge, an oven from decades past, one double-section sink, and no dishwasher. Melissa stands over the sink, looking out the kitchen's one window, and thinks she might cry.

"Don't worry—part of my job is to help with the dishes," Dove says, smiling from the doorway.

"Done with your phone call?" Melissa asks, wondering if maybe Dove was calling home to check in with her parents.

Dove smiles just enough to show she's hiding something. "Yup—just a quick one." She watches Melissa wander around the small room, touching the ancient ladles, the crusty pie pans. "Not quite what you were imagining, huh?" She watches Melissa's shoulders slump as she examines the contents of each cabinet.

"Cookie sheets, Pyrex pans, double boilers . . . what's this for?" She holds up a blue pot by its wooden handle.

"Fondue," Dove says. "Easy dinner. Just chop up some veggies, cubes of bread, and mix some cheese with kirsch—and you're golden."

Melissa sighs. "Remind me to serve that sometime. Actually, remind me the first night. . . . I have no idea what I'm doing. Everything always sounds easier in the description, doesn't it?" Melissa says this thinking about her guidebooks and pamphlets.

Dove hears this and thinks it could be applied to the rest of life. Books like *What Color Is Your Parachute?* made choosing a life direction sound gentle and easy, as if struggle never entered the picture. And when parents said things like, "I can't make this decision for you," it gave the impression that they'd be there no matter what and that whatever choice you made was okay. Long-distance romance sounded simple and filled with passionate long-ing. *No,* Dove thinks, *not easy at all.*

"Well, of course it's true that reading about something and doing it aren't quite the same thing. But we can't complain too much, right? We did choose to be here." Dove bites her top lip, considering where she'd be if she hadn't chosen the chalet life, and displays her small hands for Melissa to see. "See? Calloused already. My hair reeks of bathroom cleanser, my skin will be itchy and red by the time I'm done wiping the windows, my eyes sting, and my back is aching like you wouldn't believe. But you know what?"

"What?" Melissa looks out the window again, only this time she sees someone in an orange and black striped jacket. Could it be that cute guy, JMB, the one who talked to her by the Main House? She scolds herself for being here such a short time and already finding a crushable guy. She could get distracted, but in-stead turns back to the task at hand—familiarizing herself with the small kitchen.

"But it's worth it if you get what you want out of the experi-ence. Look—I'm totally out of my element, okay?" Dove says. "I can't explain it now, but let's just say that I never expected to be learning the intricacies of dusting and mildew."

"And I totally exaggerated on my application," Melissa says. She takes a ladle from the utensil pot and uses it like a magic wand. "I have to prepare gourmet meals with no recipes. . . . It's not like I can serve pancakes for dinner." She frowns.

"Unless you spin it . . . ," Dove says. She goes to a drawer by the fridge and finds a notebook and pen. "Here—you seem like the kind who takes notes."

"Is it that obvious?" Melissa takes the pen and paper. "I just like to know how things are, or what to do—which as I said, I don't right now."

"We're all just doing the best we can. People come here for a holiday they'll remember. They want to feel they've gotten their money's worth, right? So . . ." She takes the ladle from Melissa and returns it to its nest with the other spoons and spatulas. "You were correct; you can't serve the guests pancakes for dinner. But . . . if you call them Evening Flatbread with Sweet Berry Sauce, you can. It's all in how you say it. If I say, 'This place is a shit hole,' it sounds bad. But if I sweetly say, *'Ça fait un peu bouiboui, mais il y a de la jolie moisissure . . .'* "

"Meaning?"

"Definition—'It's kind of a dive but it has some nice mould . . .'," Dove laughs. "It sounds better in French. It's all how you spin it here." Then she covers her mouth as though she's given too much away. "At least, that's what I hear. . . ."

Melissa laughs. First, just a small laugh, then with a belly laugh that lets out the relief she feels. "So maybe life here won't suck?"

Dove shrugs. "Who knows how anything will turn out? All I know is that no matter what, do this."

Melissa watches her. "Do what?"

Dove's grin spreads wide across her face. "Smile. Big. If things turn to hell, it might be the only thing to save you."

4

Get rest when you can.

"What the hell is wrong with you?" Melissa asks the question into the dark as Harley comes in. "It's two in the morning."

"And your point is?" Harley slides out of her jeans, boots, and sweater and slips into the top bunk. The mattress is thin and lumpy; she winces, not because of the discomfort but because the feeling reminds her of home. *I might be the only person out tonight who came home alone,* she thinks, glad she's finally in bed. "The point of going out is to stay out, right? You should have seen the scene—talk about hookups—more like scoopups."

"The point is, we were sleeping—after working hard all night," Dove says, her English accent muffled by her pillow. She lies on the bed, amazed at how uncomfortable the bed is—but afraid to say anything about the bumpy mattress, the damp linens, lest she sound snobby.

"Well, maybe the maid should oil the door hinges," Harley

says, leaning down to look at Dove. Harley's long hair trails down from the top bunk and Dove turns away to avoid her impulse to pull on it. "Anyway, whatever I missed here, I'm sure it was worth it."

"You missed the meeting with Matron," Melissa says, drifting toward sleep again. She wants to go back to her dreams of skiing with JMB, her pockets filled with succulent fruit tarts she prepared just by thinking about it. "And PS, if you were thinking she'd be like Julie Andrews . . . in *Mary Poppins* . . . she's not." More like a soldier than a nanny, Matron lectured Melissa and Dove about cleanliness and expectations until they could hardly keep their eyelids from snapping shut. Matron gave Harley an official warning.

"She left the guest log for you," Dove says. "It's on the dresser. We weren't allowed to look at it." She sticks a pale white arm out from under the covers to point.

"Yeah." Melissa nods into her pillow. "Matron said only the host needs to know the details—all I got were the dietary instructions—no dairy for the dad."

"And all I qualify for is knowing that the wife doesn't like lavender-scented things, so I had to redo the bathroom and switch the candles to pine-scented ones."

"A guest log," Harley says. "Let's see." She swings her legs around on the bed so she can grab the piece of paper. By each of the beds are colored lightsticks. Harley's is red and she takes it out of the socket in order to see. She squints and reads softly to herself, then puts the paper back on the dresser where she can deal with it in the morning.

The cramped quarters are quiet now, with only the wind audible from outside. The first night in their new quarters and all three roommates are half in bed, half in their own minds.

Despite jamming a towel into the windowsill, Dove couldn't stop the drafts, and the room is cold. Melissa pulls the blanket up to her chin, wondering how cold it will get when there's more snow. She remembers last year, during the storm, and the whole debacle that went down. No matter how much time has passed, it still haunts her. Only when she reminds herself that no one here knows about that does she relax. There are other issues to consider, anyway: the food shopping she has to do in town in the early morning and the fact that she has to heft the groceries back up the hill to the back door and prepare a "welcome buffet" before the guests arrive, whoever they are.

Dove lies with her face to the wall so neither of her new roommates can see the tears that threaten to roll down her face. She doesn't give in to the feelings, though. After the phone call tonight, she's sure she made the right decision—no matter what the cost. If everyone she knew could see her now, with her matted hair, her bleach-puckered skin, the bags under her eyes, no one would believe it. Well, one person might—but he's not here. With thoughts of him, Dove falls asleep, hoping that she can squeeze in a shower before doing one last tidying up. She wants to place a chocolate on each of the guest beds—she knows this trick—it's only to get tips, but then again, that's the reason she's here.

Harley stretches her long lean legs out in the bed, thinking this is the farthest away from home she's ever been—and it's still not far enough. Maybe if she gets out there on the mountain she'll feel free. Harley closes her eyes, and smiles—she never thought she'd be the kind of person to have a drink with a celebrity, but she did. Tonight, shirking her duties, at the small bar near the snowboarding shop, she sat with Celia Sinclair and her cronies, talking about resort life as if she knew it. *Well,* Harley thinks, *I do know it—too well.* Only she knows it from the other end. She won't go back, and she won't let her past catch up to her. Besides, she's on a mission—James. James Marks. She can see his winter Olympic snapshot in her mind, the one of him at the end of the Snowboard Cross when he knew he'd won. He didn't cheer for himself or make a scene; he just stood there, quietly proud. She imagines she's at the finish line with him and right as Harley pictures leaning forward to kiss him, she falls asleep.

5

Look everyone in the eye— even if you make a mistake.

Clutching her armrest, Melissa is sure the van will careen over the steep mountain ledge. She's got plenty on her mind without having to worry about the precarious position on the Cliffside: shopping, settling in, befriending Dove and Harley, making sure last year doesn't revisit her, and all while perfecting cooking skills. She has to create a sweet treat that will be The Tops' signature snack, and by the end of the week, have a themed party, as described in the information binder.

"Hey! Can you slow down a little?" she asks for the third time, her grip tightening. She can just see the headlines now: "Incompetent Chalet Girl Falls Off Cliff on Way to Buy Weekly Provisions." And for what? So the Trois Alpes' shuttle van driver can make out with some random glamour girl. Granted, the driver is shockingly attractive, enough so he could be a heartthrob spewing French on-screen, but still.

"Chill out," the girl says, and it's only when she takes off her sunglasses that Melissa realizes she's face-to-face again with the tabloid princess Celia Sinclair. Celia gives Melissa a pointed look, then goes back to nuzzling the driver's neck, which causes the van a momentary lurch sideways on the road.

"Ahhh!" Melissa can't help but respond. Every time the guy shifts the wheel to the right, Melissa slides one foot closer to the abyss. "There's got to be a better way."

Celia pulls her lips away long enough to ask, "Paul, is there a better way to get to town?" She makes a baby-face pout that inspires rage in Melissa. *What did I ever do to deserve this famous girl's attitude? Nothing.* Paul is clearly so overwhelmed with being attached at the mouth to Celia Sinclair that he can't speak.

"Umm . . . ," he says. "Another shuttle?"

Melissa shrugs—it's not as though she had a choice of transportation into town. The supplies have to be purchased by eight in the morning, and this shuttle was the first one. Any van would be better than this one. Even walking through the snow alone would have been better. Anything would be better than dealing with dangerous driving on sickening hills with Celia's bitchiness. Up ahead, the hill leads into the small town of Les Trois—all of its shops, bars, and elite clubs, except for the supermarket, are closed in the early morning sunlight.

As the van screeches to a halt outside the grocery store, Melissa pries her hand from the armrest. Celia flings her mane of hair that's triple processed to look very natural and gives Melissa a fake smile. "Glad we could give you a lift this morning."

Melissa counters with an equally plastered-on smile. "Thanks for the ride . . . really. It was eye-opening." She doesn't add that it could be eye-opening for the rest of the world with the photos she snapped of Celia in lip-lock with Paul. She tucks away her phone.

She slides the van's door open and hops out, glad to be on firm ground. In her pocket she has a shopping list and the week's petty cash, which Melissa counted twice before coming, nervous about losing it after Matron warned her about having to cover the cost of food herself if she went over budget or lost the money.

"So you'll wait for me here?" Melissa asks before closing the door.

Celia snorts and laughs. Paul can't focus on anything other than his movie star companion. Celia leans out the passenger window. "You clearly got up early this morning to do your . . . chores." Melissa nods, feeling the fatigue sink in a bit more. "But we haven't even been to bed yet—so you'll have to make your own way back."

And with that, Paul turns the key, rumbles the ignition, and drives away with Celia close enough to be in his lap. Melissa stands there wondering what she's supposed to do now—where's her ride back? How is she supposed to get a week's worth of food and drinks back up to the mountain and up the path to The Tops? *Okay, don't panic,* she thinks. *First things first, right?* She looks at the grocery store and decides that worrying about step two doesn't make sense if she's yet to deal with step one. With money in her pocket she sets off across the narrow cobblestone street to Chez Vous to pile items in her cart and deal with later, later on.

If I have to vacuum behind her one more time, I swear I'll scream, thinks Dove as she trails Harley with the rug attachment. "Sorry, could you just . . . can you try not to track sand in here?"

Harley, in her underwear and tank top from the night before, touches the soles of her feet and shrugs when she feels the grit of sand. "I had no idea it would stick to me so long," she says and helps herself to coffee in a white mug as she surveys the clean kitchen, the empty living room, and the guest quarters, which look much better than her triple-bunked room.

"Where did you even manage to find sand?" Dove asks. With her foot she presses the button to silence the vacuum. *Some people need tropical waves, a massage, or a fancy four-star dinner to relax,* Dove thinks. *For me, all it takes is the peace I feel after the vacuum noise is gone.* She feels pleased with herself about this—it's a change for her—but then again, when she thinks about waves, and beaches, that sounds pretty good, too.

"I went to Beach last night." Harley says this as though it's no big deal and sips her coffee. On her thumbnail, bits of red nail polish remain and she quickly picks at them, making a note to find some remover. If only there were something that removed all evidence of the past as well as paint. "It was decent."

"Beach?" Dove coils the vacuum's hose up and takes one more look around. Provided Harley doesn't make a mess, everything's pretty much set for the guests' arrival. Dove wonders for a minute who the guests will be—maybe a happy family with toddlers or a nice older couple with their grandchildren. She imagines people sitting around the fireplace and playing board games. Then she reconsiders—it could be a group of rowdy college students coming to Les Trois for a week of debauchery, skiing, and snogs. Which would be worse: baby spit-up everywhere or students who've had too much to drink heaving on the deck? Dove grimaces, realizing either way she's the one to have to clean it up.

"Yeah, I kind of wandered around, hung out with some people over on the big deck? At the inn? And then just wound up at Beach—it's a really cool place to . . ." Harley finishes her coffee and puts the mug in the sink without washing it.

"I know what Beach is," Dove says, her mouth small and tight.

She turns the water on and soaps Harley's used mug, not minding the washing up so much as the fact that this classless girl—this boot-wearing, model-tall but mannerless person assumed that Dove wouldn't even know what Beach is.

"Oh, you know about Beach?" Harley asks defensively, with her hands on her hips. She's met people like Dove before—people who come from nothing and need to pretend that they've seen it and done it all. With a brief blush, Harley realizes *she's* one of those people, not that she'd ever admit it. Beach was cooler than Harley'd even thought it would be—a club built to look like a seaside resort with white umbrellas, glistening waves, tall drinks with mint stirrers, free white linen sarongs, and posh people dotting the shoreline—and all inside. Harley thinks about spilling everything to Dove, right now. She could say how until two days ago she'd never set foot out of Breckenridge, that the triple-bunk room is nicer than her whole trailer at home, that she left in a hurry—leaving scandal and a scare behind her—but she can't let the words out. It's easier this way, she figures, just gliding along, being someone else, someone different than she was before. But to do that, she'd have to admit why she wound up at Les Trois to begin with—why this certain mountain is her escape hatch. And Harley isn't about to put herself and her past on the line.

Dove, too, considers saying something—about how she knows what Beach is, how to her, Beach is nothing now. How all of this has happened and why—and how it's just temporary until the day after New Year's when her future will begin. For now, she has to keep the chalet in pristine condition—dust behind every decorative plate in the dining room, continually plump up the pillows in the living room, make beds, change sheets, keep the showers mildew-free, the bathrooms spotless, and be discreet about picking up after the guests. Dove sighs, thinking about the endless slog of work she's done, and how she'll be on a continuous loop with her mop, rag, and trash bags for companions. Unlike Harley, who seemed to already be enjoying the perks of her hosting position.

"Well, I hope you had fun, anyway," Dove says. "But next time—wipe your feet with the white towels they give you—they'll let you take one if you want." Dove calmly walks toward the bunkroom to change into her required uniform—white shirt tucked into slim-fitting black pants—before the guests ring the front doorbell.

"I did have fun," Harley says. She slicks a brush through her hair, twists it into a loop, and fastens it up with a hidden clip, going from morning-messy to prom-ready up-do in a matter of seconds. Dove wonders how Harley—with her unmade-up face, her faded jeans, her no-frills walk and mannerisms, knows how to do that. But Harley won't say. "But not that much fun. Celia Sinclair was there, though, so that was cool." Harley drops Celia's name so she won't have to mention who wasn't there—that she keeps to herself. Harley gives Dove a smile, grabs her guest log, and goes upstairs to wait for the guests. She should feel nervous about hosting her first round of people, but she doesn't. She knows from experience that all you have to do is smile, say what the judges want to hear, and look people in the eye.

"We're in for a long day," Dove says. Her own hair is long and shiny blond over her shoulders. She thinks about what Melissa asked, if her hair was real. Princess hair, she called it. With this thought, Dove quickly pulls the locks into a low ponytail and ignores the rest of her reflection.

Harley looks at Dove, thinking that at any American high school, this girl would be prom queen, or lead cheerleader, or whatever the highest social ranking would be—except she doesn't know how to carry herself. She's too shy, always looking down and keeping quiet. Maybe that's why she got the dreaded cleaner's position. "I don't know how the day'll be," Harley says. She looks out the window and sees the smallest number of flakes begin to float down from the milky sky. "If the snow picks up, I've got to get out there. . . ."

"You have to host, Harley," Dove says, pointing out of their room to the rest of the chalet where work awaits them both. "Remember, your job, the reason you're here?"

Harley spins around and looks directly at Dove. "Oh, I remember the reason I'm here, Dove, believe me. But it's not the job." Dove raises her eyebrows—maybe there's more to Harley than meets the eye. Harley slides the guest log papers out of the brown envelope to look again at the information.

"Hey—check it out," Harley says. "The guy's name is Earl."

"Interesting," Dove says, smirking. At least she doesn't have to memorize everyone's name. All she has to do is clean up after them.

"And the wife's name is . . . Countess!" Harley full on cracks up. "Countess? How cheesy is that?"

Dove's smile fades as she looks at Harley. "You don't know much about Europeans, do you?"

Harley smirks back. "Why—what'd I do now?"

Dove tries to grab the guest registry, but Harley's height keeps it out of reach. "This is my domain—the bathroom? That's yours." Her tone is playful—Dove feels like they'll eventually be friends—maybe—but the hierarchy of their jobs might get in the way.

"Just so you're aware—when you're about to make an ass of yourself? Earl is not his first name. He is *an* earl. She is *a* countess. As in titled."

Harley's tough act shows just the slightest crumbling. Her hand holding the guest log comes down. "I'm hosting an earl and goddamn countess? Who even knew people like that really existed out of fairy tales?"

Dove looks away at the rug, keeping quiet, then speaks calmly. "Oh, it's not such a big deal, Harley. Titles abound in Europe. You're hosting an earl and countess—that's below a marquess and above a viscount." Harley stares at Dove, who rattles on in her quiet manner, her hands clasped politely all the while. "In Britain, you're an earl; in Europe you're a count. In Italy, there are so many you just don't bother. . . ."

"I'm never going to pull this off," Harley says. Her wide mouth and full lips slide into a frown, her eyes hinting at tears. "I don't belong here." The wind seeps into the cracks, chilling the room and reminding Harley of where she really longs to be—outside on the slopes, with nothing but the sound of skis on snow and the wind rushing by her cold face. She wants to be there right at this moment, with—

"You'll be okay, seriously," Dove says, pulling Harley back to the present. "All you have to do is . . ."

Harley does each action as she says it. "I know—smile, say what the judges—I mean the people—want to hear, and look them directly in the eye. Even if you screw up."

"*Especially* if you mess up." Dove nods, remembering when she didn't look someone in the eye, and what that cost her. They look at one another for a minute, feeling their first sense of camaraderie, and then Dove points to the guest list. "Now, which earl and countess do we have the pleasure of hosting?"

Harley corrects her. "You mean who do *I* have the pleasure of hosting?" She doesn't mean to be obnoxious, but she likes—for once—being the one who isn't slugging around after people with a bucket and mop. She checks the list again. "We have the earl and his countess, their kids, and a couple of friends."

Dove nods. "Kids are good—if they scream and fuss, the guests sometimes tip more."

"It doesn't look like the kids are very young," Harley says, looking at the information packet. "They didn't ask for a nanny. I guess that's good—it leaves an extra bunk free in our room." Harley thumbs to the unused bed.

Dove can't take the suspense anymore and grabs the list from Harley. "Oh, shit," she says, reading the names.

"What?" Harley says, giggling. She pokes Dove on her shoulder. "Did you suddenly realize it is a big deal having royalty here?"

Dove tucks in her shirt, smoothing out any wrinkles, and bites her lip. "No. NO, it's not that . . ."

Harley's glad—she's not alone in feeling freaked out about the incoming titles. Does she bow? Call them sir? What? "It is—you don't know what to do, either. Here you are acting all calm and cool, but really you're just as nervous as I am."

Dove takes in a deep breath through her nose. "You're right, Harley; I am just as petrified as you are. More, maybe."

"Why? You scared you'll say the wrong thing? Forget to make their beds?"

Just the thought of hearing the word *bed* in this context makes Dove feel sick. "No," Dove says. She pauses on her way out the door, taking a box of individually wrapped chocolates from Roccoco, her favorite place in London. "I'm not scared of anything like that. . . . Let's just say I know them. Or one of them. Well."

6

Flirting is not a crime, but it's not going to get the job done, either.

What's the difference between jams, jellies, and fruit spreads? Melissa wonders as she roams the narrow aisles, pushing one cart and pulling another. She realizes she looks like a donkey or some other work horse, caught between the one trolley that's already piled high with all manner of pasta, tins of tomatoes, fresh greens, cheeses with names she can't pronounce, and baguettes, and another that's nearly filled with bottles of wine, seltzer water, and the thick fruit purees that the guests requested. Each one is expensive and Melissa knows she's nearly at her budget limit, but she can't ditch the one item the guests asked for specifically.

"Come on!" Melissa grumbles at the cart in front of her as its tilted wheel makes it bump into the cereal boxes. Three boxes of Alpine Muesli fall down, two on the floor, one on her head. *I signed up for this, why, exactly?* Melissa wonders. But when she stands up, she has exactly the opposite thought. Oh, this is why I signed up. In front of her is the guy—that guy—JMB, his black and orange jacket unzipped to reveal a plain white T-shirt. She stares at him, taking in his dark jeans, heavy snow boots, and his perfect mouth. Aside from being tall, winter-tanned, with high cheekbones and a sturdy presence, JMB has something else, Melissa thinks, watching his every move. He's got a casual grace. Confidence without cockiness like so many guys have to have. The combination of all of this makes Melissa aware of each of her limbs, her heart, her face blushing, aware of an invisible current of energy tying her to him.

He runs a tanned hand through his dark hair, eyeing the bakery selections set on the wooden counter in front of him.

If this moment were scripted, Melissa thinks, *he would turn around, see me, and we'd instantly connect—mind, heart, and lips.* Instead, Melissa's cart takes off again, this time forward. She grabs the cart behind her and then tries to steady the one in front, while still contending with the cereal boxes. She gives up with them, adding them to her cart, and chases the trolley as it heads down the aisle. *I'm supposed to cook gourmet meals for fifteen when I can't even shop for the food without injuring myself?* Melissa grabs for the cart's red handle while the clerk behind the cash register clucks his tongue in disapproval. *Knowing my luck, I'll be banned from the store and have to make meals out of snow,* she thinks. She succeeds in getting the cart to stop moving, only to be bashed in the butt by the other one. "Ow!" she yells, louder than she wanted the sound to come out. The clerk shakes his head and mutters something in French at her, while Melissa crouches down, imprisoned by her own clumsiness and the metal carts. "I'm an idiot," she says to herself.

"And you're talking to yourself." JMB stares down at her, one of his hands on each of the carts. He steadies them while managing to cause a small avalanche in Melissa's chest.

"I'm not insane, by the way," she says and stands up. "I'm just . . ."

"New at this?" he suggests, smiling at her. His eyes crinkle at the sides, making his grin appear wider, softer. Melissa notices a thin scar over his top lip and can't stop herself from staring at it. She wonders what it would feel like to touch it; she nearly allows her hand to wander there until she blushes and clenches her palms into fists to keep them under control.

"Yeah, new at this," Melissa says. "Obviously, I've shopped before but not for so much at one time." She looks at the contents of both carts—piles of paper towels, an oversized bag of basmati rice in a burlap sack, hoards of apples and carrots—enough for a week? What if the guests love carrots and eat through them? Or what if she hadn't figured the correct amount of pasta? "Honestly, I have no idea what I'm doing—I just hope it turns out okay." She looks directly at JMB. He looks back, the scar on his lip rising as he speaks.

"That's a refreshing perspective. Most people around here pretend they know everything. You know, 'fake it till you make it' sort of thing."

"I don't think I could do that," Melissa says.

"Too honest?" JMB asks.

Melissa shrugs. "Either that or just not a very good faker."

"Well, don't be surprised if you find you're in the minority here." JMB steadies her carts and helps her wheel them to the cash register where she hands over almost the entire wad of bills from the petty cash allotment. Melissa wonders if maybe he's warning her about specific people, or if maybe even he's guilty of faking something. *Certainly not his appeal,* Melissa thinks, *that's too real.* She knows if she stays around him too much longer, she'll like him, and that would be risky—she can't have a repeat of last year.

By the doorway, Melissa zips her coat and stands with her huge amounts of boxed groceries, wondering how the hell she'll get back to Les Trois now that Celia Sinclair has made out with Paul, and off with the van. What she does know is that the carts take up space, causing JMB to have to stand either too far away to converse with her or in between the carts, a bit too close to her to be unremarkable. *I have to get away from him,* she thinks. *Or it will be too late and I'll officially have a crush on him. And that can't happen.*

"Thanks for helping me with my clumsiness," Melissa says. She crosses her arms over her chest and feels bulky. *So maybe the down jacket doesn't downplay my semirounded physique, but it's warm,* she thinks.

JMB reaches into his pocket and pulls out keys. He's near enough that Melissa can feel his breath as he speaks. She looks again at the scar and in her fantasy she's cool enough, brazen enough that she reaches out to touch it—then he kisses her. But no such luck in reality. "So you're all set then?" he asks.

Oh my god, please leave before I like you, love you, jump you, or make an ass out of myself like last year with my former crush. Melissa slides some Chapstick on her lips to keep her hands busy and nods. "Yup, I'm good to go." Where? Nowhere, since I'm stranded, but never mind.

"All right—see you around then." JMB waits there as if she's supposed to say something. "Mesilla, right?"

Melissa is caught between cracking up and feeling dumb, and he's so close to her, so kissably near, that she just shrugs and nods. He looks at her a second longer and gives a guy-nod, pigeon style out and back, and steps away from the store and out into the town where the sun is rising higher.

Why didn't I say something? Melissa questions her brain power. *Not only am I stranded here with no ride and twenty minutes until I'm due back, but I'm also forever going to be Mesilla to him. Fantastic. At least I didn't get sucked into some unrequited crush situation.* She calls the chalet house phone, hoping Harley will pick up and come get her in town. Hosts can sign out vans without prior approval, but no one under the host can, so Dove wouldn't be any help. After six rings, Melissa shakes her head, wondering why no one is picking up. She thinks about using some of her money for a taxi, but it would leave no room for buying any provisions during the week—and what if they run out of milk or one of the kids hates pasta? Melissa sighs, hating that she feels both stranded and paralyzed—why can't she just make a decision?

Out the glass doorway she sees JMB and decides that getting back to The Tops is more important than potentially entering so far into the crush zone that she can't get out.

"JMB! Hey!" Melissa opens the door and shouts to him. When he turns, she waves at him and when he returns the gesture, her heart pounds. So much for trying to remain uninterested.

"You need a ride?" He strides to her. "Why didn't you just sign out a van?"

"I didn't think I was allowed to," she says and feels instantly like she's thirteen and unlicensed.

JMB frowns and shakes his head. "No—cooks can drive the vans as long as it's business-related." He eyes the stacks of boxed-up foods. "Which this trip clearly is." It seems to Melissa that in one motion he offers her a ride and helps her wheel the carts out onto the street to his car where they pack everything into the trunk and backseat. "I'll be right back," he says and leaves her buckling herself into the passenger seat, warming her hands on the heater. Melissa wishes she were one of those cool girls who looked stunning all windswept and out of breath from the panic of almost being late and stranded, but she's not. She knows she probably looks the way she feels—discombobulated by the bumpy ride with bitchy Celia Sinclair, frayed by the shopping and planning, and still nervous from the upcoming cooking, guests, and trying not to dwell on her hot ride home.

"Thought you might want this." JMB slides behind the wheel and hands her a mug of coffee. Not a paper cup, a real pottery mug.

"Don't you need to give this back to the coffee shop?" she asks before she sips.

He shrugs, his jacket crinkling. "I know the people who own the place—they'll let me bring it back later."

Wedged into the car with enough food for a week, with a guy who brought her coffee, helped her with the hassles of shopping, and who makes her whole body feel on the edge of something, Melissa lets the forthcoming stresses go for just a few seconds. *Who cares if he thinks my name is Mesilla? Who cares if he's a ski guide and therefore way above me in the totem pole of jobs and social circles? Who cares if I have to make a welcome brunch for fifteen people and I have to learn as I go—it's not as if I'm cooking for royalty, right?*

JMB has one hand on the wheel, the other on the manual gear stick, and hums to the song playing on the radio.

"I can't believe they still play ABBA here," Melissa says, listening.

"That's the thing about places like this," he says as the car turns back up the hill toward Les Trois. "It's timeless. Music, fashion trends, famous people, they all just come and go so easily—it doesn't matter what decade it is, or anything."

Suddenly this makes Melissa feel tiny, unimportant. "So what does matter, then?"

"Living in it, I guess," he says. "Hang on—it's way too early for philosophy." He moves into third gear to get up the steepest part of the hill around the curve. He continues to hum. "You know this song?"

Melissa shoots him a look as if to say everyone does. "Voulez-vous . . . ," she sings quietly enough so he hears her but not enough so it sounds like she's up for karaoke right now.

Voulez-vous. She thinks about the translation. Even in sappy disco tunes it's still worth wondering. "Voulez-vous," she sings again, looking at JMB's scar. It's shaped like a crescent moon and just as silver against his tan skin. "Voulez-vous? Do you want to?" the lyrics ask over and over. JMB doesn't answer.

7

Be yourself—but not too much.

Fifteen minutes into the welcome brunch, Dove finally emerges from the depths of The Tops. She's put off saying hello to the guests as long as she can manage. *It's best just to deal with unpleasant things, anyway,* she thinks, wishing she didn't have to be in the obvious maid uniform all day and night. *But then again, what do I care?*

In her black trousers and crisp white shirt, Dove slips quietly into the kitchen, watching Melissa take muffins out of the oven.

"You *do* know how to cook," Dove says.

"Eggs, yeah. These muffins? I'm not so sure. . . ."

Dove looks around the kitchen. "Can I teach you a little trick?" She doesn't want to step on Melissa's toes. "Not to say you need my help . . ."

"But I do." Melissa waits.

"Okay, so the muffins look nice . . . but plain. So—you can do a couple of things. One is you could take some brown sugar and sprinkle it on top." Dove mimes her words using one muffin as the example. "Then you stick it under the broiler for about twenty seconds—less, even. Then they have a lovely crispy sugary top." Dove remembers eating them by the fireside while wrapped in a blanket, next to William, and instantly feels a tug in her stomach.

"And tip number two?" Melissa watches Dove pluck a warm muffin from the tray and slice off its top. "I need those! There aren't extras . . . at least not yet."

"Can you trust me?" Dove raises her eyebrows at Melissa. "You cut off the top, spread jam or whipped cream—yogurt if you have nothing else—on it, and then put the top back on." She spreads thick raspberry jam on to demonstrate. "See? Now it looks all fancy, but it's nothing. That's the trick to a lot of cooking."

"How do you know so much?" Melissa asks. She starts slicing the tops off all the muffins and alternating peach preserves and raspberry. "I have to bring these out soon."

"I always liked cooking," Dove says. "At home I . . ."

Melissa watches Dove's mouth twist as she cuts the words short, and for a second she looks really sad. "Did you cook a lot at home? Like with your mum or dad?"

Dove shakes her head, her corn husk hair swaying in front of her eyes. "No. It's a long story . . . but anyway." She shrugs and hopes Melissa doesn't press her for answers.

"Ahh," Melissa groans as she finishes rearranging the muffins. "What if they hate my food and I get fired? Or worse, demoted." Then she catches herself. "Sorry—foot into mouth yet again."

Dove laughs and licks jam from her finger. "Look, I'm totally okay with my job, so don't worry about that. I . . . I chose it, actually."

Melissa makes an exaggerated face, wrinkling her nose.

"Why? What could make you want to scrub loos and change soiled linens?"

"New experiences?" Dove's smile spreads light all over her face. "Believe it or not, I like a challenge. Anyone can have fun being the top dog—but it takes . . . I don't know, strength of character to enjoy and excel at something like this."

"That's really cool," Melissa says. "Admirable." She wipes the crumbs from the counter with a sponge. "It's just weird that . . . it's like I saw Harley polishing her boots, and it's clear that she's done it before. Did you see her bed this morning? Hospital corners and everything. The girl knows how to clean, even if she's kind of . . . scruffy."

Laughter erupts from the other room, startling Dove, who dreads having to see the earl and his family again—or at least certain members of his family. She makes sure her shirt is tucked in and follows along with what Melissa's saying. "I know what you mean, Melissa," Dove whispers, suddenly realizing maybe they can hear her from the other room. "I know how to cook, and Harley's hardly the most welcoming of hosts." Dove turns to Melissa. "You'd be a really great host. You're warm, and friendly, and conversational."

"She didn't even say 'welcome,'" Melissa says. The words are just out of her mouth when Harley's frame fills the kitchen doorway.

"We need more food out there," Harley says.

Dove nudges Melissa. "Make mimosas. Champagne and orange juice—trust me, the more they drink, the friendlier they'll be about your food."

"Thanks, Dove." Melissa swoops up the basket of muffins and grabs a glass carafe of juice to which she can add ginger ale or champagne in the dining room. She hopes Harley didn't hear the criticism about the lack of welcome.

Standing back, half-hidden by the thick double-silk curtain that masks the dining room door, Dove surveys the scene. *Typical,* she thinks, narrating in her head. *Refined glamour from the countess, with her cream-colored cashmere top and off-white thin wool trousers. The earl, in jeans and loafers, stands by the window, looking out at the slopes, probably keen to get out on the slopes to ski and check out the other titled beauties in their tight black ski outfits.*

"Here are some baked goods," Melissa says, thinking that sounds more upscale than muffins. "And some mimosas."

At the offering of an alcoholic beverage, the earl turns around and smiles. "Perfect." His accent is understated and elegant. *He sounds just the same,* Dove thinks. Then a group of people bluster by her, knocking her to the side.

"So glad you can join us!" the countess says to the group that's come in. Then to Melissa and Harley she adds, "Mention champagne and they come running." She smiles demurely and stays seated with her coffee and eggs. "These are our children." She describes them without pointing, and they each look up or smile as they're introduced. "Jemma is my daughter—she's thirteen and a wonderful skier. Luke is fifteen—and Diggs is just a year ahead of him at school."

Harley checks out the kids—so much for them being toddlers and needing nannies. Jemma looks bored with the breakfast, and reaches for a glass of champagne until the earl stops her with just a look and she sulks in the corner. The boys, Luke and Diggs, laugh about something with each other and sit at the table with plates of food. *Leave it to the aristocrats to give their kids normal names,* Harley thinks. *Diggs? Fine, so it's one of many names he has (Charles Wainwright Digby Mathers) and Luke is Lucas Mattias Ridgefield, and so on, but Diggs and Luke sound like they could be friends from home.* But when she looks at their refined crisp clothing, their easy manners, their relaxed grace, she knows they are far, far from that world.

Thank God, Dove thinks, *they didn't bring the whole family—what a relief.* She emerges from behind the curtain to introduce herself. The cleaners were supposed to say hello, so Dove takes this opportunity to get it over with but Harley, oblivious to Dove's intentions, interrupts.

"I'd like to give you a big welcome," Harley says, her voice steady and smooth. She shoots a look at Melissa, acknowledging both that yes, the greeting had gone unsaid before, and also that Harley would learn as she went along. *I may not be the smoothest host in the world—or the most natural—but I'm a fast learner.* Just about anything Harley sets her mind to do, she makes happen. *I mean, I'm here, aren't I?* She looks smug as she goes to pour herself a drink. Melissa intercepts the carafe and pours drinks for the countess first. *Damn,* Harley thinks. *I should've thought of that—always serve the guests first. Next time.*

Dove decides now's the time for a quick hello. "I'm Dove, your cleaner." Dove speaks calmly and in an American accent that surprises Harley and Melissa. "If there's anything you need during your stay, just let me know."

When the earl and countess and their kids nod at her, Dove knows she's pulled off her fake-out. *They never even looked twice,* she thinks as she heads to the kitchen to start the dishes. *Then again, they only met me a couple of times.* With her hair pulled back and partly covered with a wide black headband, her uniform, and her American accent, she hardly resembles the girl they'd met.

Next time no scrambled eggs, Melissa thinks, watching as the guests bypass the eggs and head for the muffins. Dove was right—good drinks and muffins and they're happy. *Next time I'll make something more unusual and memorable.*

"We plan on spending the day on the mountain," the countess says to Harley. Harley has a mouthful of food, crumbs on her lips, and Melissa wishes just for an instant that Harley was the one who'd have to vacuum the crumbs.

"Sounds good to me—if we get out there early, like in the next half hour, we'll beat the new arrival rush." Harley looks past the countess to the wall of windows, eyeing the three mountains. *Somewhere out there,* she thinks, *is the reason I'm here.* The earl feels Harley's gaze and smiles at her. *Oh, crap.* Harley bites her lips. *He thought I was staring at him.*

The earl raises one eyebrow at her, looking like he wishes she were older or he were younger. "I'm off to get changed. I'll be in my bedroom should anyone require me."

Um, that'd be a no, thinks Harley as she drains her coffee.

"I'll join you," the countess says. "Boys . . ." Diggs and Luke are halfway out the door. "Be back for dinner."

Diggs turns around, hoping to catch Harley's attention. "Where can a guy prove his worth on the slopes here?"

"Which run, you mean?" Harley asks, her mind searching for something, anything to say back so she doesn't come up blank. I wish I'd studied the trails like the guidebook suggested, or read the chalet literature. "Well, there are so many. . . ." She smiles, trying to distract him.

"Well, maybe you'll show us then." Luke grins and Diggs waits.

Harley nods, pleased that her ploy has worked.

"I'm already changed," Jemma says to her mother and partially to Harley. "Can't I just go?" Her voice is whiny, urgent.

"You're too young to be out there alone," the countess says. Then to Harley she adds, "But too old for a nanny. Caught in between."

Harley nods, not interested in chatting, even though it's part of her job. She wants to change, too, so she can search the slopes. *It'll feel so good to be on the hill,* she thinks, *to feel the wind rush at my face.* She can almost feel the thigh-ache she'll have after a day of downhill. And if she has to let Diggs and Luke tag along, then so be it. She can ditch them on a difficult run if need be. The countess waits for Harley to say something more, but she doesn't. "See you out there!" she says and leaves.

"Well . . . ," the countess says. Jemma huffs with her arms crossed over her chest. Melissa can't take it anymore and tries to problem solve. "If you'd like . . . I could show you around. I'm finished with brunch now." She checks her watch. "I just have to be back by two to make some afternoon treats."

The deadline for creating The Tops' signature baked good looms over Melissa's head. She knows she has to bake something so delectable and irresistible that people long for it. Matron mentioned that there's an unspoken competition between chalets—and at the end of the week, on Changeover Day, an afternoon feast of all the leftover foods when nannies, hosts, cooks, cleaners, and ski guides alike gather at the Main House for a taste test of treats. *I wonder what the winner gets,* Melissa thinks, *a prize? Or is the prize just knowing your pastry or cookie is the best?*

Jemma sighs and looks at Melissa. "Getting out with you is better than being trapped here," Jemma says. "I'll even help you think of ideas for that party."

"What party?" Melissa asks.

"I overheard Matron talking about it—aren't you supposed to come up with a food-based party or something?"

"I guess," Melissa says. "Just add that to my list of stresses. Now, are you coming or what?" Melissa accepts the pouty girl's shrug as a *yes,* clears a stack of dishes, and runs off to change.

Dove reappears in the dining room after everyone is gone. Her body feels loose and free without anyone around, and she lets her hair down as she wipes the long table free of crumbs. She figures since she's the one vacuuming later, it's okay to swipe everything onto the floor. "Floor," she says aloud, first in her regular, English accent and then again in the American one she used for the guests. *Not bad,* she thinks. Then again, she and William practiced it all the time. He'd imitate her voice, studying her soft vowels, and she'd say start with the American *r*. Start. Art. Heart. He had hers. She checks her watch as if it has the countdown until she sees him again. A day or two after New Year's Eve and they'd be together, making all this—the scrubbing, the scent of bleach, and continually being left out of the chalet happenings—worth it. Despite the cold, and the new snow drifting down, coating the balcony and one of the hot tubs, Dove can conjure up the warmth of Will's presence; his deep, contagious laugh, his slim surfer-boy physique, the tattoo that made her swoon and her parents cringe. With her hand on the damp sponge and her mind drifting to palm trees, beaches, and aquamarine blue water, Dove smiles thinking about reuniting with Will. *I just have to clean enough, well enough, cater enough to the guests' wishes that they have no choice but to tip big.* Her heart pounds as she considers the reality: If she doesn't get the money to buy the ticket, she'll miss Will completely.

"Am I too late for brunch?"

Dove hears the question with her hair covering her face as she looks down at the table, wiping the last of the crumbs. "The food's been put away, I'm afraid," she says, hearing her English accent the way Will does, thick and proper.

"You're English."

Shit, Dove thinks. She expects to find one of the fifteen-year-old boys, Diggs or Luke, there for more food, and quickly comes up with an excuse for the accent switch. *I'll just say I'm studying drama,* she thinks. *And that I need to practice for various roles.* She flings her hair back and opens her mouth to say this, but stops when she sees the person in front of her.

"Lily." He doesn't ask her; he just says her name. "Lily de Rothschild."

Dove stares at him. "So they did bring the whole family," she says.

"Of course—did you think I'd stay home?" His eyes travel the length of her from black shoes to white shirt, to her hair, her mouth, and her now blushing cheeks. "Aren't you going to say hello?"

Unfriendly staff—the biggest offense in the chalet book. The tips Dove needs to buy her ticket suddenly seem like they could evaporate, so she forces a smile where there is none and stands up, clutching the sponge so hard it drips onto her shoe. "Hello, Maxwell." Her face doesn't betray the building pulse inside her chest. *I won't give in,* she thinks. But her eyes can't lie. They lock on to his.

"So we're formal now?"

"Fine, hello, Max."

"Hello, Lily," he says and stares at her with the same gaze he'd had at school last year. She remembers sneaking looks at him over her papers in class—way before the maid job, before Will, before graduating and then taking her year off. Before all of this. Once, he'd caught her looking at him and locked on to her, challenging her to see who would break the look first. The class bell had sounded, calling it a tie.

Dove stares at him—tall Max with his green eyes, brown mop of hair, and quiet intense presence. He looks much the same— better, if that were possible. Still with that cool detachment that simultaneously pulled her in and pushed her back. *I won't get sucked in again,* Dove thinks. *He means nothing to me—not now.* She remembers his eighteenth birthday—a huge fete with white tents, dinner jackets, and the girls vying for his attention in their brightly colored dresses. *Not again,* she thinks.

"You can call me Dove now," she says, feeling powerful. *It feels good not to be in school where you're trapped with the same people,* she thinks. *He's here for a week and it means nothing, anyway.* Dove stares at his hands, thinking how weird it is to see someone out of context—this guy for whom she'd longed for two years at school, is now out of the classroom and surrounded by mountains. It had been so hard to shake off her feelings the first time. How do you just move past liking someone so much you can feel them in every cell of your body? *But I did it,* she thinks, and clamps her heart shut.

Max shoves his hands in his pockets, making Dove remember, too, the way his hands had felt on her back, on her neck, and just how quickly they—and the rest of him—had disappeared that night of his birthday.

Max breathes in deeply. "I can call you Dove or Lily, whatever name you like," he says before sauntering out.

"Good. Then call me Dove. It's what people called me at school, anyway." She watches him go down the hallway toward the front door.

"But you're not at school anymore, are you? Looks like you've chosen a different sort of path." He stops and looks over his shoulder at her before going outside. "No matter what you call something, it doesn't change what it is." He opens the door, letting in a wash of cold air that finds Dove's arms and gives her chills. "Anyway, it's good to see you again, Dove." She stands there, chills and all, as he leaves her alone with a house to clean and more than enough to think about.

8

Days are long, nights are longer.

Gabe Schroeder's blond tousled curls, dark blond at the base and white at the ends, announce his presence even in a crowded room. Nameless, the bar is designed to feel like a mountaintop at night. Track lights in various shades of blue illuminate the room only partway, and scattered pinpoint lights resemble constellations. *It's very romantic in here,* Melissa thinks, *if you take away the hot, sweaty, scantily clad girls and the ski bum guys wedged in so tightly it's tough to move.* Harley is so intent on not losing her space—and her view of Gabe Schroeder—that she has to pull Melissa through a swarm of people to keep pace with him.

"Remind me again what we're doing in a packed bar when we have to get up early tomorrow," Melissa says to Harley, elbow-to-arm tight in the full bar.

"It's called experiencing what resort life has to offer," Harley says. She keeps looking past Melissa, over at someone.

"What are you looking at?" Melissa asks, trying to see.

"No one. Nothing." Harley scans the room again. *Gabe Schroeder—live and in the flesh,* she thinks. *And better than I thought he'd be.* Harley gives Melissa a look that conveys *don't ask me again, play it cool,* and Melissa nods, massaging her fingers and palms. Her hands are sore from chopping carrots and kneading bread, and her brain aches from the thrashing Matron handed out postmeal when she did an impromptu drop by to check up and she learned that Melissa's first dinner consisted of beef and vegetable stew and rolls. "What's so wrong with it? I mean, it's hearty and yummy," Melissa questioned aloud after Matron had stomped off, leaving an official warning notation in her notebook. Too many notes like that and she'd be dismissed. "You should have called it braised beef with root vegetables and honey loaf," Dove said. She mopped the floor while Melissa laid thin sheets of buttery pastry down for morning croissants. She thought about Max, whom she'd successfully avoided since their initial run-in, and how he'd probably disagree with this philosophy on spinning words—he'd said that names meant nothing. Then she thought about William and how he'd been so taken in by her birdlike name. Which was better? Dove thought about this, then revised her words to Melissa. "You know what it is? Words can't alter what's really there, but they can change people's perspectives."

"Like?" Melissa placed the tray of dough in the fridge and wiped her hands on a checkered kitchen cloth.

"Like . . . if you call food by simple names, it sounds as though you didn't make something nice enough. Beef stew with carrots and potatoes, regular. Braised beef with root vegetables in a demi-glace, fancy." *And which boy is better?* thinks Dove suddenly. *One who's here or one who is far away? One you've liked for years and then tried to forget, or one who grabbed your attention and then took off for the seas?*

"But I don't know what a demi-glace is," Melissa said, then realized she was being too hard on herself. "Okay—I know what it is, but not how to make it. I'm from Australia, from the beach, okay? I surfed before I could run and my meals all through school were basically cereal eaten on the go and tuna sandwiches. Hardly gourmet."

"Open-faced tuna salad with watercress and endive," Dove said, holding out her hand with an invisible meal for Melissa. "Get my point?"

Melissa nodded. Phrasing was everything. She recalled the debacle of last season and cleared her throat. "Do you think you can do the same trick with nonrelated foods?"

"Such as?" Dove could give her own example—but was edgy knowing she had so much to do before getting some rest: turn-down service, arranging the guest rooms with fresh flowers, water for the bedside tables, and her own touch, daily fortunes printed on long slips of cream-colored paper with specialty chocolates. Dove would write the fortunes, somewhere between horoscope and inspirational messages, with a special fountain pen packed in her bag—after all, it was the extras that supposedly brought the big tips.

"Such as . . ." Melissa untied the chartreuse apron and looped it on a hook in the cook's closet, wishing she had longer than nine hours before having to wear it again. Already the pads on her fingers were raw from using Brillo pads, and she knew many nights of aching legs and shoulders lay ahead. "If, say, you'd done something stupid, or—let's just say been caught doing something."

"Hello? Specifics would be nice here," Dove said. "Not that I'm pressing you for info, but it's difficult to know what to tell you about putting spin on things if I don't know what the thing is."

Melissa exhaled quickly. Harley was waiting for her outside—they would go out on the town together. "Last year, I liked someone, okay? A lot." She looked at the floor, the pattern of light wood and darker knots. "And I wrote about it, and kept all my thoughts in this book."

"A journal?"

"Something like that. And . . ." Melissa thought about saying the whole thing, but she couldn't. Not then. She was tired but wanted to meet Harley, explore the supposedly wild nightlife in the village. It was walking distance, and felt quainter than town where she'd done her shopping. Melissa eyed her uniform and realized she'd need to swap her cooking clothes into a more presentable outfit. "And let's just say this guy wasn't shy, he wasn't a small personality. He dated a . . . anyway, everyone found out."

Dove looked at her, perplexed, and leaned on her mop, her whole body ready for bed. *If William were here, he'd rub my shoulders and massage my calves,* she thought, wishing he was waiting for her downstairs in the bunkroom. She checked her watch—he'd be just finishing up for the day, tying the boat to the dock, waves lapping the sides, maybe. Her insides clutched when she wondered if there were any bikini-babes nearby threatening to lap, too. "I don't know, Melissa. It sounds as though you're uncomfortable telling the entire story. It's still kind of vague. But if it comes up this season, just say some stock phrase, like 'the past is in the past,' and hopefully people will buy it."

Melissa took this advice with her and went to change.

The village is night-coated and cold. In the bar now, with the blue lights overhead, and various languages uttered all around her, Melissa hopes the past stays well hidden, totally out of sight.

"I'm so glad to be out of the kitchen," Melissa says when she and Harley are finally at the bar. The bar is made of dulled steel and when Melissa leans into it, she can feel the cool metal on her stomach. "If I had to chop, rinse, or sauté anything else tonight I swear I'd lose it." She tries in vain to flag down the bartenders—tanned women with hair so blond it's white, outfitted in stark white tank tops and tight white pants. Completing the look is metallic white lipstick. "I could so never pull off that look." Melissa points to one of the women who breezes by to serve someone else. "Not that I'd want to."

Harley, taller by half a foot with her coltlike legs and boots, looks at Melissa. "Tomorrow's only a few hours away. I guess you should enjoy right now." She smiles and bites her lower lip. "Hey!" With a quick raise of her hand, Harley snags a bartender and orders two Fizzy Blues. "Let's have a toast to the lowered drinking age in Europe. No IDs needed." Harley grins. Once that's accomplished, she goes back to searching the crowd. "Wait here—I'm going to see if I can talk to him."

"Him who?" asks Melissa. She's not interested in the drinking age or in being out. More interested in recipes and measuring and, hopefully, sleeping soon. Someone steps on her toe but it's too crowded to even bend down and rub it. *Why'd I even come out?* she thinks, looking at the anonymous but unanimously good-looking crowd of moneyed skiers and their hot friends all looking for a hookup—either one night or one week. *I must stick out terribly in the land of Barbie girls and movie-star guys. Harley can fit in fine—glam her up and she'd look like one of these people, anyway. She's got the outdoorsy tough thing happening, but she's just as gorgeous as the bartenders or the famous—and I'm . . . what am I?*

Melissa doesn't know how to sum herself up; only that she knows she's not like the rest of the crowd.

"Him!" Harley says as though her thoughts are common knowledge. "Gabe Schroeder."

Melissa's face reddens when she hears his name, and all the feelings rush back to her—heart palpitations, shaky palms, quick breath. "I'm dizzy," she says.

Harley looks over. "Probably just the temperature in here."

Melissa tries to regain her composure. *After all, he hasn't seen me, he doesn't know I'm here, and Harley doesn't know about me and Gabe Schroeder. Not that there's much of an* us *to tell—more of a me and my own humiliation.* "So *he's* the reason you're here?" Accepting her Fizzy Blue from the bartender, who ignores the thank you, Melissa takes a trembling drink as she looks back to where Gabe is standing. He looks better than Melissa remembers, better than last year. "You came all the way from Colorado to the Alps to chase after Gabe Schroeder?" His name sticks in her mouth.

"First of all, I'm not chasing anyone," Harley says, raising her eyebrows to reinforce her message. "I'm following my destiny. Wait—that sounds too new agey. But it's just . . ." She glances back to Gabe. "I know what I want, and I'm destined to get it. Haven't you ever felt certain of something? Like you know inside that things will work out?"

Melissa frowns. "I don't know. Maybe I wish I did, but I think I'm more the doubt-everything-until-it-happens type."

Harley slugs back the Fizzy Blue as though it's plain water—which, when Melissa sips it, she realizes is far from it. "Anyway, Gabe Schroeder is *not* the reason I'm here. But he can lead me to the person who is." Harley finishes the drink and sets it on the bar, licking a bit of blue ice from her top lip. *Now's the time,* she thinks. *I'm going to do it—finally.* "Will you be okay here by yourself?" Harley surprises herself by asking this—normally she'd just bolt without thinking—but Melissa's got a gentle spirit, and kind demeanor, and Harley doesn't want to make enemies. Not here. Not again.

"I'm pretty much anything but alone here," Melissa says, pointing to the throngs of people. "Do what you need to do, Harley. If I get bored or too tired, I'll make my way back to the chalet."

"Thanks!" Harley squeezes Melissa's arm as a good-bye and immerses herself in the bevy of beauties and buff bodies all clamoring for the dance floor, the bar, or the bathrooms.

Melissa takes a few more sips of her drink, wincing at the sweetness and accepting the fact that it will leave her with a headache tomorrow morning if she finishes it. She knows from prior experience that she's not the best match with stiff drinks— in fact, that's one of the details she left out when speaking with Dove. *How could I phrase that?* she wonders. *I got wasted, confessed my adoration for someone, and puked in public while people read my personal journal into the resort-wide speaker system. Or, Dove's way—"Let's just say that I prefer my drinks without alcohol— too much indulgence once led to an unfortunate incident"—much better.* Melissa stands on her tiptoes trying to see Harley and Gabe, but then looks away thinking it's best not to watch, that it's best to avoid any and all contact with Gabe, even if it means hiding out.

Up ahead, Harley sees Gabe Schroeder's blond head and the incredible person attached. *He's just like in the* Sports Illustrated *photos,* she thinks, tugging on a tendril of hair so it falls into her eyes from her messy ponytail. *Hopefully this gives me the disheveled and sexy look rather than just slobby.* Gabe is surrounded by three model-type women, each with tight-fitting shirt and enhanced cleavage and all vying for his attention. *How to get in there?* Harley chews on her thumbnail and thinks.

She walks close enough to Gabe that he sees her, but past him so it looks as though she could care less about his presence. Carefully, Harley elbows past the women but manages to bump one of them just slightly, spilling the woman's icy drink across Harley's chest. Harley doesn't give in to the cold slush, figuring it'll dry. She's not one to get fazed by little mishaps. Gabe sees this and smirks—most girls would have made a scene.

"Watch out!" the woman huffs and looks to her gaggle of friends to pout with her. "And PS, nice shirt."

"Est-ce que vous êtes ivre?" Harley asks, offering one of the only French phrases she knows, thanks to slaving too many hours at the International Burrito Shack—home of the fifty-ounce margarita—her mother's greasy dive back in Colorado. Working there you had to know how to ask people if they'd had too much to drink—and in a variety of languages, so you could cut them off, or order a taxi for them, or just avoid their nasty advances.

"No, I'm not drunk—just coordinated, which is more than I can say for you," the model woman says. "What do you have to say to that?" Her accent is unrecognizable to Harley—is she French? Italian? Croatian? Scottish? Who knows. Obnoxious, definitely.

During the exchange, Harley doesn't once look at Gabe, but knows he's watching the whole thing. Harley shrugs at her and offers the only other French phrase she knows, also from the menu at the International Burrito Shack—or IBS as it was known locally—which had a frog as its mascot. *"Votre grenouille a mangé mon déjeuner,"* Harley says, her lips in a convincing French pout, and walks away. She counts to eight, and sure enough, Gabe is beside her at the far end of the bar.

"Her frog ate your lunch?" he asks, repeating Harley's odd phrase back to her.

She laughs. "Hey—it made her stop bitching, didn't it? And besides, it's one of the only things I know how to say in French." She looks at Gabe—his eyes are half-closed in a semisleepy, but wholly alluring way. *No—I am not here for him,* she reminds herself. *I'm here for—*

"So, what's your deal?" Gabe asks. "You're not French—that's pretty obvious."

"Really is it that obvious? I'm American," Harley says. The icy drink has slicked her shirt to her chest and stomach and she tries to air it out without calling attention to her body. "What about you?" She asks this to make it seem like she has no clue who he is, but the truth is, Gabe Schroeder is a well-known entity, especially among the skiing crowd. *The trick to famous people is letting their fame slip by you, coming up with an immunity to their celebrity,* Harley thinks. *It worked with Celia Sinclair and her posing film posse last night and it'll work all season.*

"Canada. I'm a skier," Gabe says. "British Columbia."

"Whistler." Harley nods as though she's been to that mountain. Gabe stares at her and rakes a hand through his mess of curls. Photographers are always snapping pictures of him in that kind of pose—hands in his hair postrun, or with his arm around some girl, or with—

"So, what brings you to Les Trois?" Gabe leans toward her. He smells good, slightly minty, and Harley has to move back a little to avoid touching him. *Not that touching Gabe would be bad,* Harley thinks. *In fact, it'd be great, but only a distraction. Plus, Gabe is legendary for his wine and dump, always written up in the sports mags as "Romeo on ice." That's it,* Harley thinks. *I'll just call him on it. If I put it out there, he can't try his moves on me, and I won't have to deal with saying yes or no; I can just move on to the real purpose of talking with him in the first place: to get to James.* She allows the five-letter name in her head for the first time since arriving at Les Trois but doesn't let it leak out. *James.* World-class skier and snowboarder and Gabe's best friend.

"I'm a host—at The Tops," Harley says.

"Ohh—the coveted host role," Gabe says, his eyebrows up.

Harley imagines Gabe is thinking back on the vast number of his past acquisitions in the host arena. "Yes, I'm one of the lucky ones. But be warned—I grew up in a ski town, so I know all about sly skiers like you."

"I'm not sure what you mean," Gabe says, downplaying a smirk.

"Definition: Player—see hookup artist. Also known as sex on sticks—skiers—sex on a board—snowboarders or—"

"How about *former player?*" Gabe asks. "Can't a person change their ways?" His mouth leaves the smirk behind and his tone sounds serious.

"Don't try the *all in the past* game with me. Once a hookup artist, always one, as far as I'm concerned." She faux-yawns and rolls her eyes, then laughs.

"Oh, okay then, I guess I'm off the hook." Gabe combines sarcasm with a touch of self-mockery. He touches Harley's arm on the bar, pressing his thigh into hers. Half of her wants to move away from him, but the part that doesn't want to wins, and their legs remain touching.

The only part of the bar that isn't amassed with bodies is the serenity tent. Melissa, desperate to get away from people, especially Gabe Schroeder, but unable to find the door out, weaves her way past the dance floor. As part of the outdoor sky at night theme, the tent is open air—a thick drape of white canvas hangs from the ceiling on the other side of the dance floor. The floor under the tent is filled with strings of white lights, which makes Melissa feel as though she's stepped inside a constellation; a welcome reprieve from the pulsing music, incessant chatter, and elbowing people. She sighs and sits on one of the plump white pillows. *In my fantasies, I stretch out like a beach goddess on this thing,* she thinks, but then the pillow slides out from under her. *But probably I look just drunk and clumsy.* Despite being on the floor and alone, Melissa has a good view of the dance floor and a small bit of space all to herself. *I'm so tired I could fall asleep right here,* she thinks. She takes another white pillow and makes a pillow bed for herself. *I won't really sleep,* she thinks, remembering the croissants that have to bake at six in the morning, the coffee that has to brew, the frittata recipe Dove was going to write down for her, the request for apple turnovers from the countess. *I'll just rest and try to ignore the scene—and him. I won't fall asleep or anything. Just a short nap.*

Harley's had about all she can take of Gabe's mellow stoner-skier-dude persona. *He's hot, but not why I'm here.* "So," she says, her hand on Gabe's forearm, "what kind of accommodations do you guys have?"

Gabe's eyebrows rise as he finishes his beer. "Chalet? Hotel? Tent? Who cares as long as there's a hot tub, right?" Harley finishes her drink, aware she's had more than one, and also aware that the crowd has started to thin out. *It must be late,* she thinks, picturing the breakfast table and how she'll have to make pleasant conversation with the lascivious earl and his brood before her morning caffeine has kicked in. "Do you have a hot tub at The Tops?" Gabe has the disarming habit, she notices, of staring right at her, not around her like so many guys who feel the need to check out every other girl in a ten-mile radius. *Not him,* Harley reminds herself through her beverage haze, *his friend. Must. Get. To. James.*

"I'm more about the ski scene than the après-ski," she says. Back home, she'd watch the rich and rugged after the lifts had closed: groups in front of the fire with mugs of hot chocolate, or sloshing around in the in-ground hot tubs. Every year, tons of articles were written about the après-ski scene at the various resorts, but Harley tossed those aside in favor of the hard-core athletic articles that detailed the ski conditions, which trails had powder, which were black diamond, and—most importantly—who skied them better than anyone else. "Anyone can hot tub—but it's a rare few who can fly down double diamonds with grace."

Gabe looks pensive, considering Harley's words. "So what you're basically saying is that you're not up for a late-night hot tub fest." He grins. "I can take rejection."

Even though he's not the object of her interest, Harley takes some pride in the fact that she's rejected Gabe Schroeder—*the* Gabe Schroeder who, with James Benton, graced the inside of her locker at school all last year. "It's not a flat-out neg," she says. *No one could completely shrug him off,* she thinks, taking in the silvery blond hair, the slope-toned body, his wit—and mainly, his dedicated stare. *Of course, he's probably used that stare to woo countless girls, but it's a tough thing to pass up.*

"So, just a partial rebuff. Got it." Gabe pushes off from the bar as if he were in a swimming pool and looks around for the first time since they started talking. "The scene is dying here. We have to bail before we're the last ones left."

Harley can feel herself crumbling just a little inside with Gabe but immediately patches up the loose feelings when he points across the room. "At least I'm not the only bum left—there's my friend." Harley follows Gabe's point. "My best friend—James."

It's a terrible cliché to compare this feeling in my legs to jelly, but it's true, Harley thinks as she nudges Gabe toward James. *James Benton.* Harley shakes her hair in front of her right eye, her shy stance. It doesn't come out often. Near the door, James is in a plain white T-shirt and old jeans, far from the slick-dressed European crowd's dressy duds—and as far as Harley is concerned, he looks better than in the magazine photos. She clipped the pages for years, following James and his rise from random kid doing tricks on the slope to his trendsetting skills now. She'd discarded all of those pictures except for one: James on his board traversing the half-pipe. It wasn't a complicated move—not like the Air Toe Reverse Generation in which he circled through the air, kicked up the toe of his board, spiraled, and then twisted back around—but it was the photo that Harley first saw of him. The one that caught her attention. In it, James is steady and solid, but airbound.

"Hey—did a feline grab your mouth?" Gabe asks her, poking her ribs with his finger. He's led her to James and they stand in a huddle.

"Huh?" Harley is dazed, staring at James, and blushing— which she never does.

"It's a thing we do," James says. "Schroeder and I keep a record of the badly translated phrases we hear. Some guy last year kept saying that—rather than, 'Did the cat get your tongue . . .' "

Gabe finishes, "He was all . . ." Gabe puts on a bad French accent. "Did ze feline grab your mouth?"

James nods, laughing. "I'm sure we sound just as lame when we speak Italian or French or whatever. What's another one? Oh—'Dude, don't jump in my mouth!' " He looks at Harley, who can't help but wish she could do that very thing. "Instead of 'Don't jump down my throat.' "

Harley laughs, totally swept up in the reality that she's with a living, breathing version of the guy whose picture she's kept in her locker, and now in her backpack here. Even last night, when Melissa and Dove were sleeping, Harley had taken the picture from its place in her bag, smoothed the wrinkles out, and gazed at it for just a minute.

"So you've found a new friend?" James asks Gabe.

Harley comes to her senses and decides she can't daydream—or nightdream—the conversation away. "If *friend* is your way of saying *gal pal for the evening,* you can guess again," Harley says, leaning back on her boot heels for emphasis.

"Looks like you've finally met your match," James says while Gabe zips his jacket.

Harley is quick to disassemble the idea of her and Gabe being a couple. "Gabe is so not my match."

Gabe looks more wounded than she thought he would. "Gentle there, grizzly." Gabe pats her on the back to show he's cool with it. He and James exchange a look. "Besides," Gabe adds, "you know my mantra, right, James?" James nods. The bar is emptying now, the last few people drifting out into the cold night, looking at the real stars rather than the representational ones inside.

"So what is your mantra, exactly?" Harley asks.

"Just 'cause I'll hook up with you doesn't mean I'll ski with you." Gabe looks smug in his ski jacket and curls, his eyes half-shut in that sleepy sexy way. "I'm beat. I gotta hit the sack if I'm going to be good for anything tomorrow."

James looks at Harley. "Yeah—we're training all morning. At Grand Blanc." He pauses. "You should come by."

Gabe shrugs. "She's a host." He says it as though *host* were synonymous with *princess*. "So she might not be able to find the time."

Harley smirks, focusing on James instead of Gabe, hoping that James will memorize her face the way she has his. "I think I can manage five minutes or so."

James nods. "Sounds good. You headed home now?"

This is it, Harley thinks, her chest pounding. *He's going to walk me home. We'll be on the pathway, surrounded by falling snow, cold air, and then he'll say he knew it the minute he saw me. That we're a fit.* She imagines the two of them on a chairlift together. "Yeah, I'm heading back. . . . I should've been out of here a while ago."

James takes a glove from his pocket as the bar lights flicker. "It's really late."

"Same old, same old," Gabe says. "We say we'll just go out for an hour and it turns into six."

"So, shall we?" Harley motions to the door, still looking at James.

James nods and takes a step with Gabe and Harley. "Oh— wait—I lost a glove."

"Why do you even bring them out with you? A real mountain guy would go barehanded." Gabe laughs.

James explains to Harley. "It's another of our jokes—sorry. We were stuck on a bus one time, reading articles out loud to pass the time. One of them was called 'ways to spot a real mountaineer' or something."

"So we keep adding to the list with stupid things," Gabe says. "It's basically puerile but amusing."

"Real mountaineers walk their friends home," Harley says. She looks away from James, thinking maybe deflecting some of her adoration on to Gabe will pique interest.

"Of course," James says. He puts a hand on Harley's shoulder. *He touched me. His hand is on my body. I always thought those girls who touched famous people and said they'd never wash again were disgusting and lame, but when your crush touches you—well, keeping your shirt as-is does have appeal.* "Which is why Gabe is going to do the honors."

"But . . . ," Harley stammers. The alcohol has mostly worn off, leaving her with a sour taste in her mouth—or maybe that's just the sting of not getting exactly what—or whom—she wanted.

"I have to locate my unmanly glove," James says. "See you."

"Tomorrow," Harley confirms. "I'll definitely see you tomorrow."

9

There is nowhere to hide.

n her dream, Melissa hears Matron's voice, doling out advice and scorn, and Gabe Schroeder looks on with his trademark smirk. "Mashed up berries are simply not a proper breakfast." Using Dove's twist of words, Melissa comes back with an answer. "Actually, these are individual mixed berry crumbles." She holds one out to Matron, who tastes it and approves. Only then the crumble turns into a Fizzy Blue, sloshing out of the cup and onto Matron's clean outfit.

"Oh shit!" Melissa says, startling herself awake. For the first thirty seconds she has a grace period, that hazy feeling of being half-ensconced in sleep, and half newly entering the waking world. She licks her dry lips and stretches her legs out on the comfy pillows. Wait. Comfy pillows? Not lumpy? And no draft of freezing air? She bolts upright.

"Where the hell am I?"

Next to her, still lying down, is a body that is turned away from her. Both she and this person are surrounded by the mass of pillows that lured Melissa to nap in the first place, last night— or this night—which is it, she wonders. Above them both is the white tent, the fake night sky switched off, replaced with the dim natural light from outside.

"Long night, huh?" The body rustles, instantly nudging Melissa to deal with the fact that she fell asleep at a bar and apparently slept the whole night next to someone she's never met.

"Look, I have to go," she says and tries to pull herself together.

The body turns over, facing her, and sits up so they are side-by-side, staring at the vacant space. It seems bigger with no one in it—the empty dance floor, the unpeopled bar, the quiet. "There it is!" he says and leaps up from the floor.

Melissa watches him walk and when he bends down she gets it. "JMB! It's you." Cue an instant reddening in the cheeks and a flutter inside.

"I can't tell if you're glad or horrified," he says, smiling.

Melissa stumbles on her words. "No. Yes, not horrified. Wait—yeah, that's what I mean. I think I need coffee. I'm just glad it's . . ." She stops herself. *No admitting anything,* she reminds herself. But inside, she thanks the switched-off stars that she didn't wind up fawning over Gabe Schroeder last night.

JMB crouches on the dance floor and looks back at her. Under the tent, Melissa looks cozy, knees to her chest, hands attempting to tame her springy curls. He smiles. "Of course it's me. You think a total stranger would just haul off and crash next to you? Ah, actually, that wouldn't be unheard of here." He swipes something from the ground and stands up.

Melissa walks over to him, feeling on the inside the wrinkles displayed in her clothing. "I'm so freaked out. I had no plans to fall asleep—seriously, I don't make it a habit to lie down just anywhere. . . ." She stops, tripping over her words. "I don't sleep with random guys." She puts her hand to her mouth.

"So you sleep only with unrandom ones?" JMB asks.

Melissa shakes her head, trying to clarify her unintentional slip. "No. What I mean is . . ."

"I know what you mean—I hardly take you for the kind of girl whose typical night includes shutting down the bar, sleeping there, and waking up next to a guy. . . ." Suddenly his grin disappears and he stops. "Just so you know, nothing happened."

Melissa swallows. *Of course I never thought something did, but he doesn't have to sound so adamant about it, like it would be the worst thing ever if something had.* "I know. I never said it did." Melissa pulls her jacket on and takes a step toward the door. "I couldn't even find the way out last night—that's how lost I got. That's why I wound up under the tent. Just in case you thought I planned on camping out there."

JMB smiles as he silences the alarm on his watch. "Man, it's really late." He sighs. "I mean, it's really early. Or whatever your perspective is. I have practice this morning."

"Oh my god—I'm so busted," Melissa says.

"You? Mesilla? Late for work? And here I was thinking you were so together. . . ."

Melissa laughs, both at the fact that he still has her name wrong, and also remembering this time yesterday, when he'd been witness to the cereal boxes falling on her head. "Yeah, every time you see me I'm just looking more and more like a klutz."

"Well, maybe next time I see you, you can prove me wrong. Not that there's anything terrible about being a klutz."

Melissa's thoughts come rushing at her: *Next time. So he thinks there'll be a next time. Or, no. He's turning into my friend. I'm NOT someone he'd want to wake up with in* that *way, just a buddy. A buddy who will be unemployed—if I don't get to work.* Twisting a loop of hair around her finger, Melissa suddenly realizes that if she were to get fired today, she'd have yet another embarrassing situation associated with her name. First last year's debacle, and now "the girl who fell asleep at the bar." "I have to go," she says, pushing past JMB. Her shoulder hits his chest and Melissa can feel the emotional wind sucked out of her. She wishes she had some sort of immunity to him. But she doesn't.

"Anyway, hope you got enough sleep back there," JMB says, thumbing to the bar, the open tent, the remnants of a night Melissa doesn't really want to end.

What if this is my only night with him ever? The tower bells clang out in the distance, breaking the quiet morning. Melissa counts seven. Coffee is due to be served in a half hour. And she hasn't even prepped the croissants, let alone baked them.

"Looks like snow." JMB pulls a hat out of his inside jacket pocket.

"I hope so." Melissa tilts her face skyward, letting the air wash her clean. If only air took away crushes and wasted evenings. "Guests are always in a better mood when there's fresh snow."

"Yeah, as long as there's not too much." JMB looks at her. "Zip up—you don't want to catch cold."

"Did you know that studies have shown that rapid changes in body temperatures have nothing to do with getting sick? It's all viruses and germs." Melissa grins at him. *A buddy wouldn't be so bad.* JMB steps closer to her and zips her jacket for her. *A hot buddy.*

"Point taken," JMB says. "At least I found what I was looking for last night."

Melissa's breath halts in her throat. Blush creeps over not just her cheeks but her chin—a sure sign she's enraptured. "And what was that, exactly?"

JMB meets Melissa's gaze. "This." He's close enough to kiss her, and Melissa allows herself the indulgence of thinking he will. But right then—when he could bend down, moving his mouth to hers, he bends down and pulls something from his jacket pocket. "My glove! I dropped it somewhere in the vastness of the bar and found it on the dance floor this morning. That's what I picked up—remember?"

Melissa nods. "Right. Your glove. Of course. Well, I'm glad you found it."

JMB pulls the glove on and puts a palm flat on her back. She wishes they could stay like that, connected, for longer, but the stress of what she has to do lies ahead, propelling her to look at him one more time, and walk away.

As she enters The Tops, the back door's squeak alerts Dove and Harley to Melissa's late arrival.

"So, do you have a story to tell or what?" Harley asks, brazen as ever. Fresh from the shower, her white turtleneck clings to her torso, highlighting every curve.

"Ignore Obscenely Dressed Girl over here," Dove says, apron-covered and calm with a streak of flour on her cheek. "Just get your butt upstairs and help me."

Melissa blushes for what feels like the tenth time today and changes from last night's clothing into her uniform, feeling like she's been caught doing something risqué. "Nothing happened, just so you know," she says to Harley. Harley raises her eyebrows and grins.

"You have such a great smile," Melissa says, just a little envious. Not that I want to be her, but just for a day—to see what it's like to be tall and effortlessly gorgeous, without a care in the world.

"Shame I don't show it, huh?" Harley rakes a brush through her wet hair, letting it dry this way and that, which only adds to her natural appeal.

Dove shrugs, tapping her foot as she waits for Melissa. "Ninety seconds and the croissants are burned. Not a threat—just a fact."

Melissa nods, shoving her legs into black pants, her feet into socks and clogs. "Dove, I'm completely indebted—thanks for starting breakfast." She looks at Dove, expecting her to take full credit and ask for a favor, but she doesn't.

Dove sighs, flopping onto her bed while Harley continues to glow. "And to just what do we owe this rapid change of facial expressions? Yesterday you were all pout and attitude—and now suddenly you're super-smiles?"

Harley's lips curl up at Dove. "Nothing."

Melissa's ringlets are full enough that she needs only to place a hair elastic around a ponytail once—no twists. She does this now, in keeping with her job's rules—cooks shall wear hair back at all times. "Ohh—that's the kind of nothing that's fun to hear about. Who is it?"

Harley shakes her head. "Go make your bread products. This trap is staying shut."

"Suit yourself," Melissa says, semiglad Harley didn't spill. If she had, Melissa might have felt compelled to tell her own interior slush.

"Fifteen seconds," Dove says. Melissa darts past her, up the stairs.

"See you," Harley says.

"Where are you going?" Dove asks, sitting up on her bed. To the right, tucked between the mattress and the wall, is the photo she looked at all last night when the chalet was empty. The earl and countess had been at the first of their formal drink parties, Diggs and Luke had gone off in search of girls whose command of the English language was slim, and Harley had deposited Jemma at the Main House Films—better known as a holding pen for the younger set. Finally, Dove had the place to herself—with the beds turned down, she'd gone to sit in the living room to watch the twinkling lights of the village below, but felt out of place in the guest areas. After retreating to the bunkroom, she curled up in her pajamas, too tired to do anything other than stare at the photo of William. *We look so right together,* she'd thought before falling into a heavy sleep.

"I'm out of here." Harley ducks into the back mudroom.

"Don't you have to do the pleasantries at breakfast? As in, be the host?" Dove sees Harley's appeal—her wild side, her energy—but doesn't want to be the one covering for anyone else right now. Probably half of this year's ski guide crop and snowboarders were already trailing after her.

"Oh, I'll be back soon enough—just checking out some necessary ski info," Harley says. "And PS—we all have to show up at the Main House to get the holiday decorations." She twists her mouth. "Let's hear it for tinsel." *Let's hear it for mistletoe,* she thinks.

Dove doesn't inquire just what all this means—where Harley's headed now—but hears the door squeak as Harley leaves.

Dove slides her hand next to her mattress and pulls out the photograph. Sweet William with his uneven smile, his rough-chopped hair, jacketless on the mountain next to her. In the frame, they stand close enough to each other that no space shows. Dove remembers reading that you never know what you'll miss about someone until you're away from them, but she knew right away with William that she'd lie awake for hours missing his low, scratchy voice. Often it sounded as though he'd been yelling, or running—out of breath—and talking to him yesterday had given her the same twisted feeling inside, making her miss him more.

"I take it that's not a family photograph?" Maxwell's voice breaks Dove's morning reverie.

She immediately presses the picture to her chest, and then slides it back to its hiding place. Not that there's anything about William she needs to hide—not anymore. Not since her parents found out about him and threw a fit, the words and threats flying fast, their disappointment in her choices coating everything. "It's just a holiday picture, that's all," Dove says. She feels the need to be ultracalm around Max, to prove to herself she can be the collected one now, that he might have seen her at a time when she was vulnerable, but that she's not like that now. She can't bear the thought of having any part of her still like Max. Not like she did. But being around him starts to make her feel the old sensations rising. "You're not meant to come back here." She stands up. "Staff quarters and all."

Max regards her with amusement. "Forgive me if I offend." He gives a small butler bow. Dove remembers him bowing to her the one time they'd danced—at his eighteenth birthday—under the canopy, while her dress was still unstained and she didn't know yet that the night would end poorly.

"You can't offend me," Dove says. With businesslike manners, she tidies her hair, coiling the blond rope of it back onto itself and pinning it up. Very prim, she thinks. Though she wishes she didn't, Dove has accurate recall for the way Max's hands felt in her hair. She thinks back to standing on the terrace at his parents' country house, the formal gardens lighted by torches, music floating up from the dance. She'd wished he would kiss her for the longest time, but instead they talked while he combed his fingers into her hair.

"I can't offend you because you're immune to any offense—or specifically to me?" Max leans on the door frame, his hair morning-ruffled, his arms crossed over his polar-fleece–clad chest.

"I don't know how to answer that," Dove says. She wants him to leave so she can go back to thinking about William. It's too easy to get sucked into witty repartee with Max. She'd fallen for that before—banter that convinced her he liked her, only to be rudely surprised at his party. In her mind she superimposes William into the memory of Max. Their looks don't overlap at all—Max is tall and dark, lanky and brooding where William is open, smiling, lean and shorter—lighter all around. In her mental snapshot, William is with her on that balcony; it's his hands in her hair, not Max's. "I have to go clean." She tries to keep her face neutral, her whole self detached and cool.

Max stands up straight, clearing his throat. "Right. Sorry." Now he sounds genuinely apologetic, as if his morning plan had been to stand here chatting with her.

Dove is close to him now, waiting for him to move out of the doorway so she can attempt to make the beds. "If there's nothing else . . ." She lets the sentence go unfinished.

Max steps aside. "Actually, there is one thing."

"Yeah?" Dove stands in the doorway now, thinking that if they'd already done the holiday decorating, they'd be right under a sprig of mistletoe, and due for a kiss. She wipes the thought from her mind, focusing on how many bedrooms she has to clean, how much wood she has to haul in for the afternoon fire.

"Don't bother with my room," Max says. He licks his lower lip and puts his hands in his pocket.

"Don't feel sorry for me," Dove says, locking his eyes to hers. "You don't . . ."

Max holds his hands up as if she's an officer. "I'm not. I don't. That's not what . . ." He steps out of mistletoe range and into the darker corridor.

"Oh." Dove suddenly gets it. "You don't want me seeing you in there." She waits for him to disagree and gives a dismayed laugh under her breath. "Don't worry—I won't interrupt any of your—romantic pursuits."

"Lily . . ."

"Dove. Call me Dove, for god's sake. You know full well it's a real nickname." Dove had been her nickname as a kid—due to being pale and ultrablond, and small—Max had known her then, too. They met first at primary school and then again at boarding school. He was the year ahead of her, and at Oxford University now. How had she summed him up in her journal? *Max is my big missed opportunity—or if I give myself the credit—I'm his.*

"Just . . . I don't go by Lily anymore." She sighs, feeling stupid. Of course he doesn't feel bad that she's the maid when she should be his equal—skiing, being catered to. After all, only last year she'd been doing all of that: partying at night, leaving wet towels on the floor to be picked up by the sorry chalet girl. Now she's that girl. Wistful, Dove gives him one last look.

"Lily. Sorry—Dove. I meant to say Dove. I only came down to see you this morning to say thanks—for the chocolate. I haven't had one since—"

Oh damn, she thinks. *What a careless error.* The Roccoco chocolates she'd left out. It never occurred to her that Max would interpret his as anything other than a standard good-night treat. "Everyone got one," Dove explains.

"I know." The light from the bunkroom swells from behind

him, illuminating Max until he appears even larger than his height. "I just . . ."

"Don't." Dove says the word and wishes she'd left anything else—a flower, the weather report, anything except a chocolate from Roccoco—the one place they'd gone together. One date. One food. One kiss. Lots of talk. Dove shakes her head, trying hard to shove the past where it belongs—away and closed. As she walks past Max, he reaches for her arm.

"I'm serious, Dove. You don't need to pick up after me. It'll be one less thing you have to do, okay?" He looks at her and then breaks away, offering her a self-effacing smile. "I'm a slob, anyway."

Dove feels the glacier in her melt just a little at his burst of smile, but then chides herself, knowing he's just covering up his hookup intentions with his charm. "Whatever kind of mess-maker you are, I'm sure I've seen worse. Or, if I haven't yet—I will." She moves down the hall at a fast clip, hoping that he won't follow and knowing if he did, she'd probably have to pinch herself to walk away again. By the staircase up to the main floor, she stops just for a second, waiting to see if Max is following—and Dove kicks herself inside and out when she hears the back door's squeak again, knowing he's left her again—and that she didn't do anything about it.

"I'm ruined. I suck. I can't do this." Melissa repeats the phrase to herself as she flurries around the kitchen trying in vain to get everything prepped on time.

"Problems?" Dove rummages in the cleaning pantry for the brass polish. The kickrail that surrounds the fireplace is tarnished and she needs to finish that before breakfast, just in case the countess wants to relax in the living room. "Oh, here it is." She holds the Nevr-Dull in her hands and looks at Melissa.

"No—no problems at all, if you take away the fact that I feel completely insane and unqualified for this job."

"The croissants look great," Dove says as consolation, gesturing to them with her chin. Melissa notices that Dove doesn't point. She doesn't curse, really. She doesn't fumble or blame.

"Impeccable," Melissa blurts out.

"Sorry?" Dove asks, her lilting accent going up at the end of the word.

"You. It's like... since I got here I was trying to find the best word." Melissa slides a tray of apples into the oven under the broiler for fast cooking. Maybe at some point, she'd have the timing down—or at least wake up in her own bed and have a few extra minutes—but for right now, there are no minutes to spare. Each one is cut-side down, and when they emerge, soft and cooked, Melissa will top them with cinnamon, raisins, and brown sugar, and a dollop of vanilla yogurt. I hope the countess appreciates this, Melissa thinks, stirring the yogurt so it thins out. The countess had mentioned in passing that she has a digestive imbalance, and Melissa knows from her parents, who are big health nuts, that since yogurt is acidophilus-intense, it might help. Melissa pours the yogurt mixture into a small glass pitcher, thinking that while she's only creating more dishes to wash, everything seems nicer, more elegant when served from proper tableware. Dove doesn't interrupt her, but watches, patiently waiting. "See?" Melissa says. "You're just standing there while I've taken too long doing this. And you have work to do."

Dove nods. "Yes. But you were in the middle of saying something. So I'm being patient."

"But most people aren't. Or, not all the time." Melissa wipes her hands on the kitchen towel and furrows her brow. Eggs? No. They had them yesterday. What would complete the meal? "We have something bready, something fruity; now we need something indulgent . . . ," she mutters. Then, to Dove she adds, "Your manners are impeccable. It's like nothing fazes you."

Dove accepts this praise—if that's what it is—and takes a new rag from the cabinet. "It's just how I was raised." Then she plucks at a stray hair. "Some things faze me, believe me."

"Oh," Melissa says. "Not that I was born under a rock or anything, but . . . maybe it's just in comparison to Harley. Or not. I don't know." Melissa touches Dove's hair. "When I was little I had a doll—and I hated dolls, by the way, but my mother insisted on giving me them in the hopes it would make me perfect or pretty or something. So I did weird things with them like throw them in the sea to find out if they'd come back with the tide—and had the dog play catch with them. . . ." Melissa washes her hands for what feels to her like the millionth time, feeling the skin on her fingers pucker. "Anyway, I had a doll called Silver. She had your kind of hair."

"So I'm like a doll?" Dove wrinkles her nose. "Just because I'm short, people always do that—you know, compare me to an animal or a doll—like I'm so fragile."

"I never said you were fragile," Melissa says. "Don't take it the wrong way. It's only . . . I mean, you have fairy-tale hair, the kind that should be trailing down from one of those pointy hats with the veils." Melissa mimes this and Dove sighs.

"I'm kind of sick of it, to tell the truth," Dove says, swiping a lock of it against her cheek and looking at it. Then she drops it and fiddles with one of her earrings—a plain diamond stud—and opens her mouth to explain everything—how she got here, what she left—when the oven timer goes off. "I have so much to do. Sorry. Good luck with the meal . . . it looks lovely, really." Any impetus to give Melissa her whole story fades with the ding of the bell, which also serves as a reminder that the entire chalet awaits with rumpled linens and dirty bathroom sinks for her to scrub.

"Thanks again for the croissant help, Dove. I owe you." Melissa gives her a pointed look. "Really—I always pay back favors." She takes the tray of apples out from the oven, their fragrant scent filling the kitchen. "I'll save one for you?" Melissa puts the tray on the stove top and begins moving them to the serving platter with silver tongs. More dishes, more serving tools. But at least it looks nice.

"Great—it'll be my postmorning work reward." Dove leaves the kitchen's good smells and takes her rag and brass polish out to the living room, hoping to be able to clean in peace.

"Good morning," the countess says to her from her posture-perfect stance by the window.

"Morning," Dove says and tucks herself up as small as possible by the fireplace railing. The pot of polish smells strong, but it works well. Dove dips the rag in, glad she remembered to choose a soft one lest she scrape the finish. William taught her that, how to polish brass with a firm arm, pressing hard into the metal to ensure a proper sheen, how to wipe it without leaving any streaks. Dove sees her warped reflection in the railing and worries just for a minute about William—he said he'd wait for her, called with dates to meet him there, but what if he changed his mind? What if she'd taken all these huge risks for nothing? Dove's hands slack with the thought.

"Something wrong, dear?" Matron's voice cuts through the morning calm. With her shirt so ironed that bending in any direction seems an impossibility, Matron comes over to inspect Dove's polishing. "You need to go back. You've missed a section."

Dove doesn't refute this, even though Matron is incorrect—*I started here, not there,* Dove thinks. But instead of putting up a fuss, she nods. "Of course."

"And the beds?" Matron's fists rest on her hips.

"The guests are still in them," Dove says. Out the window, the sun rises in between two of the three mountains. Early skiers appear as tiny dots on the wide white trails. Dove wishes she were out there, too, instead of trapped inside polishing. *I am a fairy-tale girl,* she thinks. *Just like Melissa said. Only, I've trapped myself.*

Matron leans down, pretending to inspect further, but really so she can speak without the countess hearing. "Just because certain guests choose to waste the day in bed, doesn't mean you can get out of cleaning the rooms."

It doesn't? Dove thinks. "How would I—"

"You simply wait for them to leave their room—for dinner or whatever they desire—and dash in for a very quick tidy-up."

Dove blushes, even though she's done nothing wrong. "I'm not . . . I didn't think that—"

Matron cuts her off. "I'll be back at noon. I want everything finished by then."

Dove wrinkles her brow, knowing there is no rule stating a time by which everything has to be done. Some of the guests might decide to sleep until eleven—then she'd have only an hour to take care of their suites. "Matron, I believe . . ."

"You're not employed to believe, Lily. You are employed to clean." Matron surveys the railing again, this time leaning on it with her hand, leaving a full palm-print. "Looks as though you have more work to do here."

Just call me Dove, damn it, Lily thinks—justifying the swear in her mind after Matron's rudeness. Matron goes to check on the kitchen and Dove worries for Melissa, about the food inspection, about her newness to cooking. *Which am I, anyway? Dove? Lily?*

Does it make a difference? At least I don't need to waste time wondering why Matron gave Melissa the cook's job and stuck me with the cleaning. Punishment. Dove has a feeling it's not only that Matron wants to penalize her for past behavior—she suspects that her own parents had a word with Matron, and asked for the toughest job assignment.

10

Want tips? Put your head down and do the work.

"Here's what I know so far," Harley says. "We all work these fifty or sixty hours a week...."

"With just one day off," Melissa says. "Which can't come too soon, as far as I'm concerned." She changes out of her black pants and into jeans. "Can I say how good it feels to leave my grungy clothes behind?"

"You're only going into town for an hour," Harley says. "Why bother?"

"Because at least then I feel like I have an hour off." Melissa shrugs and checks out her reflection. "So much for glamour," she says, tucking a sprig of curl behind her ear.

"Glamour's not everything it seems," Harley says.

Melissa laughs. "Oh, yeah, this coming from Miss Outdoor World herself."

Harley smiles. "Really? You think I'm, like, rugged or ..."

"You're a camping advertisement. You belong naked, in the

woods, with lascivious hikers watching you or something." Melissa studies Harley's thick hair; the rough chop of it falls to her shoulders. "Did you cut your hair yourself?"

Harley swallows, picking up Melissa's lip gloss as though she's considering sliding it on, but then puts it back down. "Yeah. On the way here." She touches her hair. "It was long." She looks at her reflection. "But now it's not—anyway."

"Anyway, yeah—our hours are long, the work is hard. . . ."

"Well, your work is," Harley says. "I thought for sure it'd be more intense, but the guests seem pretty mellow so far. Maybe I just lucked out for this first batch, huh?"

Melissa shrugs. She pulls on a tight-fitting light blue shirt, and a navy blue vest. *My hands still smell like onions,* she thinks. *They probably will all day.* "Could be."

"Yeah," Harley says. "Maybe European royalty is the most laid-back kind of guest."

"Or maybe we just want to get laid." Diggs and Luke stand at the doorway, poking their heads in and laughing.

"Hey!" Melissa grabs her scarf close to her as if the boys have caught her naked. "You're not supposed to be in here."

"Hey!" Diggs imitates her. "We're paying to be here, so we can be just about anywhere we like."

Harley sighs. *Maybe it was too good to be true, having quiet, easy guests who take care of themselves. At least I got to see James practice.* He and Gabe had both waved to her, seen her, registered that she was there, but hadn't been able to break away to talk. Harley had stuck around drinking coffee, chatting to other early morning onlookers, and felt her breathing rate increase when James waved from the top of the run. The thought that James, who had lived in photo form in her locker for two years, whose face and ski slope statistics she had committed to memory, knew she existed was so amazing, so surreal, she didn't even notice that Celia Sinclair was next to her. They'd both stood watching until Celia posed for a couple of paparazzi shots, and then nudged her way in front of Harley, smiling in a way that wasn't true to the action. Harley tried to catch another glimpse of James and Gabe but they were halfway through their runs, so she'd drained the last of her coffee and come back for breakfast.

"So, what is it you two boys are looking for?" Harley turns to Diggs and Luke.

"You'll do," Luke says, all lanky limbs.

"Not likely." Harley squints at them with fake anger. So much for privacy in the rooms. There were already rumors circulating around Les Trois about late-night sessions between staff and guests—which were highly frowned upon by the higher-ups.

Diggs lets a goofy grin appear on his face. "If I were older? Come on, you know you'd have a thing for me."

Harley nods. "Okay, okay, boys. Yes, Diggs, if you were older, perhaps you'd be the object of my affections. . . ."

"So you're saying there is someone already in that capacity?" Luke intervenes, using his hand like a microphone, pretending to interview Harley.

Melissa watches, amused. "Yeah, Harley, is there some ace skier you've got your eye on?"

Harley looks down, blushing, then grabs Luke's hand and speaks into it. "Why yes, folks, there is someone. The old ace up my sleeve . . ."

"Or in your pants," Diggs adds, funny with his ultraserious voice. "Okay. Now—just who is this lucky guy?"

Harley pushes Luke's hand away and shakes her head. "No comment."

"Well, for god's sake, women, help us find some resort-bored hotties for ourselves then," Luke pleads.

"Really, Harley, that's what a good host does, right?" Diggs says. Then he turns to Melissa. "What about you? Are you look-ing for love with a younger man?" Diggs' comedy routine contin-ues with an outstretched hand to Melissa.

"Don't mess with me." Melissa smiles back. "Haven't you ever heard that? Don't bother the person who cooks for you. . . ."

"Dude, she could poison us or something," Luke says, all drama as he pretends to choke. "But actually, can I make a re-quest? Could you do a chocolate dessert tonight? I'm kind of addicted."

"Chocolate. Sure." Of course she had been planning to poach pears, to impress Matron who told her that poached fruit was an elegant ending to a meal, but chocolate is more fun. "I'll come up with something." Melissa wraps her gray fleece scarf around her neck, remembering when she'd bought it. *Last year, at this time, I was only just falling for him. Him.* For the first time in ages she conjures up his face and name—but doesn't say it out loud; it's too much to contend with. She sighs, smells her oniony hands again, and breezes past Harley, leaving her to deal with Diggs and Luke. "I'm off for my one hour of peace. During which time I have to come up with not one but two sweet recipes—one for you"—she points to Luke—"and one for the chalet. Those signa-ture treats."

"How about a tart?" Diggs suggests with a grin. "Not as the signature treat, but for me, I mean." Melissa gives a sarcastic smile back. Diggs hands her a plastic doorknob sign. "Hang this around your neck. Do not disturb."

"Ha hah. Very funny. I'm sure you have legions of women just waiting for your mastery of the well-timed prop." She hands the sign back to him and he promptly tries to hang it from his belt loops.

"Don't be late for decorating," Harley reminds her. "Not that I'm one to talk about being late. . . ."

"Right," Melissa says, imagining herself alone under a sprig. With a shudder, she remembers seeing Gabe Schroeder last night—from a distance, but still—just hearing his name makes her queasy. "Mistletoe. I can't wait."

At the small café, Melissa sits at a round table, looking out the window. The café faces the bottom of one of the mountains where many ski runs pool into a large flat area where people can leave their gear on racks outside before going to the Hot House for coffee and hot chocolate or sit at the outdoor tables or just head back over to the lifts for another run.

Melissa fiddles with her pen and notebook, doodling swirls and angled shapes, trying to think of clever names for treats. A signature treat. But what kind? And a party, too. *What should I plan?* Past ideas included pita parties, where guests got to stuff their own fillings into wedges of pita bread—boring and messy. There's always make-your-own-sundae, but that feels clichéd. Melissa doodles on her paper and stares out at the Hot House.

A cluster of people are gathered by the small Hot House building—snapping photos of Celia Sinclair and some other big-name guests. She can see Harley with two guys, all three of them skiing over to the lift line. She checks her watch—only forty minutes until decoration time. When she sees JMB walk by, Melissa sets down her notebook and goes to the door, quickly debating whether to call him over—to wave—or to do nothing. Without stepping outside, she holds open the door to the café, letting in a gush of cold air. "Hey! J—" She gets out only the first initial when he turns around.

"Mesilla!" He immediately comes over. "Want to come for a run?"

Melissa takes in JMB's ruddy cheeks, his layers of clothing—long-sleeved green T-shirt, short-sleeved one on top, fleece vest—the essence of laid-back warmth. "I thought you had to practice," she says, remembering their conversation. Was it only this morning she'd woken up next to him? She wants to kick herself now for not taking advantage of that situation. Not that she'd necessarily have done anything differently, but looking back, it seems to her as though she's missed an opportunity. "I'd love to." Melissa looks at the double chairlift and wishes she were on it—with him. "But I can't—duty calls. Or, it will in about a half hour."

"Oh, more gourmet meals?" He steps inside, following Melissa back to her table.

As soon as she sits down, Melissa breathes a sigh of relief that—owing to last season's debacle—she hasn't written anything incriminating in her notebook, which is splayed open on the tabletop. "We have to help decorate—you know, get the festive feelings started with all the tinsel, red, and green anyone can tolerate."

"Sounds kind of fun, actually," he says.

Maybe he wants to go with me, Melissa thinks. She sips her coffee to buy time and muster the confidence to ask him. *If I put it out there, it's not breaking the pact with myself not to chase anyone—it's just being friendly.* Then she looks at him again. *There's no way he'd be into me, anyway. We're destined to just be friends.* "You can come if you want," Melissa says, chucking the proverbial ball in his court.

"What kind of invite is that?" JMB breaks off a piece of the cookie Melissa has in front of her and samples it. "I hope your baked goods are better than these."

"It's just a friendly invite—you know, feel free to stop by," she explains. "And yes, my cookies will be better." She pauses, then opens her notebook to show JMB her doodles. "Maybe. These swirls are all I have for ideas so far."

"That's right—today's treat day." JMB licks his lips. "Last year, I was here and I went from chalet to chalet collecting every single signature treat on offer."

"Isn't that a bit much?" Melissa asks, thinking how fun that sounds—parading from place to place, sucking up cookies, brownies, and laughs with him.

"Oh, man, I was hurting afterward—way too much sugar. But I guess you burn it off on the slopes." He takes Melissa's pen from her. "Okay—so, you have swirls—so start from there."

Melissa smiles. "Good idea. I like swirls; I always draw them. I think they remind me of waves. Of surfing."

"So you're more of a beach person than a sloper?"

"Do I have to be one or the other?" Melissa watches the way JMB holds his pen, wondering if he's ever written his thoughts down on paper, if he's ever revealed himself too much. "Okay—so—back to business. Yes, swirls are good."

"I like vanilla and caramel together."

Melissa looks at the baked goods for sale and considers her words. "I just want guests to rave about them, you know? Not that I need to be hugely popular, but . . . the countess would like a yogurt bar. Luke and Diggs—the teenage boys who are girl-obsessed—like chocolate." She pauses, thinking that brooding Max hasn't mentioned a preference for anything. "And the earl has more interest in anything in tight pants than food."

JMB laughs and the corners of his mouth crinkle. "Sounds like you have your hands full."

"Kind of. I guess I do—it's totally overwhelming in the

kitchen, and frantic. But then, there's this calm afterward, when the meal is done."

"That's pretty much how competing feels." He looks out the window to the snow. "You're all wound up, this crazy mass of emotions—nerves, excitement—and then the jolt of making the run or doing the trick . . . and when you're done, standing there at the end. . . ." He looks at her. "You know you've made it. Maybe you've won, maybe not. But you're there, and it means something."

Melissa swallows, wishing she didn't find JMB attractive, or that she had those model looks that Harley has—something to grab his attention. "I'd like to see you in action," she says, then puts her hand to her mouth and shakes her head. "That came out wrong."

JMB laughs again and points to her paper. "How about this? Caramel and vanilla swirl bread."

"Not bread, brownies—no. Individual brownie cakes." She waits for him to say she can watch him sometime, but he doesn't, so Melissa covers the slight by writing the ingredients down in her notebook. *It's like writing in code,* she thinks. *I'll be able to look back on the recipe and know that it's like a journal entry about JMB and this conversation—but only I'll know about it.*

"Sounds perfect. Save a couple."

"A couple?" Melissa swats at his hand playfully. "Didn't you learn your lesson last year?"

"Oh, I learned plenty last year," he says.

Me too, Melissa thinks. *More than you know.* She wishes she could rewind last season and go over it. *If I worked here, at Les Trois, I'd never have met Gabe Schroeder, never have written about him, never been exposed. And I would have met JMB a whole twelve months sooner. Not that that would mean anything, but still.* "So I'll just save you one brownie treat then. I have to think of a name, too."

JMB stands up just when Harley comes in. She doesn't look left, so she misses Melissa's wave. Melissa watches JMB, who looks at Harley. *Who wouldn't check her out,* Melissa wonders, not really blaming JMB for looking, but wishing she had that kind of magnetism. *She's the kind of girl he'd go for,* Melissa thinks. *Legs, attitude, and brazenness.* JMB puts both palms on Melissa's table and looks at her. "Save three of your unnamed brownie things at least—a, I can easily down a couple and b, my best friend is a total sweet fiend, too."

Melissa's mouth twists into a small swirl. "Your best friend?" she asks.

"Yeah." JMB smiles at her. "Last year we trained at different places but our coaches figured we'd do better together— competitive edge, that sort of thing. So we're here at Les Trois. You'd like him," JMB says. Melissa watches Harley at the café as she orders a cocoa and flirts with the guy behind the bar. "Gabe Schroeder. My oldest friend."

Three syllables. Hearing Gabe Schroeder's name aloud, and from JMB's mouth, is all it takes for Melissa's queasy feeling to return. "I should go," she says.

JMB nods. "I think I'll do a couple more runs and then swing by. Maybe I'll see you there."

Maybe. *Guys are full of maybes,* Melissa thinks. *That is, if they're not that into you, which obviously JMB isn't.* As Melissa stands up to vacate her spot, Harley saunters over, registering JMB and Melissa together.

"Hey." Harley plops down in a chair despite the fact that Melissa and JMB are zipping their jackets and heading out. "What's up?"

"Lights, holly, mistletoe—that's what's up," Melissa says. "Or what will be—after we hang them."

Harley nods and sips her drink as though she has all the time in the world. "Right. The infamous decorations. Rumor has it there's a drinking game involved. . . ."

JMB butts in. "I can confirm the verity of that hearsay." He looks at Harley. Melissa twists her fleece scarf around her neck, nerves tightening as she watches how easily Harley converses with JMB. JMB waves out the window as he explains. "Some people do shots each time they hang holly; then there's some complicated rule about sugar shots—which are so sweet you don't know you've done too many—and you have to swig those while you string lights."

Melissa looks to where JMB has waved and to her horror sees none other than Gabe Schroeder making his way toward the café. "I can't be late—Matron already has it out for me." She pauses, not wanting to miss any conversation, but also can't deal with the thoughts of slamming face-on into Gabe. "Harley—you coming?" Melissa taps her foot by the door.

JMB pauses and nods and looks out again at Gabe. "We're headed for the gondola run. Want to join us, Harley?"

Melissa feels her chest dip. He asked her to ski with him. *Isn't that the truest test of his feelings? If his passion is on the slopes and he wants Harley to experience it, I really have no romantic future with him.* Determined not to let this brush with rejection get her down, she shrugs and smiles. "Have fun."

Harley nods. "I think I have time for one quick run."

"Cool." JMB nods. And to Melissa, he gives a head tilt. "Make sure to save one for me now, right?"

Melissa heads out the door, wondering if she'll ever have time to ski this season. This makes her long for her day off, hoping the weather is decent enough for a long day of swishing down the slopes, trying the intermediate trails, and—at all costs—avoiding Gabe Schroeder. As he approaches she wraps her scarf in front of her face as though protecting herself from the cold when the reality is she's protecting against more embarrassment.

With Melissa gone, Harley plays it cool, snapping into her skis next to Gabe and James. She can see staff people walking to the Main House for the required decorating session, but she's not about to give up the opportunity to ski with James.

"Here we have him, folks," Gabe says, sports-announcing his friend as the three of them head to the lift line. "Master of the Slope, James Benton."

Harley realizes she hasn't said his full name out loud yet. *It's like if I do, he'll evaporate,* she thinks.

"And here we have Master of the Slop, Gabe Schroeder."

"That's Gabriel P. Schroeder to you—or better yet, just call me Lord," Gabe says, threatening his friend with a pole.

"Your initials are GPS?" Harley laughs. "As in Global Positioning . . ."

"As in many kinds of positioning," Gabe jokes. He stares at Harley the way he did at the bar—full-on attentive. "Anyway, it's better than his initials."

"Why?" Harley moves up in the line, keeping both guys close. "What's so wrong with JB?"

"Well, those aren't my real initials," James says. "But I won't bore you with that story."

Gabe seconds his opinion. "Yeah, wise choice. It is boring."

"You're boring," James shoots back. Then to Harley he adds, "Okay—the deal is that I have one of those silly hyphenated last names. My parents are British. Anyway, I was born James Benton-Marks, which then was shortened to JBM, which then—as you can probably guess, if you've spent any time around prepubescent boys—got chopped to BM."

Gabe laughs. "Those were the days. Ah, Mister BM."

James rolls his eyes and continues to Harley, "So then, before I went pro, my coach signed some form *JMB,* which I see now was a fortunate typo. But most people call me James."

"I call him JMB," Gabe says.

"I think I'll stick with James," Harley says, thinking again how amazing it is she can call him anything. For a second, she imagines herself on the cover of a magazine with James—that she's the girl next to him under some Olympic banner.

"Just as well," James says. "Only a few close buddies call me JMB—it's more of an old friend thing—you know, just buddies."

"Fine," Harley says. She wishes she had a history with him that made her part of the inner circle, able to call him JMB. But then again, she doesn't want to be his buddy—she wants much more than that. "Okay, James—let's hit the slopes."

11

Beware of tangles as you decorate.

"I miss him so much I just don't know what to do." Dove finally admits this to someone other than her boyfriend. *It feels good to let it out,* she thinks, just to unload her wallowing. "William's thousands of miles away—but he's the reason I'm here. It doesn't make sense, really."

Melissa and Dove work together trying to untangle piles of Christmas lights. "Long distance seems really tough. . . ."

"It is." Dove's glad to have an understanding ear. "Who put these away last season? They're a mess. It's all knotted." She sticks her tongue out at the lights.

"But then again—my brother met a girl when he traveled and they wound up getting engaged." All around them the other chalet girls—hosts, nannies, cooks, and maids—are grouping ornaments for the huge fir tree in the Main House and getting ready to loop pine branches around the railings outside. Some arrange large silver bells for the annual Christmas Eve concert the following week; others study guest lists, tallying how much eggnog, how many prizes are needed for Games Night. As JMB suggested, the drinking game is in full swing, with some staff sneaking sugar shots and others swaying as they try to hang mistletoe.

"What about you?" Dove tries to distract herself from feeling blah by turning the tables on Melissa. "Is there someone you're finding hard to resist?"

Melissa looks around—too many ears could hear if she admitted the truth. "I can't name names, but . . ." Then she remembers her vow to herself not to get involved, not to open herself up to any possible issues like last year. "You know what? I think I learned my lesson and despite part of the reason people love these jobs— the potential for hookups and heartthrobs—I'm backing off."

"Backing off from whom?" Dove slows down with the lights, hoping Melissa will answer.

JMB. JMB. JMB. All of him—his crinkling eyes, his solid presence, how he makes me laugh, how he seems genuinely attentive to what I have to say, and how he doesn't care that cereal boxes dropped on my head. How he's just a friend. "No one. There's absolutely no one who does anything for me."

Dove shrugs. "Well, there's someone who might be into you."

Melissa drops the coil of lights, fumbling. "What—wait— who? What do you mean?"

Dove gestures with her chin. "Over there. That guy. He's been looking at you."

Melissa looks to the far wall, near the door, and just for a second locks eyes with him, sending ripples of confusion and anxiety through her body. *Gabe Schroeder. Staring at me.* "Shit—we have to go. Now."

Dove sees the panic in Melissa's eyes and pulls her into the crowd of decorators. "This way. Let's go outside."

Melissa nods, coiling another strand of white lights around her wrist. "We should hang these from the balcony—it'd look really nice." *And get away—as far away as possible—from Gabe Schroeder.* Melissa feels better, thinking about leaving the building, getting away from him. But then she realizes that if he's here, that leaves Harley and JMB alone together. "Let's go," she says to Dove, her shoulders slacking.

She grabs a box of red velvet bows and the rest of the lights and motions for Dove to follow. They go out the side door of the Main House, leaving the confusion and mayhem of holiday festivities to decorate their own chalet.

"You okay?" Dove tugs on the lights, freeing a strand from the twists.

"Fine," Melissa says, willing it to be true. "Tell me more about you and William."

Dove fiddles with a red bow and then secures it with wire to the posts on either side of the walkway. "I wonder what he's doing all day long, and even though we've been talking almost every day, and I write . . . it just doesn't seem like it's enough. I mean, how can it last like that?" She fights back tears, wishing she didn't have all her emotions so close to the surface.

She looks back at Dove, wishing she could make her feel better. "Look, you guys haven't been together that long. . . ."

"What's that supposed to mean?" Dove instantly raises her voice.

"Don't get defensive," Melissa says. "I'm not saying anything you don't already know—but all I'm pointing out is that you don't have patterns yet."

"What do you mean?"

"My mom's a shrink, right? So she's always pointing out relationship patterns, like how we all repeat things over and over again, due to our own psychology. I, for example, have a tendency to like guys who don't like me back. I know this, yet I convince myself I have some shred of hope, and I keep liking them until I do something stupid." The sky ushers in hues of blue and gray as clouds roll in. "Case in point—back at school I liked this person who never liked me back, I finally confessed, and poof—our friendship disappeared. Then . . ."

Dove walks next to Melissa, watching the puffs of white breath escape her mouth. "Then what?"

"Then last season—not here—it all blew up in my face again. So you see . . . now I'm trying to flip the pattern. Not do it. And you can change the pattern with William. If you miss him this much, maybe you should go see him. Cut off the inevitable pining and longing associated with long-distance love."

Dove kicks her boots into the snowy path as she walks. "How is it that I'm here, in air so cold it turns my breath, and William's someplace where it's hot enough for shorts. He probably sleeps naked."

Melissa laughs. "And is that a good thing?"

Dove shrugs. "It's good as long as he's alone."

"Don't you trust him? I thought you said the minute you met him you knew it was right—and that he felt the same."

Dove stops in front of a large pine tree near the path to The Tops. "Let's hang a strand here—we can twist it on the lamppost and run a cord into that outdoor outlet." She points to a brown box sticking up from the ground. "It's not that I don't trust him . . . it's just—he's really personable, you know? He's the first person to make a joke and put you at ease, the person who helps out without being asked."

"He sounds perfect," Melissa says. *Not for me,* she adds in her head. *But for Dove. Who would be perfect for me? JMB. But I will not repeat that pattern—ever. Maybe I just can't pick them—after all, I picked Gabe and that was the worst choice.*

"He is perfect—except for the family issues." Dove and Melissa stretch the coiled-up lights over the lower part of the lamppost and then Dove shimmies up to fling it over the top.

"Nice work," Melissa says. "So, what exactly are the family issues—if you don't mind me asking?"

Dove looks down from her precarious perch on the lamppost. "Long story short is that he's got a dodgy family background—Dad ran off after accruing serious debt, and he's kind of rough around the edges."

"Which is kind of sexy, right?"

"Utterly," Dove says. "Wait—don't let me fall. I have to shake that thought off." She grips her legs around the lamppost and twists the lights so they'll stay on. "Anyway, we were here . . . over there, actually." Dove holds on with one hand and points to another chalet with the other. "We stayed at Le Roi—my parents and I. And everything was great—until they caught me with him."

"They caught you doing what, exactly?" Melissa asks. She figured Dove for an innocent, not a prude—but a hand-holder.

"Not like that," she says. "William and I didn't . . . we haven't . . ."

"Got it," Melissa says. "Here—take another one—it'll look better all done up." She throws a second strand of lights to Dove.

"So my parents caught us—in the living room with wine, in a state of undress—not bare or anything, but rumpled . . ."

"Rumpled. I like the sound of that. And they freaked out?"

Dove slides down the lamppost and goes to plug in the cord. "No. That's the thing. They didn't care that we'd taken wine—they didn't care that I was snogging him in the public place."

"Oh," Melissa says, recalling the original tour Dove had given her of The Tops. "No wonder you told me there's nowhere to hide."

"All my bloody parents cared about was that he—William Bennett—wasn't one of their crowd."

"That he's poor, you mean?"

Dove shakes her head, the long silvery blond hair flowing evenly over her shoulders. "Poor doesn't matter. In my parents' minds, class is the most crucial element to having a good life. And that's the one thing William doesn't have."

"So your parents just kicked you out?" Melissa can't believe how harsh that sounds. "My parents are the other extreme. They're really into this idea that life just unfolds as you go, without any planning."

"Isn't it funny how different they are? I mean, what would you be like if you'd been born into my family?" Dove laughs, her arms over her chest. "So to answer your question, no—they didn't give me the boot. That would've been too easy. Instead, they gave me a choice." She puts on a deep voice, mimicking her father. "Lily—you've reached a crossroads." Dove switches back to her own voice. "I mean, he made it sound as though I'd driven myself to the fork in the road and it was my fault they were being close-minded. Anyway, I had to choose between home—meaning parents, my early acceptance to university, and my private financial trust—money that's always been there. And being here—with him."

"So you made your decision."

"I did. And I don't regret it. I mean, I don't know. Maybe a small part of me wishes I could have had it all—my trust fund, great school . . . but they'd never be able to get past it. My parents have said from day one that the most important thing is that I live a life they can be proud of. Not me. Them. And when I'm with William, that's how I feel. Like I'm proud of myself for being my own person. For standing up for myself." Dove feels the unease rise up in her chest. It's one thing to make a temporary decision to stay with William and skip enrolling at Oxford, but another thing entirely to do it forever, which is now her reality. *When did it get so complicated? When I stepped off the path they chose for me. And what if it doesn't work?* Dove pushes those thoughts away, focusing instead on seeing William in the bright sunshine on the beach.

"No wonder you miss him so much—it's like you gave up everything to be with him and he gave up nothing," Melissa says. The wind blows a strand of lights free and it droops. "Here—cinch that tighter."

Dove does and then drops to the ground, bothered by the way that sounds. "It's not like that. William has committed to work the winter season in the islands. I was already here and figured getting a job at Les Trois would be the easiest thing. He didn't want to back out on his word. So he's there, I'm here."

Melissa smiles. "And soon you'll be together, right?"

Dove puts her cold hands in her pockets. "Right."

Up at The Tops the front door opens and the countess and earl step onto the balcony. The countess waves down to the girls. Dove waves back, hoping Maxwell isn't anywhere up there. That he's gone off and found someone else or just plain gone off and disappeared—that's his pattern.

"Can I ask one thing?" Melissa says, not wanting to hurt Dove, but honestly confused. She waves to the guests, and Jemma waves back, hopping up and down. "Crap—I just remembered I promised I'd show Jemma how to make pretzels. Of course, I don't know how to either, so we're bound to make a mess."

Dove and Melissa start walking back to the Main House to finish decorating and get on with the rest of their work. Before they go inside, Dove turns to Melissa. "What'd you want to ask?"

Melissa pats her curls into place and slicks on Chapstick. "How do you know when it's more than just a fling? Something that's worth putting yourself out there?"

"I don't know," Dove says, thinking back to her days and nights with William—his words, the way he liked to rest his palm on her thigh and sit in the quiet watching the sun sink between the mountains, the way he knew what she needed—a hug, a laugh—a cracker—without her even having to ask. "Maybe it's just this switch that goes off inside you—and you know then that there's nothing you could do to feel differently. That being with this person is worth giving up—not necessarily money, like I did. But letting go of that part of yourself."

"What part?"

"The part that is totally afraid of being crushed."

12

Once borrowed, forever owed.

The next day goes by in a whir of routines—morning dusting, vacuuming, Harley's daily forecast at the breakfast table, Dove's fast bed making (having one less to clean made the morning faster), and Melissa's two trays of the caramel-vanilla brownie swirls, which prove addictive.

In the afternoon, the guests traipse off to an ice-skating festival with Harley leading the way.

"When we got here I wished I were the host," Melissa says when she, Dove, and Harley overlap in the bunkroom. "But now I don't so much."

Harley pulls a grey wool V-neck sweater on, topping the outfit with a bright red scarf. "Do I look festive or what?"

"You do," Dove says. "I can't believe how fast time is going. This time next week we'll be setting up for the holidays—Games Night, the winter wonderland, the formal." She pauses, wondering what it will be like to be on the serving side of the events. "It's so odd—I've been the one to make off with a bottle of champagne at the dance, and now I'll be the one patrolling to make sure people don't."

"And what are you going to do now?" Melissa asks.

Dove lies back on her bed, sighing. "I don't know—probably take a walk through town and write some letters. I have to check on tickets, too—William's convinced I should wait until the last possible minute to book my flight."

Harley raises her eyebrows. "Sounds like he's got a case of cold feet."

Melissa sits near Dove. "Aren't you worried you won't get a ticket if you don't buy it soon?"

Dove reaches for the photo of William and puts it on her chest face down. "No—you guys don't get it. He wants to make sure we get a good deal on the ticket—"

"We? I thought you were buying it?" Melissa stands up and begins to rifle through her drawers for a clean shirt.

"No—I'm buying it—but we . . ." Dove's voice dips, getting so soft it's difficult to hear her. "I don't know. I thought he'd split the ticket with me. But he can't."

"It's not like you're rolling in it," Harley says, unaware of Dove's past and the fact that she was, until recently, more than rolling in it. "When you're down and out, other people should help you." She goes to her mattress and lifts it up, pulling a maroon leather pouch out from underneath. "I'll spot you the money. You should go now and buy your ticket. If you love him as much as you've been saying you do—then you'd be a fool to miss seeing him because of a plane ticket."

Dove sits up and at first doesn't accept the money from Harley. "How'd you get this? Why do you have so much cash?"

Harley grimaces in disbelief. "Oh, what? A girl like me can't have cash flow? Am I so beneath you guys that you find it hard to believe I've got spending money?" Harley steels herself against any comments and goes on. "Just to inform you—both of you." She looks at Melissa, too. Dove looks tiny on the bed as she listens to Harley. "You want to know the reason I have this?" She crumples the bills. Forget keeping her past a huge secret. *Who cares, now that I'm here, right?* Harley sucks in her breath. "Pageants. Stupid, god-awful beauty pageants."

Melissa's mouth hangs open—rugged, brutelike Harley on a runway? "You're gorgeous, obviously . . . ," Melissa starts.

Harley gets close to her, fuming. "But what? Rough around the edges? Sure. That's me. But if I want to, I can turn into Miss Teen in a second. I might be from a trailer compound, but I can fake it with the best of them."

"So you earned the money?" Dove asks, thinking that if Harley knew the real truth about her own background, she'd probably hate her. *While she was growing up in a trailer, I was in a house that for all intents and purposes could be called a castle. Hardly fair.*

"Did you think I stole it or something?" Harley puts her hands on her hips, defiant.

"No, I'm sure that's not what she meant." Melissa steps in to defend Dove.

"Don't for a second think I didn't earn this," Harley says. She holds the crumpled money tightly as though it might disappear. It always did when her mother got hold of it—one minute they'd have crisp bills for food and the mortgage on the restaurant, and the next the bank would call and threaten foreclosure. Harley knows all too well about money slipping away.

Dove thinks for a minute, the room full with emotions, and then stands up. "Harley—thank you. Thanks for your kind and generous offer. But I can't accept it."

"Why?" Harley takes this personally.

"It's just . . ." Dove takes a deep breath. "I want to stand on my own and prove I can do it—you know, support myself."

Melissa opens her mouth to butt in, getting out only, "Do you think your parents would . . ."

And then Dove cuts her off. "No, Melissa, my parents have nothing to do with this."

Harley offers the money again. "Just think—you could know for sure that you have the ticket. That you're going."

"That would be nice . . . ," Dove says but shakes her head again. "What if I don't make enough tips this week to pay you back?"

Harley shrugs. "Look—I have room and board and I get to ski for free." She doesn't add that she's getting closer and closer to her real goal—landing James Benton—but thinks it as she talks. *James sat next to me on the triple lift with Gabe yesterday, and when Gabe took off to help at the main house with decorations, James didn't mind. He waves whenever he sees me, and he certainly has invited me to enough things—come along and watch me practice. It means something. Tomorrow—tomorrow I'll tell him how I feel. Or show him.* "So I don't exactly have a need for the money at this moment."

Dove swallows, twisting her hair in her fingers. "If I had a ticket, I could do one of those countdown things—you know, when you get to say 'ten more days and I'll see him,' then 'six more days and I'll be with him.' That sort of thing." Dove imagines peeling calendar pages off, each one bringing her closer to William.

Melissa collects a pile of dirty pants, shirts, and underwear, amazed at how fast the wash piles up; the shirt she wore on the bus ride here—that seems so long ago already, the black pants streaked with honey from the biscuits she made—at least now she knows the oven cooks unevenly. And the fleece scarf. Even that needs to be washed—partly because it's a little dirty and partly because it reminds her of last season and throwing herself at Gabe, only to be turned down. And now this year—she had it on when she was at the café with JMB. It's so easy to like him—too easy. So Melissa takes the scarf and all the feelings tied up in it, and adds it to the pile of things to wash clean. "Maybe you should take the money with you and decide at the travel shop."

Dove smiles. "Yeah—that's a good idea. Is that okay, Harley?"

Harley nods, glad that her offer to help has been accepted. "Just . . . you know—don't say anything about what I told you."

Melissa looks up from her laundry bagging. "What, you don't want word of your glamorous history getting around?"

Dove pulls on her coat. "I think Harley feels like the rest of us, right? Let the past stay there?" Harley nods. Dove contemplates explaining her own past—but she can't—not to Harley, who worked so hard to get here.

Dove pockets the cash from her friend. "Looks like snow."

Harley nods. "The forecast report I gave this morning said just a few inches, but I'm betting on more."

"Then I'd better go." Dove makes her way to the back mudroom. "I'll be back in time to refresh the living room before the cocktail hour."

Melissa nods. "Have fun!" Then she sighs. "All my clothes look like shit—either stained or wrinkled or just ugly. Looks like I'm spending my free time Chez Soapsuds." Laundry is all the way on the other side of the resort, coin-operated and slow. "This is so annoying." She pulls out a T-shirt, finds it stained, and puts it back.

Harley tosses a pair of jeans to Melissa. "Do me a favor and wash these?" She makes a prayer sign to Melissa and completes the look with a frown. "Please? I have to escort the horny boys again."

"Did we hear our names?" Diggs and Luke appear at the doorway. Melissa rolls her eyes at them but smiles—they're harmless and sweet. And true, in a few years they'll be the ones with a legion of swooning fans.

Harley barely acknowledges them, which Melissa can tell only makes the boys like her more. *I'm just not like that, though. She knows how to play it cool and I know how to play it tepid. Oh well— you can't change who you really are. No matter what you leave in the past, you can't entirely be free of it.*

With a face that gives nothing away, Harley turns to Diggs. "How long have you been standing there?"

"What's it to you, Host?"

"Hostess Cupcake, is more like it," Luke adds.

Harley stomps over to them. "I humor you. I trot you around. I let you cling to me. In return I ask you one simple question— what did you hear while you were standing there?"

Diggs looks slapped. "Nothing."

Luke shakes his head. "Really, Harley. We just got here."

Harley stares at them a second longer. "Okay—then let's head out. Skating party, here we come."

She leads and the boys follow, but Diggs shuffles behind. He turns to Melissa, giving her a look that informs her he might have heard quite a lot before announcing his presence.

13

Don't let your dirty laundry pile up.

n the dank basement of the concrete slab building, Melissa hefts her laundry bag over to the counter and begins sorting. Another chalet girl folds her clothing into neat stacks and smiles at Melissa.

"What a boring thing to do, huh?"

Melissa nods. "Not exactly how I'd like to use my downtime."

"Are you a nanny?"

"No—cook," Melissa says. "Actually, that's the first time I've said that aloud and not felt like an idiot—or a fraud."

"I know what you mean. I'm a nanny down in the Cluster Huts." She points behind her as though the small group of luxurious cabins—primarily hired out by families for reunions or stars with an entourage—are right there. "And I'm only just getting the hang of it. Who knew kids could wear you down? I thought it'd be all finger painting and cookie decorating."

"I'm Melissa." She walks over and shakes the girl's hand. "You're a good folder. Sorry—that sounded lame."

"No, it's true—I am an excellent folder. It's on my resume under special skills." She puts down her most recently folded item and looks at Melissa. "I'm Charlie."

"Short for?" Melissa looks at Charlie—she's fair with lots of freckles, bright strawberry-gold hair and eyebrows that are even lighter.

"Short for Charlie," she laughs. "Everyone always asks me that. But it's just my regular name." She looks at her watch. "I have to run. I'm due back right when nap time is over—of course. Anyway, nice to meet you."

"Good to meet you," Melissa says. "Good luck with your charges."

"Yeah—Lord and Lady Sinclair—otherwise known as the evil toddler twins."

"Sinclair?" Melissa asks, thinking back to Celia Sinclair and her famously rude smirk, and how she deserted her in town at that first shop.

"As in the nephew and niece of the starlet." Charlie stacks her clothing in a plastic laundry basket. "I am a good folder—I worked retail every summer. But now—ah, the glamour of watching Celia Sinclair stumble in at dawn with a new guy and the same old hangover."

"Is she as mean as she seems?" Melissa starts to toss her whites into the washer. In goes the shirt stained with prunes from that breakfast, and the underwear she wore the first day, bras, and another shirt—the one she wore shopping when JMB gave her a ride home. *It'll be good to clean these,* Melissa thinks. *Start fresh.*

"Celia's not that bad—just squirrelly. She wants to egg you

on, get you to chase her but then dart away. Something like that. But she's not all bad."

"And you're assigned to her clan for how long?"

"Oh, she's here for a while—through this week, and Holiday Week, and then into New Year's. Not sure where she goes after that." Charlie lifts the basket toward the door. "But I heard that this one girl last year was offered a job traveling around—she got attached to the kids while they were here, and I guess just wound up leaving to follow them." She pauses again.

"Would you do that?" Melissa adds the detergent and reaches into her pocket for change.

Charlie packs up her stuff, shifting the weight of her clean clothing to her hip, tilting her head as she considers her options. "Depends—let's just say I wouldn't turn down the chance to go to Paris with the Sinclairs—or back to LA—or island-hopping. But who knows."

"I guess you have to wait and see what happens." Melissa wishes she were a patient person, someone for whom this advice wouldn't be maddening.

"Right. Exactly." Charlie lifts her fingers in a wave. "See you!"

"Bye." Melissa watches Charlie walk away and goes back to sorting through the colors, turning her shirts right side in, her jeans inside out to avoid too much fading, and her socks so they aren't balled up. With the taste test night, she does a quick calculation about how many swirled cupcakes she'll need—enough for the guests, figuring Diggs and Luke will consume more than their fair share—and that people from other chalets can stop by to test out the sweets. *I'll need to counteract the sweetness with something not so sweet—maybe mulled cider. That's easy—just stick a few cinnamon sticks and cloves into a pot of apple cider and warm it up. Maybe I should do candy apples for my party theme. Matron made it clear that it doesn't have to be huge and elaborate, just something memorable—food and conversation.*

"Easy, sweet, and tasty," she says aloud and hears her voice echo back as it bounces off the concrete walls.

"Now that's the kind of pickup line I like." JMB drops a bulky bag onto the gray floor and starts shoving the contents into a washer.

"Hey," Melissa says, determined to resist the part of her brain that yells out to her *you like him, you like him* when she sees his face.

"What's a girl like you doing in a place like this?" he asks.

"Oh, are we trading lines now?" Melissa puts the colored clothing into the wash, adds detergent, and slips coins into their slots. The room fills with the pleasant hum of machines, the gentle whirs and clicks of laundry. *It's okay being with him. Really. He's a buddy.* I'm his buddy. JMB hoists himself up on the counter.

"Okay—right now. Worst lines you can think of." He leans his forearms onto his thighs. Melissa sees the cuff of his gray waffle-weave shirt is ripped, and fights the mental image of being in that shirt—not necessarily with him, but in it—borrowing it the way girls do in the movies, sexy and comfy in their boyfriends' clothes. *But he's not my boyfriend!* the other half of her brain shouts to the first.

"My friend bet me that you wouldn't take off your shirt in public," JMB says.

It takes Melissa a second to realize it's just a line. She shoots back with, "Is that a mirror in your pocket? Because I can definitely see myself in your pants." She cracks up and so does JMB. *This is good, healthy,* she thinks. *I'll break my pattern by saying all these things that I kind of feel, and then they'll be out of my system.* She takes a few steps closer to JMB, not touching him, but right next to him so she's leaning on the washing machine in front of him and he's up on the counter. With her legs stretched out at an angle, his feet nearly make contact with her knees.

"Should I call you in the morning or nudge you?" JMB gives her an overtly sleazy look.

"They call me *coffee,* I grind so fine."

"I'm conducting field research to find out how many women have pierced nipples."

Melissa crosses her arms over her chest instinctually. "That'd be a no." She thinks, then does a strut to him. "The voices in my head told me to come talk to you."

"Oh, that's a good one. Then you can be semipsycho and make face time." JMB drums his fingers on his knee. Then he hops down, getting so close to Melissa she sucks in her breath. His chest presses against her. He leans in, with a Russian accent whispering into her ear, "Are you my contact? Code name: Natasha?"

"Da," Melissa replies, her whole body tingling with his touch. She wants to keep him close, but the part of her that knows better pushes him away with an outstretched palm. "If I could rearrange the alphabet I would flip the *m* and *w*."

"What?" JMB wrinkles his brow.

"You know, flip the *m* and *w* . . . ," Melissa explains and realizes it's the perfect solution—if there were two JMBs there'd be one to be her buddy and another to be her unrequited crush. "You're not a twin by any chance?"

JMB shakes his head. "Okay—lewd."

"I like cringe-worthy ones better." Melissa takes his place on top of the counter. JMB stands in front of her, in the perfect position for her to wrap her legs around his waist and have him kiss her. "Lewd. Okay." She looks at him and he stares at her, grinning.

"Am I going to offend you? Really—I don't want to piss you off."

"Are you making excuses for not having any lewd lines?" Melissa asks. "What're you going to do when you're at a bar and want to pick some hottie up?"

"I'll just fall asleep next to her," JMB says, laughing.

Melissa looks to see if he's serious or joking, thinking back to waking up next to him under the white tent. "Why did you do that, anyway?"

JMB shrugs. "I couldn't leave you there—and despite trying to rouse you, you were pretty out of it. So I just figured . . ."

Melissa cuts him off. She can't bear the thought of hearing from him directly that he wouldn't leave a *friend* alone, that he wouldn't want a *friend* to wake up in a strange place, that of course he didn't want someone else to bother his *friend*. "I'm feeling a little off today; would you like to turn me on?"

This halts him and his train of words. "Hi, my name is Milk. I'll do your body good." He steps in, just a little closer to her.

Melissa looks at the scar on his lip, focusing on it so she won't lean in and be tempted to kiss him. "If your right leg was Christmas and your left leg was Easter, would you let me spend some time up between the holidays?" They stare at each other in mock drama and then—right as it's getting intense—Melissa cracks up. Heaving laughs ripple through her stomach.

"Oh my god." JMB laughs so hard tears well up in his eyes. "Okay. One last one. You go there." He positions Melissa by the three washers. "I'll be here." He stands across the room by the washers. He acts like he's just seen her and does a double take, then walks across to her. With his hands on her shoulders, he leans down.

Oh my god, he's going to do it—he's going to kiss me. Right here, with the laundry. *And that will be our funny slash cute story about how we got together.* She stares up at him, at his smile, his scar, the way his eyes seem to hold her. He leans down. "Do you mind if I stare at you up close instead of from across the room?"

No kiss follows the words, but JMB keeps his grip on her shoulders for a few seconds, waiting for her to laugh. *Why do I do this to myself?* Melissa thinks, unable to push away from him. *How can I be expected to have no feelings for him when . . .* She opens her mouth to respond to his lame line.

"I . . ."

JMB looks at her, waiting. "And what do you say back?"

A voice from the doorway interrupts both of them. "How about 'Do you have a map? I just keep on getting lost in your eyes.'"

"Dude, that is SO cheesy." JMB drops his hands from Melissa's shoulders and gives a head-tilt acknowledgment to Gabe who stands in the doorway.

Melissa wills the washer to finish so she'll have something to do. *At least the revolting fluorescent lighting in here hides my blushing, even if it accentuates every pore and flaw.* She avoids looking at Gabe.

"This is Gabe Schroeder—the guy who needs no introduction," JMB says. Gabe enters the room, keeping one hand in his pocket; the other he rakes through the blond mop of curls.

"Hi." Melissa looks at him finally. Same Gabe. Same gorgeousness, same appeal, same feeling of humiliation.

"Hi."

"Do you two know each other?" JMB looks first at Gabe and then at Melissa, cocking one eyebrow in confusion.

"No," Gabe says.

Melissa echoes, overlapping with Gabe. "We don't know each other at all."

The three of them stand still with the washing machines and dryers churning their own soft music. *This is too much, too weird, too crazy. I have to get out of here.*

"Oh, look how late it is," Melissa says. "I have to go cook."

"I'll change your load over for you." JMB smiles, breaking the tension. "God, even that sounded like a line." Melissa laughs. Gabe looks on, studying the scene. "Good luck with the swirls."

Melissa smiles, both at the fact that he remembered and that Gabe might potentially wonder about this inside joke. "Yep—swirls it is. I'll save you one—or more than one, right?" Melissa says and, patting JMB on the arm—a very buddy gesture, she figures—leaves her laundry to spin around and around like her own insides.

Outside the room, she braces herself against the cool concrete walls, catching her breath while her hands shake. *It wasn't as bad as it could've been.*

From inside the laundry room, she can hear JMB and their muffled talking.

"She's hot," Gabe says.

"True," JMB agrees.

Me? I'm hot? Cool. I mean, hot. Melissa's shaking hands cover her smile. Maybe the past is past, getting washed clean with her clothing. *And the future is open—Gabe doesn't think I'm a loser and JMB thinks I'm hot.*

"So, are you going to see her again?" Gabe asks. Melissa leans in, waiting for the answer.

"Who, Charlie?" JMB answers. "We'll see."

14

Check the weather every day.

"What the hell happened to you last night?" Harley demands of Melissa. Outside, the air is calm, the ground warm from yesterday's higher temperatures. The resort is in a fluster—with guests annoyed at the semitepid conditions that made the snow's surface icy, and the freezing temperatures today that are causing windburn and air too cold for snow.

"What happened to me?" Melissa asks rhetorically. "What about you, Miss I-didn't-creep-in-until-four-this-morning."

With her chestnut hair flipped down toward the floor, Harley runs her fingers through it, never one for the dryer. She's fresh from the shower, clean, on her way to watch James and Gabe in a mock race—if the conditions are decent enough. They want to ski the double black, take a break from boarding, and Harley has visions of paralleling next to them.

"Yeah—late night . . ." She smiles to herself, remembering.

"You tell me first," Harley says. "Did you leave that good-girl image behind and go around the world in a tub?" Harley makes a reference to the loud hot tub parties that start at one chalet and then move on to the next hot tub whenever the noise complaints get too many or the wet bar runs out. In the morning, Dove and the other cleaners pick up the stray suits—the bikini tops tossed carelessly over the railing, the high-cut one-pieces left to soak all night in the bubbling tub. Stopping by to collect something at the Lost and Found at the Main House is a notorious admission of guilt.

"I'm not a good girl," Melissa says, then realizes it's a stupid thing to debate—and a lame label to want to shrug. "Fine— maybe I am. But not in the way you make it sound." Next to the clean host, Melissa feels even gooier than she looks: Her hands are coated in sticky dough—remnants from her most recent culinary attempt.

Before Melissa can answer what she did the night before, Harley blurts out her own exploits. "Can I just say how much of an exhibitionist Celia Sinclair is? I'm guessing she doesn't know when the camera's rolling and when real life takes over. She was there—at this party last night, flirting with some guy who turns out to be the prince of Denmark or something. Some country up north. Anyway, I managed to get his attention. . . ."

"So you just wanted to take him away?" Melissa asks. "Not that I'm defending Celia Sinclair." *Definitely not—Celia's been throwing only mean looks and cold shoulders toward me. And Harley has every right to do what she wants, it's just that I'm wary of girls like that—ones who are in it just for the conquest of snagging the unsnag- gable guy, even if someone has true feelings for him.* "What if Celia really liked Prince Herring or whatever?"

"First of all, Celia is just buying time, waiting for production of her next movie to start—I think next week, around Christmas. The word around town is they're lining up some big scene for New Year's Eve."

"There's a ball then," Melissa says, whisked momentarily away by the thought of going to said ball in a dress with a certain guy. But no, not likely. "So you were saying, about stealing Celia's flirt from her last night?"

Harley pulls her hair into a messy ponytail, the front strands framing her face, calling attention to her light pink mouth. "I'm a pretty driven person, you know?" Harley pinches her cheeks in lieu of blush. "Old pageant trick. Anyway, there *is* a guy I want here—you know that. James. Jacques, if you're French. But . . . I'm not against finding some fun on my way to him."

"But . . . if you were really into him, wouldn't that mean other guys don't hold any appeal?" Melissa wonders how all this gets figured out, cemented into types of girls, types of people. *Jacques, James, Jean, Jean-François, Jean-Pierre, Jim, Jamie—there are tons of similarly named people here, just like there are certain types of girls. Only, which kind am I?*

"I, personally, don't think that's true. I think that's something men invented to keep women down—like if she's really into me, she'll just wait and wait until I notice her. Until I come around. It's boring, it's pathetic, and it makes you—me—women, just totally passive."

"But I thought you *were* being all aggressive and trying to get James," Melissa says, wondering just who this James guy is, and what he looks like—who would be special enough to grab hold of Harley, who didn't seem to grab hold of much.

Harley buttons her jeans, punctuating her actions with her words. "I *will* get James. I *will* succeed in that realm. And I'm prepared that it might take a while. So . . . as fuel on the romantic fire or whatever, I've given myself permission to have some fun along the way."

"Fun meaning hooking up with other people," Melissa says. She thinks back to the laundry yesterday, with JMB, and the bad lines they'd traded and how exciting it was, how despite everything, and her inner battles, she wished he'd kissed her. Maybe he would have, if bad news in the form of Gabe Schroeder had not interrupted their good time. She still hasn't gone to collect her laundry—too freaked about whom she might see there. What if Harley tried one on him? The thought makes her nauseated.

"Anyway . . . if you wanted to know what happed to me last night . . . ," Melissa starts, not really wanting to revisit the post-laundry incident hours. She'd slumped away from the basement after Gabe and JMB's comment about Charlie, figuring Charlie was the best and worst kind of beautiful—hot but in that long-term commitment way—not slutty, which meant that JMB was probably already in love with her. "Let's just say I had a renewed faith in my suspicion that guys suck. Then I dealt with the sweet treat competition."

"And I heard we won!" Harley raises her hand for a high five.

"We?" Melissa makes a face. "Not that I want to get into a whole debate over territories here, Harley, but *we* didn't win. *My* brownie swirls won. The ones made with ingredients I shopped for, with my arms that got sore stirring the batter. I made them while you were out on the slopes for the fifteenth time. I even burned my wrist." She shows her red mark as proof. Harley stares at Melissa, first with her hands on her hips, about to protest, then just taking it in. Melissa goes on, feeling glad about defending herself. "I mean, do you realize it's been almost a week and

I haven't even been out there once." She gestures *out there* to the mountains.

"I didn't realize. . . ."

"No, of course you didn't realize," Dove interjects from the doorway. The dark circles under her eyes are in sharp contrast to the rest of her creamy complexion, highlighting her long hours, her fatigue. "You're too busy having a grand old time playing matchmaker for Diggs and Luke and ignoring the rest of your job description."

"Hey—those boys asked me to and I'm their host."

"But that's left me to deal with the countess and earl—on top of my cleaning. Not to mention their other son . . ." Dove bites her lip as she says his name. "Maxwell . . . who . . ."

"Just what is the deal with Max, anyway?" Harley asks.

Dove looks at her and suddenly gets a jolt of jealousy. What if Harley had a hot-tub evening with Maxwell? Not that he's mine, but still. And if I feel that way, what does it mean? "So you're aware, Maxwell is a deep . . . he's just quiet. And probably best left alone." She sighs and looks at Melissa. "And Melissa's done an incredible job on the fly—just learning all this as she goes. And . . ."

"And Dove has, too," Melissa says. "You think it's easy slopping around other people's mess? Dove reeks of bleach, she's picking up . . ."

Harley butts in, "So you guys think I'm slacking? Fine. Then I'll show you . . ."

Dove overlaps, her voice rising with emotion. "With every wet towel I pick up from the floor, with every disgusting pubic hair I wipe away from the toilet, all I can think is I'm one step closer to William."

"With money you borrowed from me," Harley says, forgetting her intent to stay calm. Why should she? After all, she worked hard for that money. Hours of pancake makeup, bright lights, Vaseline on her teeth to keep her lips from sticking, and a hundred other tricks of the trade. Now Dove, tiny, pretty Dove, who somehow seems so entitled, has to complain about her job.

Dove stands in front of her, arms crossed defensively across her chest. Leave it to Harley to throw that back in her face. "Oh, so that's supposed to cushion the blow? That's why I didn't want to be indebted to you. I never used your money—it's back in your drawer." Dove is about to drop it when Harley makes a face and rolls her eyes. "What's that supposed to mean, Harley?"

Harley shrugs. "Nothing . . . only, I don't get why you can't just make it happen. I mean, when I want something, I just do it. If your guy—Will—is so great"—she pauses and sighs as if to prove William isn't worth the hassle—"then why wouldn't you just take my money?"

Dove looks in awe, wishing she'd never mentioned William or any of it. "It's a true judge of class, isn't it, that you need to bring it up so much? Only those without any need to mention their heroics."

Harley looks like she might slap Dove, opening her mouth and clenching her fist until Melissa steps in between them.

"But you did get the ticket, right?" Melissa asks. She pats Dove on the back and shoots Harley a look to say *cool it*. "Let's just take it easy here." The tension stays elevated but Harley backs off.

Melissa undoes her soiled maroon apron and eyes herself in the mirror. She looks the part, anyway: flour streaks, honey in her hair, chocolate on her forearm.

"I did. So thanks. And I will pay you back," Dove says. She sees Max in his black jacket exit the front door and make his way down the path with a strawberry blonde. She fights the urge to check who it is.

Harley sighs and smiles, putting the financial fiasco behind her. *If Dove wants to shoot herself in the foot, so be it. It's just a reminder that we're all in it for ourselves.* "Well, at least I have bragging rights. Last night I got kissed by a Norwegian prince—me a girl from a trailer park who wore bright pink taffeta and tried to win Miss Junior Mountain USA."

"I thought you said he was from Denmark."

"Whatever. The point is—a prince kissed me. A prince that Celia Sinclair had all but labeled for herself." Harley smiles at her reflection. "I'm not trying to sound conceited—really. It's just . . . I was this pageantry girl in high school." Harley ties her hiking boots without looking up, and admits, "I cleaned these crappy motels for spending money, okay? I was Dove—but worse. Roadside, run-down motels. Like you wouldn't even have stayed there. Ever."

Melissa looks at Harley, feeling bad for her past, but wondering how it all fits together. "Why?"

Harley shakes her head, looking just a little wounded. "My mother made me. She was the one who forced these competitions—like she needed to win. I was going to fix everything wrong with her trailer world."

"And did it work?"

Harley shakes her head and licks her lips, her eyes a million miles away. "Between lugging giant bottles of tequila, which is technically illegal by the way since I'm underage, at my mother's dive restaurant and cleaning up after truckers, the last thing I felt like doing was getting sewn into a tight scratchy dress and smiling for the judges. But I did it." She looks away, out the window to the blank sky. No snow is falling, but the air is bitter cold. The bell in the town center that doubles as a weather advisory gives three solid clangs. "Maybe it was the old saying—like if you do what your parents want, they'll love you more. . . ."

"Well, that doesn't work," Dove says, interjecting from the doorway. "But maybe I'm not the best judge."

"So . . . ," Harley puffs out loudly, breathing away the pessimism. "So basically, I took off with all the money I'd earned—money my mother was keeping from me and spending every chance she got, just so you know, and came here. Following my bliss or whatever."

"Bliss in the form of James?" Melissa asks.

Harley grins from one side of her mouth. "That—and the slopes. I'm a good skier. Not the best, but decent enough to do more than just keep up. Ski team was my only break from cleaning, shows, and waitressing."

"With all that on your resume, you should have more sympathy for me," Dove says to her, her face open, waiting for a nice response.

"No, see, you've got that wrong. I don't know where you come from. . . ." She eyes Dove's face, her long shiny hair, her placid demeanor, and squints as though something's not quite right. "Sure you clean shit up now, but where were you last year? I bet you used to be the one leaving mascara wands on the kitchen counter—you know, so the black gets into the tile grout and it takes forever to clean?"

Dove blushes, remembering doing exactly that at the time she met William. It seemed easy then—staying at a hotel or resort, affording the luxury of dropping towels and coming home to find a well-made bed. "But I'm doing it now."

"Well, that's true. Credit for learning." Harley looks outside and puts her hand to the glass. "Freezing. Not good for conditions . . ."

"Your guests are restless upstairs," Dove says. "Just as an aside."

Harley sighs. "Really?"

Dove nods. "This is the moment for good face time. If you want tips, you better go amuse them. And not just Diggs and Luke, though I'm sure they're still asleep after that not so quiet session last night."

"Yep—I got them a couple of California girls. . . ." Harley smiles. "They were cute together, actually. What if I wind up being a matchmaker?"

"More like hookup facilitator," Melissa laughs.

Harley looks at her. "Are you done for right now? In between meals?"

Melissa nods. "Finally. I've been on my feet for seven hours straight."

"Well," Harley says, untying her boots and grabbing her clipboard that comes complete with game suggestions. "How about you go in my place. I'm sure James wouldn't mind. In fact, maybe it'll look good. You know, play up my hard-to-get factor."

"So I'm your stand-in?" Melissa says.

"If you want to see it that way," Harley says. "You just mentioned that you haven't skied yet."

"The conditions are poor," Dove warns. "Three bells—that means take care. Precaution. Four bells means serious advisory."

"And five?" Harley asks.

"Major storm," Melissa says. "But I think I will ski—it'll give me a break. Plus, I'll get to check out your special one and only James!"

"I think I'll tag along," Dove says, anxious to vacate after her fight with Harley. "I need to replenish my rose water supply, anyway. I dot the bed pillows with it at turndown."

"No wonder everyone's been raving about you," Harley says, trying to smooth things over. "I'm off to entertain the masses."

"Yeah," Melissa says to Dove as they get ready to leave. "You're sure to rake in the money this week."

"I hope so," Dove says. "I need to pay Harley back for the ticket. Maybe I'll get a nice envelope," she says, referring to the red envelopes guests are given the option of leaving as they check out.

"Matron said tips can't be split." Melissa twirls her hair so it stays put behind her ears. "Is that true?"

Dove nods, thinking. "It is. And some people try to get around it by pitching in and saying they'll pool all the tips, but you can get well and truly screwed. . . ."

"Hey, that just might be the first time I've heard you use improper language," Melissa says, imitating Dove's uppercrust voice.

"Well, people give tips however they want to—and you never know the way it'll work out. I remember my parents . . ."

Melissa's mouth falls open with her realization. "You came here, didn't you?"

Dove looks at the floor and then at Melissa. "I thought I'd said as much."

"Implied, maybe, but . . ."

They exit the bunkroom, heading out the squeaky back door, leaving the mess of their room, and Harley's voice encouraging a game of charades upstairs. Outside, the frigid temps make Melissa's eyes water.

"We were part of the *toujours*—the always crowd. The people who come back year after year."

"Oh my god, that must be so weird, then," Melissa says. Her feet crunch over the hardening snow.

"What, you mean do I find it awkward picking up trash where once I dropped it?" Dove laughs. "At first—okay, maybe I still do. But when I met William, I kind of got to be friends with his crowd—the summer season people. He taught sailing on the lake and I met him . . ."

"And the rest is plane ticket history?" Melissa says. Then she calculates something. "Haven't you been apart longer than you were together?"

Dove's smile turns into a tight twist. "I'd rather not think of it like that. He's got to do his job; I made a promise to myself that I'd function and on my own—and then be with him."

"And what happens after the infamous meeting on the tropical island?" Melissa and Dove stop in front of the Main House. Melissa has to borrow skis from the equipment shed out back—unclaimed items went there at the end of the season, or damaged goods no one wanted, or castoffs from the rental shop when they turned over inventory.

Dove's eyes are wide; her face glows in the cold. "You know what? I have no idea." She pauses and sucks in, then coughs. "It's so freezing out here I can hardly breathe. Are you sure you want to ski?"

"It might be the only shot I get. . . ."

"You mean the only shot with those boys Harley's all chummy with." Dove smirks. "But as for your last question . . . I think I've spent my whole life living on this planned-out route—from nursery to primary school to Fairfax." Dove pauses, remembering the uniform at Fairfax, how once in the autumn-crisp wind Max had draped his school blazer over her shoulders. She'd loved feeling blanketed by that coat, by him. She wonders if William would lend her a jacket—of course he would. Only, the days had been warm enough when they were together that she'd never had to ask. "Anyway, now I'm free. I have no plans whatsoever beyond this week, holiday week, and then the islands. With William."

"What about college?" Melissa asks, mainly curious because she's confused about what to do next also. *I could travel, stay on here for the summer, go to cooking school? Now, there's a thought. Maybe if I had a plan beyond these next few months . . .*

"I deferred a year," Dove says. "Oxford gave me a one-year grace, and then if I don't accept by next September, I lose my place."

"Oxford? Wow—that's pretty . . . well, you know the reputation." Melissa unzips her side pocket and takes out her staff ID. "Could I look more shocked in this photo? They took it right as I was stepping onto the coach to get here." Dove nods. Melissa looks over to the Main House doors, which now all but shout "holidays"—with their swags of green and red holly, and small blinking white lights. "Hey—there's Max."

Dove is about to ask how Melissa knows Max, as if she alone has him. Then she realizes they could have spoken in the kitchen or outside at the resort while Dove's been locked in the loos cleaning and sweeping. "I feel like Cinderella, frankly," Dove admits. She stares at Max as he outfits himself by the ski racks.

"You look like her, too," Melissa says, tugging on Dove's long silvery locks. "I mean, this is total princess hair."

Dove tucks it under her ski cap. "I don't feel like a princess, I'll tell you that much."

"So come skiing—maybe that'll brighten your day," Melissa says. She scans the area, wondering when Harley's guy friends will show up. "Harley did say to meet them at the equipment shed, right?"

Dove nods. "You go. I'm going to walk and stretch my legs—and enjoy fresh air before I have to retreat to the laundry room to get the next set of towels and sheets."

Melissa perks up. "Laundry room? Oh, Dove—huge favor. Please?" Melissa stammers as she sees some guys walk toward the shed—*I have to meet them if I'm gonna take a run with them. I can't wait to see what kind of guy Harley would follow thousands of miles without knowing him.* "I left a bunch of my clothes there yesterday—and I don't . . ."

"Let me guess—you don't want the hassle of picking them up."

"It's not out of laziness, I assure you," Melissa says. "More like saving face." She pulls a bright red ski cap on over her curls, holds her ID in her hand, and starts to walk away.

"Why? Did something happen?" Dove asks. Max has disappeared from sight, and she's thankful. Not that she minds being around him, but he's a distraction, a link to her old life she doesn't want to complicate her present.

"This guy—never mind, I'll just tell you. I'm assuming your mouth is a vault, right?" Dove nods. "JMB—his name's JMB and I guess I kind of like him. Or, really do. But . . . yesterday it was like my humiliation came back to haunt me. Turns out JMB's friends with that guy from last year—the one who I liked so much and then . . ."

"Oh, that's rough," Dove says. "What're you going to do?"

Melissa claps her hands. The sound is muffled by her gloves and she doesn't see her ID card fall to the ground. Dove is too busy eyeing Celia Sinclair's posse of poseurs and paparazzi. "She's just a movie star. That's all—an actress. Why all the fuss?"

Melissa turns so she can see Celia's latest getup—an all-in-one bright white ski outfit topped by a fur-rimmed hood. "She better hope that's fake fur."

Dove rolls her eyes. "Who's she with?"

Melissa puts her hand over her eyes, shielding them from the bright light. "It's . . ." When she figures it out, her face falls. "It's JMB," she says. "I guess he gets around. First Charlie . . ."

"Who's Charlie?" Dove shakes her head. "I can't keep this straight."

"Charlie's this girl—she seems sweet, actually. A nanny for Celia's brood."

"Oh, lucky her," Dove says, reveling in the sarcasm.

"But when I left the laundry room yesterday—I don't know—it seemed like Gabe Schroeder—blech—I feel dumb just saying his name—was talking about her with JMB."

"And did JMB have anything to contribute?" Dove watches the cameras flash as Celia and JMB wave, walking toward the foot of the mountain.

Melissa starts to hurry. "Look—I have to go if I'm going to do this. I'm not going to have enough time for cooking tonight as it is . . . and yes, from what I overheard, it seems like JMB already had a taste of Charlie's sweetness and maybe now he's going in for some famous fun."

"It could've been a misunderstanding," Dove says.

"Or it could just be my bad patterns of picking guys who are ultimately lame and lascivious."

Dove smiles and sighs. Her back is sore from bending down to make the beds—though she has to admit, it's been nice skipping Max's room. *Just as well, really,* she thinks, *I don't want to see his underwear on the floor or his letters home to girls—his anything.* "Whatever happens, happens," Dove says. "I know that sounds ultrapassive, but it's worked for me so far. Three months ago I was vacationing here, now I'm working here—and so on. You just never know."

"I guess not," Melissa says. "Well, I'm off to try the green run. I figured I'll start intermediately." Dove nods. Melissa walks to the shed, asks for skis and poles, and as she's clicking into the bindings, sees Celia Sinclair kiss JMB on the cheek while Dove walks toward the laundry, figuring she'd better get a move on with her work—it's a good distraction from the muddle in her mind.

15

Check the weather every day—twice.

Melissa can't help but stare at JMB and Celia—he spins her around, laughing, faux-dancing on the snow as the wind picks up around them.

"Bit of a spectacle, aren't they?" Gabe Schroeder sidles up to her.

Melissa tries for calm, knowing she'll never achieve cool. "Fame has that allure, I suppose."

Gabe shrugs. "Been there, done that." He gives a last look at JMB and Celia. JMB starts to make his way to the shed.

Suddenly, Melissa can't hold in her feelings, all the resentment and embarrassment from last season. She remembers seeing him for the first time, how kind he'd been lifting her bags, how they'd hung out and traded stories over frozen lemonade. He'd invited her to watch his race—and when he'd won, he'd waved to her. And then, everything ended when he'd allowed her journal to be announced to everyone—and denied any of it was true. "Why do you do that?"

"Do what?" Gabe looks at her with a serious expression.

Melissa tries to steady herself on her poles so she can get her other ski on. "You know what happened last year—and God knows I've tried to avoid you. But you keep popping up."

"I do not," Gabe says. He reaches out to hold firm her pole.

"You were at that club, the one with no name—"

"You were there?" Gabe asks. He sounds genuinely interested. "Why didn't you say hi?"

"Um, hello? This might come as a shock-surprise, Gabe, but you made my life a living hell last season. I . . ." She doesn't care anymore about feeling stupid, about harboring feelings for him, and realizes it might just feel good to let it out and let it go. "You knew I liked you, okay?" Gabe nods, a blush creeping over his cheeks, highlighted by the paleness of his curls. As he watches her, Melissa recalls the intense way he stares at your mouth, which makes you feel like you're the only one in a ten-mile radius. "And yet you did nothing—no, correction. You did the opposite. You did everything in your power to see that I became a laughing stock. Reading my journal out loud? Into a microphone?"

"It was called Night of Humiliation," Gabe explains. "And if you'd stayed, you'd have learned that . . ."

"I would have learned that it is a huge mistake to ever put anything on paper if you want it kept private."

"No, wait. After you left that night—you missed my act. You didn't hear that I . . ."

"Oh, shut up!" Melissa says to him and feels redeemed. "I'm sick of sneaking around here hoping not to see you this season. I'm tired of feeling dumb for having feelings. So I had them. *Had* being the operative word in the past tense."

Gabe stares at her, his eyes still on her mouth. Then he looks at her directly, their eyes glued until he speaks. "The past, huh? I'm sorry. I—You—I never meant to . . ."

JMB dashes over, out of breath and happy as a puppy. "Hey— did I miss her?"

Gabe shakes his head. "No."

"Miss who?" Melissa asks. She feels strong, powerful, present in the here and now rather than trapped with one foot in the past.

"We're supposed to meet . . . ," JMB starts.

"Oh, wait—me, too," Melissa says. "I have to look for someone named James? James Benton?" Gabe and JMB exchange a look. Melissa shrugs and explains. "My friend Harley sent me to ski with him—I haven't been on a run yet—can you believe it?"

"Uh . . . ," JMB starts. He puts a hand on Melissa's shoulder and she's sucked right back into liking him but being determined not to. Then again, maybe the Charlie thing was just a fling, and the Celia Sinclair thing just a photo-op. Or maybe, like Gabe's reputation, JMB is just a ski slut. "I'm James."

"What?" Melissa feels her toes grow numb in her boots. Her fingers feel chilled, too. Just as she puts the pieces together, small flakes begin to fall. She takes a breath. "Wait. *You're* James? Harley's James?" She doesn't even hear the possessive slip out.

JMB makes a face and wrinkles his brow. Gabe raises his eyebrows. "I'm not *her* James first of all. And yeah—my full name is James Marks-Benton. Thus the JMB."

"Thanks for the grammar lesson," Melissa says. "Now I feel lame all over again." *Really, I feel torn and totally conflicted—I've liked JMB from the start—he was kind of mine, even if he wasn't. But now he's Harley's, which changes everything. Doesn't it?*

"All over again?" James asks. "Why again?"

Melissa looks at Gabe, urging him with a glance to speak up.

She wonders if he'll cover for her or use this opportunity to ridicule her—air out the misfortunes of last season. Gabe shrugs his shoulders, his jacket crinkling. "No reason—we were just talking about the past before you got here. How it . . ."

Melissa interjects. "How it's better kept back there."

James looks at Gabe for further info, but none is offered. In fact, Gabe switches gears. "So—funny coincidence, huh?"

"Harley mentioned she had a cool friend in the chalet." James nods. "So if you're the cook who works with Harley, you probably know her, right?"

Melissa nods. She can see where this is going. Harley will get her man, just as she said. *Only, her man is my man,* Melissa thinks. *Or was. Or wasn't. But still.* "I'm getting to know her," Melissa says. "We haven't been here long. . . ." *And I'm getting reacquainted with having unrequited crushes. But maybe it's like cooking—the more you do it, the better you get at it. After all, those first few days waking up before dawn to set up coffee and scones were hard—and now it's just a fact of life.*

The three of them ski over to the base of the mountain, lining up for the triple chair. "One quick run, okay?" Melissa says. "I have loads to do." She thinks about tonight's meal, and tomorrow's party. *Now that the brownie swirls have been a hit, there's even more pressure on me to create something fun. But what?* Still half in shock she's here, and standing with him without the urge to bolt—or without that urge taking total hold of her—she looks at Gabe. "And not a difficult run. I'm out of practice."

"Got it," Gabe says. "We'll take care of you."

With James out of earshot, Melissa whispers to Gabe, "If you're taking care of me, then I'm in real trouble."

Gabe laughs, his eyes registering a little hurt, but his mouth staying in the moment. "Give me a little credit, okay?"

JMB, Melissa, and Gabe move up in the line every few minutes, but the crowd is thick. JMB fiddles with his binding, Melissa ponders party ideas. *Tacos? Fortune telling and pizza? No—something sweet and simple, with a twist.* JMB looks over his shoulder toward the Main House where Celia Sinclair is putting on a show for some little kids, dramatically smiling and cooing at them. Melissa sees Charlie, the nanny, and waves. Charlie waves back. When she does, Melissa isn't the only one to acknowledge it—JMB waves, too.

"Hey, guys?" JMB says when the line seems to take forever. "Do you mind if I bow out? I have some errands to run and if the weather's going to be blowing in as they say, I need to go—like now."

Gabe shrugs. "You're leaving me in charge of this young thing?" With his hand looped into his poles, Gabe thumbs to Melissa.

"I'm sure you can handle it," JMB says to him. To Melissa he adds, "Keep him out of trouble. Keep him away from the nanny population. In fact, keep him away from any and all females. And let's meet up tonight—hot drinks at The Ledge?"

Melissa nods, wondering how she could keep Gabe from all females when she is one—unless, that is, JMB doesn't consider her part of the risky population. At least JMB mentioned going out. That has to mean something, right? She hasn't been to The Ledge yet—the small cabin in the center of the frozen lake. It served only hot chocolate and homemade sticks of marshmallows. "Can he really get me in there?" Melissa asks Gabe once they're next in line for the lift.

"To The Ledge?" Gabe asks. He takes his poles off his wrist and holds them in one hand. "It's invite only, but trust me—with a background like James has, he's golden."

"Cool." Melissa smiles. The chair comes around and she doesn't have time to move to the edge seat, so when she sits on the triplechair, she and Gabe are right next to each other.

"But just so you know . . ." Gabe swallows as the chair lift hoists them into the air. Melissa feels her stomach flip. From the height, she assures herself, not from being with Gabe—the Gabe who enticed her all last year, who trashed her feelings, whom she hadn't seen since. Gabe and James whom Harley had been hanging out with on the side. *All those times Harley'd gone off to watch people ski jump, or meet random people for coffee, she was probably seeing James.*

"What?" Melissa asks, taking in the amazing view. Mountains, peaks covered in snow, and below them skiers swishing down the slope. Everything seems in slow motion, with the falling snow.

"I'm just trying to help you now . . . Not that you want my help and not that you trust me enough to tell you the truth. . . ."

Melissa turns to him, trying to get comfortable on the metal chair. Her breath comes out in puffs. "Look, I'm not some fragile bird. Don't treat me like I'm going to get wounded with everything you say." Melissa can feel her confidence build the more she speaks—just like making soufflés, or dishes people said were too tricky for a novice cook.

"All right." Gabe takes off his hat, keeping his poles firmly stationed across his lap, and scratches his head. "James is friendly. Really kind. But he's also . . ."

Melissa can fill in the blanks. "Let me guess? Slutty? On the make? Into one night pickups?" She frowns. She knew it, but it sucks coming from his best friend.

Gabe grabs her arm. "That's how people used to describe me, you know."

"Used to?"

"As in the past," Gabe says. Melissa feels his hand on her even through the down jacket, thinking how last year she would have given anything to be alone with Gabe, cloistered on a ski lift, with him touching her. She looks at him. He is gorgeous still, and being with him in this context—without liking him—without feeling vulnerable—makes him even more appealing. He sighs before speaking. "Just for the record, James is taken. It's not that he's a ski slut—far from it. I'm only recently revising my ways—but James . . . he's . . . He just happens to have found someone he likes already."

This news hits Melissa hard. Hooking up, having James be the prototypical guy on the move, chasing after anything in tight pants—that's fine. But having him like someone? Really be into her? No wonder they were talking about Charlie yesterday. She's the perfect girlfriend, probably—all beautiful and sunny, with kindness that's apparent with her nannying job. *And that's how JMB met Celia Sinclair, too,* Melissa thinks. Her chest feels empty now and all she can muster is one word. "Oh."

The chairlift sways in the wind, causing Gabe to grip Melissa's arm tighter. "You okay?"

"From the wind or the news?" She looks at him, wondering if they could turn out to be friends. Wouldn't that be something to write home about. Not that she was committing anything to paper anymore except recipes.

"Both." Gabe looks in back, at the chairlift behind and then around. "The weather's picking up."

"I don't need to know who James likes—I'm not . . ."

"You don't know her, anyway. I don't think. It's a foreign name. Unusual." Gabe shrugs. "The guy's private—to an extreme. He won't even let me meet her."

Melissa laughs, glad that maybe she and Gabe will be friendly after all. She thinks for a second how cool it was of him not to spill the past to James, when he could have so easily. "Maybe James is afraid if you meet her—this amazing woman he likes—that you'll sweep her off her feet."

Gabe cracks up, keeping hold of the chairlift and his poles. "Yeah, that's right. Watch out, Mr. Benton-Marks—Gabe Schroeder's in town, lookin' for the ladies."

"I forgot . . . ," Melissa laughs and then stops herself.

"You forgot what?"

"Nothing." Melissa studies her jacket zipper, then looks down at the mountain. "God, we're really far up." She swallows. "I just forgot how funny you are, that's all." She remembers that last year she was taken in by Gabe's looks, but now he cracks her up—cracks everyone up—without that annoying habit some guys have of being a clown or having everything be about them. "You're just naturally humorous."

"Well, thanks for appreciating me, I guess," Gabe says. He sees a cloud of snow swirl around them and hunkers back into the chair.

Melissa nods. The wind whips against her cheeks, stinging her skin. "Are you sure we're okay up here? We're not going to be buried under twelve feet of snow?"

The lift creaks, moving them closer to the top of the mountain. "I don't know. They had only three rings of the bell, which isn't a true danger, so that means we're . . ."

As he says this, the weather warning bell sounds again. One. Two. "Three," Melissa says aloud, the worry building inside her.

"Four," Gabe says. "Shit—it was warm yesterday, too."

"Meaning?" Melissa gets nervous.

"Meaning—nothing. Let's just avoid avalanches, accidents—that sort of thing. Sometimes big changes in temps can signal storms, or if too much melts, it makes the packed snow unsteady." Melissa responds to this with just a worried look. He smiles and pats her back, then lifts the bar as they approach the mound. "Here we go."

Melissa follows Gabe, squinting through the snow that's now falling fast, sweeping through the area with a fierce wind.

A ski trooper stops them. "You two going down or heading to the Cliff House?"

"What do you mean?" Melissa asks. "We're just doing one quick run, that's all."

The trooper shakes his head, the fluorescent ski cap highly visible even through the snow. "Nothing's quick in weather like this. You better hurry down or bunk in." He nods to the Cliff House.

Gabe looks at Melissa. "Up to you," he says.

Melissa's voice is high-pitched with concern. "I have to cook for everyone—dinner's due and I haven't . . ."

The trooper steps up. "Look, Miss, we're preparing for a serious storm here. The food'll have to wait. Go down immediately, or stay and weather it out up here."

Melissa looks at Gabe. "I'm an intermediate skier."

"You'll be okay," he says, looking at her tenderly. Then he looks at the trail, the heavy sheath of snow.

"I haven't skied in a year," she says. Then, to push the point, she adds, "Just in case you've forgotten—the last time I skied was . . . I skied that day—the day . . ."

"The day I ruined everything," Gabe says and skis a few yards away.

Melissa straps her poles on to follow, but the trooper stops her. "You sure you know what you're doing?" She shrugs and makes a face. "It's only starting now—the run's a full twenty minutes—

in good weather. By the time you reach midsection, visibility will be almost nil."

Panic jolts though Melissa's body, and she skis fast over to Gabe. "Gabe! Wait!" He turns to her. "We should stay. I can't . . . I don't think I'm going . . ."

He sidesteps over to her. "It's okay. It's okay, Melissa." He stares at her, with the same eyes that captivated her last season; the same mouth that she wished wanted hers. "People will cover for you down there. You're right—we should stay."

She wonders if this is a hardship for him, if he hates the thought of having to spend more time with the girl who liked him before. Or if maybe he's immune to all that now. Melissa looks through the wild wind and snow to the Ledge House. She wouldn't be able to cook dinner, to make dessert—the chocolate mousse pooling in the fridge—and she wouldn't be able to meet James at the ice pond. *Not that he's interested in me,* Melissa thinks. *With my normal name and unforeign self. But still.*

"Should we go?" Gabe asks. He points to the Cliff House, a log cabin structure that served as the first ski lodge when Les Trois opened decades ago. "We better get in there and claim some space—if it crowds up, at least we'll have a bed."

Melissa blushes, despite the cold and her nerves. "A bed?"

"Didn't I say I've changed my ways? What—you think I'm on the make up here? In a storm? Give me a slice of credit cake, won't you?" Gabe shakes his head and yells through the whistling wind. "A place to sleep, I mean." He chuckles to himself and asks her again, "What're you thinking? That I'd try to make the most of a snowstorm?"

"NO. NO—I swear, I wasn't thinking that. . . ." Melissa manages a smile even though the worry of the storm and its fallout has her tense. "Well, maybe I was a little. Maybe it's not such a stretch to envision you having a romantic interlude with some storm-trapped vixen."

"I'm not into vixen," Gabe says. "At least, you don't have to worry about me running off with anyone tonight."

"Oh, well, now I'm relieved," Melissa says, enjoying the banter. "Hey! You just gave me an idea."

"Oh, yeah?"

"You said slice of credit. . . ." Melissa thinks, the wind howling past them. "It sparked something." She pictures baking, wishing she could be the official host of the party, but knows she'll have at least the joy of making the food and setting the tone. "I think I know what I'm going to do for my theme party."

"Do tell."

"I'll tell you inside—when we're sure we're safe. And when I've thought about it more."

Gabe gives Melissa one of his signature grins that shines through her cold exterior. *Make the most of the snowstorm,* she repeats in her mind. *Would Gabe want to . . . ?* She shakes the thought away. *Burn me once, shame on me . . . burn me twice . . . well, I guess we'll have to see,* she thinks, and they ski toward the Cliff House, their shelter, their safe haven for the night.

16

When you chop enough onions,
crying is inevitable.

Dove slings the roast into the stove and finishes the red currant sauce with a touch of lemon juice, letting the mixture bubble up and heat in a copper pot. In the dining room, Harley regales the earl and countess and their clan with stories of her trailer-park upbringing. Clearly, the upper echelons of society are enchanted or at least amused by her vastly different background. Dove can hear their laughter and energetic conversation, which is a good distraction to the undercurrent of worry about Melissa. Matron reported that Melissa, along with a group of other skiers whose names she didn't mention, are hunkered down at the Cliff House for the night. With the storm raging outside, The Tops is cozy, though Harley and Dove keep checking to see if there's any further word.

She'll be back by morning, Dove reminds herself. *And I'll just tell her we covered for her—hopefully everything will be okay.* Dove hears Max's deep laugh from the next room and wonders what Harley said that was clever enough to register with him.

"It's funny," Harley says to Dove when she dashes into the small, hot kitchen, "but they like hearing me talk about my real past. Not some made-up version—but the way things really were for me."

Dove nods as she stirs the sauce. "This is almost done. Think you can hold them off for three more minutes?"

"Sure." Harley dips a finger into the roiling red sauce and winces with the sting of a burn. "Tasty, though."

Dove shakes her head. "I told you not to touch my food while I cook—it's a pet peeve." She turns the gas off and arranges all the appetizer plates, then begins to ladle sauce onto each one. "You do a great job hosting, Harley. Really." She looks at Harley, who now even dresses the part—black slim turtleneck, hair pulled back to the nape of her neck, and a long pencil-cut charcoal wool skirt she bought in town.

"It's like—there's a part of me that wanted so badly to leave Colorado and pageants and working on the Martingale Ranch and serving high-hat tequila. . . ."

"You worked on a ranch?" Dove asks. "That sounds so cool."

Harley shakes her head and grins. "It was, but probably it sounds more exciting to you because you're . . ."

"I'm what, exactly?" Dove can't let Harley finish, impatient to put the final touches on the dinner. She pours the sauce so that each plate has a thin perfect circle in its center while wondering what breakthrough observation Harley's about to blurt out.

"You're a princess," Harley says and uses kitchen tongs to pluck at Dove's white blond hair, which is twisted into a bun. "And you have the hair to prove it."

Dove laughs a little, knowing Harley's only joking—or at least partly. "You know what, though?" Dove looks around, taking in the kitchen's scents and calm order. "I think if they could see me right now, my parents would be proud of me." Dove's eyes well up just a bit, though she doesn't allow any actual tears to stumble down her cheeks.

"Harley!" the earl shouts from the dining room. "Come back—we're in desperate need of your cheer!"

Harley puts the tongs down and watches as Dove begins to fry wedges of breaded Camembert cheese to go along with the sauce. "You're good at this," Harley says. "Why shouldn't they be proud? Not that I'm one to talk. There's nothing you can do to please my mother—except win Miss Rocky Mountain Teen or whatever. And probably that wouldn't be good enough. . . ." Harley looks down, wondering if her present is still in danger of being trod upon by her past.

"I *am* good at this," Dove says. "Cooking. Cleaning . . . well, maybe a passing grade. But it's not Oxford. It's not the same as university."

"Not everyone goes to college," Harley says, pausing before going back to her hosting duties. "Whether it's here or some other far-flung locale—or even back to the Martingale Ranch—or not. It's kind of beers, boys, and saddles."

Dove raises her eyebrows. "Not all bad . . ."

"Oh, so there's a wild side to you, Miss Dove?" Harley clucks at her.

"More than you know," Dove says. "Or maybe more than *I* know. Anyway, these need tending or they'll burn."

"I'll help you serve—just call me in." They stare at one another, both thinking the same thing. Without Melissa to act as their intermediary, they have to be civil. "She'll be okay."

"You sure?" Dove wrinkles her nose. "I just keep thinking of her freezing up there, and . . ."

"We'll take care of everything here, that way all she has to do is make it through the night without getting frostbite—"

Dove gasps. "Oh, I didn't even think about that. She'd want us to do the dinner really well." She puts triangles of cheese into the oil where it begins to get crispy on the edges. "Here—this one's done. Each person gets two wedges—wait till I finish another plate, then you can serve two at a time."

"Okay." Harley stands there, impressed with Dove's efficiency. "Melissa would want the dinner to go off without a hitch—which it seems we'll pull off. . . ." She pauses. "And I think she'd also like it if we didn't sit up all night worrying about her."

Dove nods, but doesn't comment on that last part. "Serve the countess first, of course." Harley nods. "If I'm telling you things you already know, just ignore me." Harley nods again. "And I set the table with the sterling cheese forks—they look odd, with a flat edge. But that's what's best for melting cheese. If the cheese were firm, you would use the—"

"Wow—you know your shit," Harley says. She takes the second plate and begins to transfer them from the kitchen to the dining room where they are met with *ooohs* and *ahhhs*.

"I take it they like what they see?" Dove asks when Harley bounds back into the kitchen.

"I said they're fried cheese," Harley says.

Dove's smile fades, her shoulders slump. "No—who the hell wants fried cheese as a starter at a fancy dinner party?" Dove finishes arranging the wedges so that each plate is identical and helps Harley serve the final four.

"These are hand-rolled Camembert done in a panko crumb served with a red currant citrus puree." Dove holds her two plates out, going to Diggs and Luke to serve them, but Harley gets there first, leaving Dove to hand one to some random friend of Luke's and the last to Max.

She places the plate directly in front of him, turning the cheese so the points face away, proper etiquette. Max turns it back to face him. She turns it away and then he turns it back until she lets out a small but audible humph. Under the table she flicks his arm and then smiles at everyone else. "Enjoy!"

Back in the kitchen, she turns the roast, readies the plates and vegetables, checks on the chocolate mousse Melissa had started to prepare, and wonders what the real cook is up to, if she'll be happy the dinner's going well, or feel as though Dove's stepped over the line, trying to be a better chef. *I just hope she's okay,* she thinks, setting all the dirty utensils and pans into the right side of the sink, which she's filled with hot soapy water. The bubbles come up to her elbows and for a second, she drifts away, imagining floating in the water—warm waters—with William. She eyes the clock. He's due to call in two hours—they've never missed a day since being apart—well, except that once when he was in transit from here to the island of Nevis in the West Indies, where the boat is docked. Last night he told her he had an important announcement—a special conversation to have—and Dove can tick down the minutes now until she hears from him. *Starters, main course, sorbet, dessert, coffee, and my phone call.*

Then quickly Max is beside her, his arm plunged into the warm water next to hers, their skin touching underneath the froth. Dove's instinct is to pull away, but something holds her there until Max speaks. "Thought I'd help by clearing."

"Don't bother," Dove says. Then she knows she sounds rude. "I mean, thanks for the help, but I've got it all under control."

She looks up at Max. He looks down at her, his body still close to hers. "Do you?"

Dove stands there in the wake of Max's intensity, her insides swirling. She washes the bubbles from her skin and turns her attention back to the roast, taking it out of the oven to rest before slicing it so that the meat will stay juicy.

"Hey." Harley clears the plates and checks on Dove's timing. She notes Max's proximity to Dove and wedges herself in between them, feeling territorial about her fellow chalet girl and her guests. "I have a story that should take about five minutes—think me, a greased hog, and my high school drama teacher chasing it with a broom."

Dove smiles, gritting her teeth as she tries to ignore Harley's hip pressing into Max. "You're an original, Harley."

"She is," Max says, his eyes boring into Dove's. He wipes his hands on a towel and then leaves.

"Thanks—listen. . . ." Harley watches Max exit and puts the plates into the soapy water and then on her way out, tugs at Dove's hair again. "Two thoughts."

"Tell me," Dove says, glazing the baby carrots with a port-wine reduction sauce. "I'm all ears. They're the one part of my body that's not overheated from the oven, sore, or busy."

Harley laughs. "One—you come out with me tonight. Not now—but later—"

"I'm not into the hot-tub scene."

"Not the tubs—the tanks—the outdoor water tanks near the Fauxcean."

"The Fauxcean—I haven't been there in a while." All the way on the other side of the resort, the Fauxcean was a once-warehouse that had been converted into an indoor ocean complete with phosphorescent waves, fish, and nighttime snorkeling—its tag line, "fake, but good."

"The party's there and out back."

"No, thanks," Dove says. "I have an important phone call." She smiles, so Harley knows it's William.

"All right, all right. But—should you change your mind . . ."

"What was the other thing?" Dove asks, slicing into a large caramelized onion.

"Oh," Harley says over her shoulder on the way to the dining room. "If you ever want to really lose the princess image? Let me do your hair."

Dove keeps working on the food, staring at the roast from behind the wisps of white-blonde fringe that have come loose from the knot at the back of her head. Max had said he loved her hair—that one time when they'd danced at his eighteenth. *I should chop it for that reason alone,* Dove thinks, then recoils from the suggestion. *No—what he thinks doesn't matter. It's what I like, how I feel.* William never mentioned her hair—he said he wouldn't care if she shaved her head or never cut her hair again—he liked her for everything else. Dove smiles to herself, then eyes the clock once more before cutting into the roast.

The meal over, the dishes set to dry on the racks, the lights in the kitchen switched off, Harley puts a quick line of brown-red lipstick on and turns to Dove.

"You sure you're not coming?"

Dove nods. "I don't feel right about it. Aren't you worried about her? What if she's trapped on the chairlift . . ."

"Or being eaten by wolves?" Harley shakes her head. "Where I come from—ski country, that is—shit like this just happens. You know—people go off-piste or they do something stupid. . . ." Harley sighs, her edginess rising to the surface. "I mean, Matron gave the radio report. There's a group in the Cliff

House—we have to assume she's in there. Unless she did something stupid."

"Don't attack her when she's not here to deflect you." Dove grimaces, wishing she could somehow be reassured that Melissa was okay. "Melissa didn't do anything stupid," Dove defends. She checks her watch. Ten minutes. She has to get Harley out of here so she'll have some privacy.

Harley considers pushing the issue, telling Dove that it's always dumb to ignore weather patterns, but then wonders if maybe her annoyance is coming from somewhere else. *Maybe I wish I were stuck away from here, or with a certain someone.* She sighs, retreating. "No, you're right. She wasn't acting crazy. She just got stuck in a storm." Harley looks outside as though the answer might be right on the frosted window ledge.

Dove sees Harley's face and thinks that it does have a small bit of tension collecting in the brow. *Maybe she is human after all, not some leggy robot who can switch off emotions at the drop of a glove.* "So you're staying positive."

"Sure. Besides, we've got to keep moving here. Do our jobs, keep up the life of the party. . . ." Harley grins. She snags her leather jacket from her top bunk, and before slipping into it, checks her bikini straps are secure under her shirt. "All set for the tropics," she says. Then, on her way out, she adds, "You gotta stay positive until given reason to believe otherwise. . . . She'll be okay."

Dove nods, watching Harley leave. She goes to the mirror and stands with her arms down, her hair fully descending the length of her back. Even in the bunkroom's dim light it looks silvery, the way it had always looked in the summer at her parents' estate. "You look like a princess," Dove says to herself, imitating Harley. "Princess hair." *It's rather a fitting image,* Dove thinks, looking at her phone and waiting for the inevitable ring. *Princesses who have no real job, no real say about what they do, no real power nor control—sounds like my life. Well, my life before.*

The minutes tick by, with each moment accentuated by the gusting wind, the silence in the room. When William is ten minutes late, Dove decides to be proactive and call him. *After all, there's no set rules about it, right? I called yesterday; today's his day, but I can try again.* She dials, waits, and the line rings over and over again, then slips into his message. She doesn't talk. Then she waits, thinking William is probably below deck and doesn't hear the phone, and will call her back. Another five minutes. *This is ridiculous,* Dove says, glaring at her own reflection, annoyed with everything, with herself for waiting, with her hair for casting an image she revolts against. She calls again, waiting for his voice, but doesn't get to hear it—just his voice mail. "Hey—this is William's phone." His short outgoing message always gave her a happy feeling, but this time it makes her scowl. *We always talk. Every day. And it's your turn,* she thinks as she looks into the phone. But she doesn't say that. Instead, Dove speaks eloquently, calmly. "It's me—hope you're okay. Call." Not like an order, but a reminder.

She places the phone down on the bureau, still hoping it will ring, or that the reason he missed the phone call is because the lines are down, though the one time that happened, he left word via ship-to-shore wire that was then printed and sent to the Main House. Before losing it completely and overreacting, Dove pulls her boots on, stuffs herself into a puffy jacket, and stomps off to check the bulletin board there.

By the time Harley arrives at the Fauxcean, the electronic wave is cranked up to full power, causing a massive drenching on the sandy shore every eight minutes. Outside, the hordes of paparazzi lurk in the cold, waiting for a shot of Celia Sinclair and whichever boy-candy she has draped on her arm. Harley walks past them, smiling and playing to the cameras with her best model pose, hoping they'll mistake her for a celebrity.

"Over here!" yells one photographer. Harley turns.

"Nice!" another one shouts.

Harley remembers reading that you're always supposed to leave them wanting more, so she hurries inside, overhearing questions about who she might be from the other photographers and loving every minute of the attention.

Inside, swimsuit-clad guests, ski guides, nannies, and random staff boogie board on the waves, lie on towels on the fake beach, or try their hand at snorkeling in the underwater dark. Stretched out on a chaise longue, Celia Sinclair eyes the door for any of her fellow starlets and sips her tall tropical drink.

"This rocks," Harley says, squeezing past a clump of biki-nied girls. She waves to Celia in a moment of solidarity, but Celia quickly dispels any notion that they're connected.

Celia rolls her eyes at Harley and then turns on her side, bla-tantly ignoring her.

Harley makes a face back, but then shakes her head. *You think I care if you notice me? I've got bigger fish to fry than third-rate movie stars who pick up boys like fast food.* And with that, Harley sheds her outer clothing, revealing her multicolored swimsuit. She smirks at it, remembering when she had to wear it at the last pageant—how she bolted right afterward and never looked back. Taking in the wealth and wonder around her, she smiles. *How amazing it is to go from one life to another,* she thinks. Then she spies the reason for being here.

"James!" She waves to him but he can't hear her over the ocean noise, steel drum music, and loud conversations. He's playing volleyball on the sport-side of the Fauxcean, and she walks to him, ignoring the looks from other guys.

James gets ready to serve, holding the ball in his right palm, his right hand in spike position. He throws the ball up and is about to hit it when Harley speaks. "Hey there, sailor. You didn't go skiing after all." She wonders why James would have skipped out on the run with Melissa and Gabe.

James gets ready to spike. "Had to take care of something." He doesn't say what.

Harley fiddles with the bikini straps, calling attention to herself. She looks incredible in the suit—and hopes it'll sway James's eyes to her. James doesn't lose focus on the ball for a second, though—and manages to score a point.

"You're not easily distracted, are you?" Harley asks, impressed. She slurps rum and coke from a tall plastic cup. Drink trays are scattered every few feet or so, color-coded by cups—red for raspberry shockers, blue for blue whales, clear for rum and coke.

James swigs from her cup, sweat beading his upper lip. "Old trick from the coach. He always says you have to be prepared for any and all distractions—weather, crowds, people shouting things from the stands—and you have to just ignore it."

"Girls in bikinis?" Harley says, her tone low and suggestive.

"That, too."

Harley sits on a long beach chair and pats the end of it, hoping James will sit there. She wonders if he's had anything to drink, as most of the people in the club seem to have. He sits next to her. "So, now you're pretty good at fending off anything that comes your way?" Harley leans forward, flirting shamelessly. She finishes her drink, feeling the warm buzz of alcohol race through her.

James tries not to look at her bikini top, but his eyes falter on

Harley's body, and she stretches out on the chair, resting her legs on his lap. "I'd say I'm pretty good at resisting whatever comes my way—if it gets in the way of my game."

Harley sits up. *Now's the time,* she thinks. *Enough flirting, enough following him around. Enough having him get to know my friends.* What did he have to take care of today that prevented him from skiing?

"Harley," James says, looking her full-on. "I'm kind of glad to see you, actually."

She gets ready, moving in a little closer. Her shoulder rubs his; their thighs touch. In one forward motion she'll be able to kiss him. "Oh, yeah?"

James pauses. "I wanted to say . . ."

Harley puts her finger on his lips, overacting the part of the sultry, bathing suit–clad girl, but liking the ambience. "Wait. See if you can resist this distraction."

She replaces her finger with her mouth, kissing him full on the lips, then moving so she's sitting on his lap. She kisses him hard, holding on to his muscled back, loving the feel of his hands on hers. Then he pulls back. "What was that?"

Harley, still in a trance from finally doing what she wanted for so long—kissing James—the James—that her normally strong voice sounds warbly. "Just the end result of years of . . ." She looks up, notices Celia Sinclair staring at them, and leans in to kiss him again.

Right as their mouths are about to meet again, a voice interrupts. "Do it."

Even Harley's taken by surprise with the command. Still in her position on James's lap, she looks to see who had voiced the idea. She looks over her shoulder and sees Dove, out of place with her puffy jacket on, her face filled with sadness.

"Hey, Dove," Harley says.

James picks Harley up off his lap and slides out from under her. In the fake sunlight, Dove wonders if the red on James' cheeks is due to being hot, or embarrassed. *Poor Melissa,* she thinks. The one guy she hoped for turns out to be with Harley. "Here. Do it."

"Do what?" Harley asks, wondering why James moved away from her, her insides still reeling from the kiss, the way he responded, his mouth.

Dove shoves a pair of silver scissors toward Harley. "Cut it off."

James stands up. "Whoa—not sure what's happening here, but don't think I need to be a part of it."

Harley stands up, nearly as tall as James, both of them dwarfing Dove. "James—don't go. Stay with me. . . ." She wishes it hadn't come out so needy, so honest. That she had more of a cover-up. But when you've liked someone for so long, it's impossible to be anything but candid.

James shakes Dove's hand and pats Melissa on the shoulder. "I have to go. I was supposed to be at the Main House a few minutes ago to check . . ."

Dove interjects. "If you're wondering about your buddy— Gabe's fine. I was just there, checking on something else, and radio word came in with a list of all the people at the Cliff House."

James looks relieved. "Oh, man, that's great."

"So you'll stay?" Harley asks him. She holds the scissors, anxious for his reply.

James slides his feet into worn flip-flops and looks beyond Harley to one of the thatched palapas—the huts where people sit drinking or talking. "No—I came here to distract myself—you know, lame attempt at dealing with the stress of having people

I care about trapped on a mountaintop." He gives a weak laugh. "Pathetic, but . . ."

Harley frowns. "I thought you didn't get distracted."

James faces her. "I don't." He looks at her, hoping she'll get his point, but not voicing it. "Have a good night, okay?"

"Harley." Dove pulls on Harley's arm. Harley refuses to break her stare—watching James walk away. He better leave now, better go home and fall asleep and dream of me. But James walks over to the palapa by the cresting wave, and stays there, talking to a girl whose strawberry blond hair is visible even from a distance. "Who is that?"

Dove looks over. "Charlie. She's a nanny—for Celia Sinclair's group."

Harley glares at Dove, looks around to glare at Celia Sinclair but can't find her. "And how do you know this?"

Dove holds up a hand. "Hey—don't shoot the messenger. . . . I'm just telling you what I know. Maids are always the one cleaning up other people's stuff; thus we know more of their dirt."

Harley sighs, responding to the stress in Dove's face. "So, what's up?"

Dove frowns, the emotion of the evening coming back to her. "I was so worried, right? I mean, first about Melissa, and then . . . the dinner freaked me out—"

"But it went great; they loved it. . . ."

"No, but—it's like—my mom's the one who taught me how to cook. And being in there, doing that job, I just felt like it was right, like I wasn't just reacting to my parents and taking the first job that came along."

"What's this about?" Harley listens but looks again at James, who has a hand on Charlie's shoulder. With her hands crossed over her chest, Harley still feels exposed, too bare in her bikini.

With a shudder, she watches as James and Charlie walk toward the fluorescent exit sign and leave together.

"This is about how much it sucks when people break their promises."

"He didn't call?"

Dove shakes her head. "And maybe you're right—waiting by the phone, being that girl? It's just silly."

Harley nods. "Right. I mean, where's the power in that? You should go for what you want."

"Exactly," Dove agrees and then puts her hands on her hips. "So, now, do it."

"What?"

Dove takes the scissors from Harley's hand and holds them next to her head. "Chop it off."

Harley's eyes widen. "Oh, no, Dove—I didn't mean . . ."

"I've decided. I do have princess hair. And a princess life. More than you can ever know. And even if it's superficial—so be it. At least it's a start."

Harley opens the scissors and then pauses. "Have you been drinking?"

Dove looks at her. "Maybe."

"No, Dove, I don't want to do this—you'll regret it. Don't act out of anger."

"Oh shut up and just get on with it." She takes the scissors back and in one quick motion cuts a long hunk of hair from the side. It falls to the sandy ground in a gentle blond puddle. Dove stares at it.

"Well?" Harley waits for Dove to freak out, to scream and say she made a mistake. But Dove just waits. "Okay . . . here goes."

After the cut blond locks pile on the ground, Dove feels her head. "I'm floating." Her hands hold her small head, feeling the choppy strands.

Harley surveys her work. "I have to say, you look incredible."

Dove shrugs. "Different?"

Harley nods. She touches the front of Dove's hair, making the short bits stand up. "You're like a pixie, but not overly cute, if you can imagine."

Dove smiles. "And no princess?"

"None."

Harley feels a tap on her shoulder and sees James. *Back for more,* she thinks. She looks around but sees no trace of Charlie. "Hey."

"Thanks, Harley," Dove says. She looks at James in his navy blue shirt, his steady presence, his magnetic eyes. She sees why Harley and Melissa like him and hopes they don't get hurt. He appears to be a player.

Harley nods at Dove.

"Want to go for a swim?" James asks them. He takes off his shirt and Dove is sure she hears a gasp from Harley.

"I have to go," Dove says. She can't stop touching her hair. *I feel free. Light. Different.*

"I'd love a dip," Harley says, focusing her attention back on James. "You'll be okay, Dove?"

Dove nods. "Have fun."

James nods to Dove. "It's just a swim, okay?" Then to Harley he adds, "We can talk?"

Harley shrugs, giving him one of her sexy looks. "Whatever floats your boat."

Dove sees them pad off through the sand toward the water, with Harley's arm on James' back. She rakes her fingers through her very short locks and wonders what it looks like, then heads outside to see for herself.

17

Keep plenty of sweets on hand.

After talking for hours about everything from pancakes to parties, childhood misconceptions (she thought every car on the highway was going to the same destination she was . . .), to music, Melissa is all but talked out. She and Gabe are sectioned off from the other overnight Cliff House guests, tucked into a corner near a stack of logs and an old oversized compass. Gabe and Melissa have worked their way through an enormous bag of jelly beans and gummy bears as well as any other candies from the Cliff House's sweets counter. On the other side of the room people sleep or huddle close for warmth. Snow has finally stopped gusting outside. Melissa fiddles with the compass and chews a sour-apple jelly bean.

"Oh, here's another thing . . . I thought the compass was supposed to point to you—like your personal direction or something." She laughs. *I can't believe I'm here, sitting with Gabe Schroeder—a year after the fact—after spending twelve months trying to ditch my feelings, my memories.*

"It's great that you can laugh at yourself," he says. He takes the compass from her and holds it to his chest. "I can see that."

Melissa takes it back, noting how their fingers touch briefly in the exchange. "West, east, who knows where I'll end up." She stares at the compass like it's a crystal ball. "How do you know what direction is the right one?"

Gabe leans back onto the logs. "I don't know." He puts his hands in his jacket pockets. "Maybe it's finding that person. You know, true north? How it's always there ... Maybe that's how you figure out where or what to do."

"Do you have that?" she asks, avoiding his eyes, instead looking at their legs, how they form a set of lines, almost touching.

Gabe lets his eyes flick to hers, then rakes his hands through his hair and clears his throat. "Isn't that what everyone wants? A person ... I can't speak for everyone, I guess...." He doesn't complete the sentence and instead stands up. "I have to stretch. Want to check out what it's like outside?"

Melissa wishes he'd finished his thoughts but stands up, then groans. "Oh, man, my legs are sore. And I didn't even ski!"

"That's what happens if you sit too long—come on, let's take a walk and then come back and get some rest."

Melissa follows Gabe, stepping around people sleeping and the few people still awake, playing cards or eating energy bars from the emergency supply box. "You sure it's safe to go?"

Gabe shrugs. "Guess we'll see."

He opens the heavy door. Outside, Melissa and Gabe crunch on the fallen icy snow, up to their knees in drifts, then up to their waists in other piles. "It's so soft," Melissa says. "To think, right now at home people are at the beach."

171

"The Fauxcean you mean?"

Melissa shakes her head. "No. My real home—in Australia. It's summer."

Gabe laughs. "Sorry, it's hard to remember sometimes that there's a real world outside of this place." He looks up to the sky, then back at Melissa. He reaches into his pocket. "Oh—here's one more. A Belgian chocolate—let's split it." He bites half, then gives the other to Melissa, placing it in her mouth for her. She lets it melt, the sweetness coating her tongue.

"Yum. . . . Anyway, the Fauxcean can't compare to the real thing," Melissa says. *I wonder what's happening there tonight, who's there, if Harley and Dove are swimming, if James is there—and who he's with.*

"I'm sure—it's like indoor skiing compared to this." He points to the mountain.

Melissa breathes deeply, filling her lungs with the cold air. "It's so peaceful now."

"Calm after the storm?" Gabe walks through the snow closer to where she is. "Come here."

He leads her over to the triplechair lift where they'd been caught in the whirlwind before. The empty lift chair sways slightly in the breeze. "Climb up."

"I don't want to go for a ride," Melissa says but starts to climb up the embankment so she can reach the seat.

"It's stopped for the night." Gabe climbs in next to her and puts the bar down.

Melissa smiles. "This is fun, actually, Gabe."

He frowns, joking. "You thought you'd be miserable with me?"

"I don't know—maybe. Considering . . ." She stops, not wanting to ruin the moment with issues. Her hands curl around the metal bar next to Gabe's. They relax back, both tilting up to the sky.

"Check out the stars; aren't they amazing up here?" Gabe says.

"They are," Melissa says, "but that sounds like a line."

Without looking at her, Gabe responds, "You think the worst of me, Melissa. First of all, I'm not the kind of guy who uses a line. Second of all, I'm just pointing out an ecological wonder."

"Oh, well then." Melissa smiles. "That's fine. And yes I agree, the stars are something."

Gabe clears his throat. "So what if it was a line, anyway?"

Melissa stares at the ink-dark sky, the millions of lights, the flickering stars and thinks about her bad line exchange with James. *He's my buddy,* she thinks, flashing back to the laundry room. How he could have kissed her but didn't. *I'm his buddy.*

"Lines serve their purpose, I guess."

Gabe nods. "And if there is no line?" He stops looking at the sky and looks at Melissa. Her hair sways in the wind, mirroring the movement of the chair. She stares at him, feeling every inch of herself in the moment now, with him.

Gabe puts one hand on the back of her neck, the other on her back and kisses her. His lips are plush, his grasp strong. Melissa feels the kiss on her mouth, but it registers everywhere. *We have nowhere else we have to be right now, no meal to cook, no race to run.* She imagines staying like that for hours, then going inside— back to their little nook in the corner of the Cliff House. *Maybe I shouldn't be so quick to write off a seasonal hookup*, Melissa thinks, kissing Gabe again.

When they pause, the stars seem brighter, the snow glows nearly blue from the sky. Melissa can't fight the smile on her mouth. Gabe puts his hand on hers on the chair rail and they resume looking at the stars. "Maybe I'll have to come back up here—on my day off.... I can't believe it's so soon. The time is flying by here."

"That's the way it goes." Gabe nods. "One minute it's your first day; the next the season's over." He points. Melissa wonders if this means relationships, too. *One minute you're making out on the chairlift; the next you're ignoring one another at the ice rink. Or not.* "Isn't that Orion?"

"I don't know—I usually just make up names for the stars. Holiday Week is next week—I hear it's hectic." She clears her throat, hoping her next question won't be overinterpreted. "Gabe? You are sticking around next week, aren't you?"

"Oh, yeah. I wouldn't miss Holiday Week for anything. Hectic doesn't begin to describe it—you'll see. But it's the best," Gabe laughs, taken in by her. "So how exactly do you make up constellations?"

"Well, they all sound fake. Like the seven sisters—Pleiades—the daughters of Atlas and Pleione ..."

"That's not made up—"

"No, that's real. But how about ... there? See the triangle thing—that's Marvin the Trucker."

"Ah, yes." Gabe nods, ultraserious. "Myth has it he was enamored of that right there—the G and B twins."

"G and B?"

"Great and Busty," Gabe says, then cracks up. "Not to be confused with that bright star there, Mergatroid."

"And way over there." Melissa takes Gabe's hand, stretches out his finger, and points to a blotch of stars on the other side of the Cliff House. "That's Stanley and Rose, the old couple who watch over everything—like their daughter Astrid the Obnoxious."

Melissa laughs. Gabe pushes closer to her, enjoying her warmth.

"What's so funny?" he asks.

"Nothing—it's just that until today, I could have done one for you. Named a constellation, I mean."

"And what would it have been called?" Gabe's eyes sparkle as he waits for her answer.

Melissa thinks of what to say, again not wanting to ruin the moment but still wanting to be honest. She puts on a deep announcer's voice. "Gabe the big mistake—note the many dots of regret, the multiple ways you can see the humiliation. . . ."

She stops, feeling like she's dredged up exactly what she shouldn't have. Gabe sighs. "Do you know why I did it?"

Melissa looks at him. "What do you mean?"

"Because . . . someone found your journal, right? They read it aloud. That was wrong. But you left before I got a chance to respond. . . ."

Melissa feels her chest tighten, the old waves of insecurity and embarrassment washing over her. She lifts the chair bar up and hops down, falling into the snow but not caring. She stands up. "You did respond—your response was the worst kind—you did nothing."

She starts to walk away, wishing the lifts ran at night so she could leave. Gabe hadn't changed—no matter what, he was still the guy who hurt her.

Gabe leaps down, marching through the snow to her. "But I did—after you left—I spoke into the microphone and said it was true—"

"What was true?" Melissa's green eyes flash with hurt, the tears threatening to spill.

"That I felt the same way." Gabe grabs her shoulders. "You

left, remember? But I said it—I told everyone. You can ask JMB—he has a letter from me stating as much."

Melissa considers this—it's all so much to take in. "Gabe . . ."

He looks at her, about to lean in and kiss her again. All the way down the mountain, parties rage into the next day, but at the top, right where they are by the triplelift, the quiet is all-encompassing. Melissa looks at Gabe, waiting for him to say something—anything—to prove the truth.

"Well?" Melissa asks.

Gabe locks her eyes on to his. "You think I wound up at Les Trois by coincidence?"

18

Seriously, there's nowhere to hide.

The next morning brings pink light that streaks through the sky in blurry waves, ripples of peach and soft yellow haze that signal the storm is officially over; skiing is at its peak with new snow, and those who spent the night away from their own beds must make the walk back to their chalets.

With the first run of the triple chairlift, Melissa and Gabe are safely deposited back at the base of the mountain, still in their same ski outfits from yesterday, only with memories of having shed some of the items in the dark of the Cliff House the night before.

Melissa doesn't know what all of it means, but for once doesn't feel the need to overclarify, to pick through each action and word to figure it out—at least right now.

"So, I'll catch up with you later?" she says, by the back of the Main House.

"Sounds good," Gabe says. He leans forward and Melissa is sure he will kiss her good-bye—thinking this will explain what exactly they are, if anything. But instead he picks something off her coat collar. "Mushed-up jelly bean."

"Yuck," Melissa says and laughs, looking down at the remnant on Gabe's fingernail. "Blueberry."

Gabe nods. "Yeah." Melissa wonders if that second he's thinking back to sharing the bag of jelly beans, how she liked the blue ones best, how every time he fished one out he'd give it to her— first putting it in her hand, then later feeding it to her with his lips.

Gabe flicks the bit of gummed-up bean aside. It lands on the snow. "Man, I've got a ton of stuff to do." Melissa smiles, liking that she made the most of being stranded. "So I'll see you."

She wants to be the first to leave, and she is, as if it proves to her that she's in charge of the situation. *And is there really a situation? I don't know.* She begins to make the steep trek back from the Main House up to The Tops while Gabe makes tracks toward the Mountain Inn. As she crunches over the snow, Melissa grows more and more aware that the ski troopers out on early patrol, the avid winter sportspeople who rise at dawn, the post-partiers who like to eat breakfast and then head to bed, are looking at her. That they saw her say good-bye to Gabe.

And when she gets back to The Tops, just before coffee is due to be set out on the sideboard, along with sterling silver spoons, sugar cubes, and mugs, she has to open the back door with a squeak, announcing to the entire house that she's coming in for the first time since yesterday.

Dove is in the shower when Melissa comes back, and heads outside with her hair still wet. *One of the newfound pleasures of having such close-cropped hair,* she thinks, *is being able to go outside and not have icicles form on the ends of your hair.* She remembers being at school, having her hair freeze, and how once Max held a lock in his hands, thawing it before the all-school assembly. Then she tries to picture William doing that so she won't feel weird about thinking about Max in the shower.

She feels her hair again—the white blond is new-chick soft, chic, and very, very different. *Just what I want,* Dove says, slipping a black cashmere ski cap on and noticing how cold her scalp is without the cover of thick locks. She fights the urge to run inside and check her phone yet again for messages from William—he hasn't called, still, and she doesn't want to give him the credit of ruining her mood.

She drags the mats from the mudroom out in back of The Tops and begins to clean them by hanging each one over a railing and whacking it with the wooden side of a broom.

On the steep steps above her, she sees Diggs, looking worse for wear, pulling himself up the path by the railing.

Dove chuckles to herself, watching Diggs struggle to stay upright. *Clearly he had a rough night,* she thinks. *Or perhaps a fantastic night only to be greeted by a rough dawn. The morning shame parade has begun,* Dove thinks, *and I'm glad I'm not in it.*

Slinking out from behind a pine tree a few yards from Dove is Luke, whose laugh echoes through the surrounding air. Dove turns to watch him as she beats the rugs free of debris. Days of mud fall off, and it doesn't occur to her that sand from the Faux-cean will soon cloak the mat again.

"Whooo hooo!" Luke says, laughing as he leaps out from a big pine tree.

"Shut up!" says a female voice, hissing at him from the shelter of the massive branches.

"Why? I want to tell the world. . . ."

The female voice hisses again and reaches out to put her hand over Luke's mouth. Then it looks as though Luke is leaning in for a kiss from whomever he's with. "Not now, you fool. Not in broad daylight," the female voice says.

Dove peers closer, tucking herself down so as not to be seen. *Luke scored,* she thinks. *Cute Luke with his future hotness. And with whom?* Dove squints. On the snow, Luke starts to wobble. "Come lie down with me," he pleads. "Let's make snow angels."

"Not a chance," says the girl. Dove thinks her voice is familiar.

"Then let's just take a nap. I'm knackered." Luke plops himself down in the snow, spread out like a gingerbread man.

"Fine—stay there—just keep quiet and pretend like nothing happened," says the girl. When she finally turns around to go, leaving Luke to take a very cold nap in the snow, she looks to make sure no one's watching.

Celia Sinclair. Dove smiles to herself. *Celia and Luke. I should come out here more often at this time of day—no wonder the maids always know the juiciest gossip.*

As she's thinking this, the earl's voice booms from the front stoop and Dove quickly hikes the small hill that separates the front walkway from the back-door area, figuring if she's going to spy, she might as well do it properly and check out the whole scene.

"Open up!" the earl shouts, pounding his fist on the heavy wooden door. After a minute, the door opens and the countess, ice-queen cool with a coffee mug in hand, stands in the door frame.

"Oh, deciding to come home now, are we?" She gives the earl a stare and then turns back inside.

He walks in and closes the door behind him.

Dove raises her eyebrows and retreats to the relative boring safety of her rugs. One down, two to go. Dove hauls the clean mat inside to the mudroom. Back at the bunkroom, she hears rustling and pokes her head in.

"You're here!" Dove says to Harley.

From the top bunk, Harley raises her head enough to open one eye. "Yeah."

"How come I didn't hear you come in last night?"

"I didn't," Harley says. Her hair is tousled and she flops back onto the pillow.

Dove checks her watch. "Not that you want to know this, then, but breakfast is served in eight minutes. And I can smell omelets."

"So Melissa got back safely?" Harley scratches her head and rubs her face.

Dove nods. "The radio report came in last night—and I heard the water running and now I smell eggs, so . . ."

"Well, aren't you just the little detective," Harley says. "Ugh, I can't get up now. I haven't even slept yet."

Dove raises her eyebrows and is about to go when she notices sand on the bunkroom floor. "God, Harley, have some consideration! I'm the one that's got to vacuum here."

"It wasn't me," Harley says. "I didn't do that."

"Oh, yeah?" Dove says. "Did it magically get transported from the Fauxcean? Or no, let me guess, the real sea—all the way from . . ." She stops herself. The real sea makes her think of the islands, which make her think of Nevis, where William is, where he is but from where he hasn't called.

"I didn't do it," Harley protests. She sits up quickly in the top bunk, banging her head on the ceiling. "Shit!"

"Keep your voice down," Dove says. "People are sleeping." Of course, she knows this statement isn't true—the earl and countess are awake, as is Diggs—though with a steady hangover—Melissa's up, and Luke is semi-awake outside in the snow. Maybe Jemma's asleep. "And next time don't track sand in here. That's what the mudroom is for."

"It wasn't Harley's fault. It was mine." Next to Harley, rising slowly, is a figure in a navy blue T-shirt with his back turned away from the door.

"Oh," Dove says, surprised at first to see Harley's not alone, but then less so once she thinks back to the entire morning's show.

The figure hops down from Harley's bed and looks at her. "Bye. Glad you got back here safely." And to Dove he adds, "Sorry about the sand."

"That's okay," Dove says, wondering what all this means. "Bye, James."

With even more juice for the gossip cocktail, Dove, though desperate to know what happened with Harley and James, heads back outside to leave them to their good-byes and to take care of the last two mats. The first is small, made of carpet remnant. Dove finishes that with just a few whacks of the stick and brings it back to the mudroom where she can hear sounds of conversation and clinking silverware. Breakfast has started.

I wonder if I should wake Luke, Dove thinks, seeing his form still stretched out cookie cutter–style in the snow. *I'll give him five minutes.*

She hangs the last rug over the railing, then proceeds to bang the dirt out. With each whack, she gets out her feelings. *Here's to William, who didn't call. Here's to cleaning up other people's crap— literally. Here's to going out last night, and coming home alone. Here's to not being able to predict the future nor control the past. Just once, I wish I could live for the moment, in the moment—the exact right now.*

When the rug is free of lint and dirt, Dove backs away. Hot from the exertion, she takes off her ski hat and fluffs out her hair, enjoying the feel of the sun and wind on her neck and head. Behind her, footsteps. *More slinking around,* she thinks.

"Hey." Max stands in front of her with no jacket, just an untucked rumpled blue button-down shirt, jeans, and thick wool socks on the paved path.

"Hey." Dove puts the broom down and looks at him. "Aren't you freezing?" She wonders if he's been out all night, at Fauxcean, or with some girl—one of Celia's friends, maybe, or some hot titled Euro—and forgotten his shoes.

"I woke up a while ago," he says and points to his room. "You can see pretty much everything from my balcony."

She looks at his sock-clad feet again. "So you didn't do the walk of shame?" Max shakes his head, a smile playing at but not formally slipping onto his mouth. For some reason, this makes her happy. While everyone else at Les Trois was off making the most of the dark hours, Max was tucked in his bed. "So what did you do, exactly?"

Max sighs, licks his lower lip, and checks out the sun at it rises more in the sky. "Honestly?" Dove nods. He looks at her. "Waited for you to come back."

Dove feels a current of emotions go through her. "You did?"

Max doesn't repeat himself and Dove finds herself tied completely to the precise spot where they're standing—to the cold ground, the chilled air, the rising sun, to Max, taking the risk of standing before her. Not thinking of the past and not worrying about the future, Dove steps forward, puts herself into Max's arms, and pulls his face down so she can kiss him. They stay like that, wrapped in one another, for what feels like a long time. With only the sun's rays—and Luke, who has woken up—catching sight of them.

19

Sharing is important.

In the cavernous front room at the Main House, Matron, in her starched white shirt and gray flannel trousers, makes an announcement to the crowds of staff gathered by her command. Everyone itches with their own plans for the day off—a blissful twenty-four hours to do whatever they like—snowshoe, sleep, ski, shop, snog, or all of the above. Seated on the leather couches and chairs, leaning with their backs to the walls and heaped onto the floor, the staff and ski teams await her words so they can depart.

"We have a problem," Matron begins. Each face in the room registers this with the fear that Matron will call attention to that person's flaws or party mishaps.

What if she's going to fire me because I interacted with a guest? Dove thinks, replacing "interacted" with "made out passionately" in her mind.

What if Matron docks my ski privileges because Coach is pissed that I was late to morning warm-ups? James considers, hunkered down with the other skiers at the back of the room. *Not to mention getting into one of the chalet beds rather than my own at the Mountain Inn.* He looks around the room. *Granted, I wasn't in her bed long enough for it to matter.*

Gabe tightens the laces on his hiking boots and side-glances at James. *What if I'm busted for wanting to pick Les Trois as our practice location for the season when I really chose it based on illegally hacking into the computer system and finding out where Melissa was signed up to work.*

Oh dear Lord, what if Matron makes me a cleaner because the guests are complaining about my meals—if I'm in trouble for missing last night's dinner and dessert, even though being stranded in a snowstorm in my mind qualifies as a legitimate reason for missing? Melissa sighs, tugging at her hair and looking at Harley, who is so busy looking across the room at the skiers that she doesn't notice.

Screw Matron, Harley thinks. *What about James? What did last night mean? The swimming, the way he held me in the water, but then, too, the way he disappeared with Charlie the Nookie Nanny?*

Matron claps her hands, calling attention to her sturdy frame. "The problem is"—she sweeps her eyes over the room's crowd—"as you know, Holiday Week begins Monday. Changeover Day is Sunday. Tomorrow is . . ."

A loud yelp from a group of male hosts brings an anonymous shout of, "Day off! Let me hear you say yeah . . ."

One lone voice echoes him. "Yeah!"

Matron glares at everyone. "Unfortunately for you—though fortunately for the resort—we are terribly oversubscribed for Holiday Week." Matron flips over a page on her clipboard.

She's so organized, so planned, Dove thinks. *Not at all spontaneous.* She bites her top lip, thinking she's usually like that, a planner.

Someone who schedules everything from dusting to phone calls. But then, sudden kisses work well, too.

"The ramification of this overbooking is that we are behind schedule for such events as the ice follies, the Outdoor Games—when cooks report for beverage or sweets duty, and the traveling dinner party. Not to mention the standard prep." Groans from the group begin, only to be silenced by Matron's voice. "Listen! What this means is that for this week, there will be no day off."

Shouts of protest ripple from the staff, rising into shouts until Matron rings a bell and begins to talk. "For those of you who see this as an injustice, might I remind you that it is also considered an injustice to break the rules of conduct clearly referenced in the resort literature."

This reminder quiets most of the protestations. Only Harley raises her hand. Matron nods to signal she may speak.

"So we have no break? Not even a half day?" She looks over to the skiers, hoping to convey her wish to spend a half day on the slopes, specifically with James who meets her gaze for a second and then looks away.

Matron marches over to Harley and hands her a piece of paper. "Just for asking, you may have the pleasure of organizing the Top of the Heap."

"The what?" Harley's lack of sleep and romantic distraction get the better of her.

"It's a Holiday Week tradition for guests—at the peak of the middle alp, with mulled wine—which you will not drink—and a gathering of snowmen. Sorry, snowpeople, we say now."

Harley leans on her boots, arms crossed over her chest, cocky and gorgeous enough to somewhat pull it off. "So, I'm supposed to hike up the mountain and make Frosty?"

Matron smiles demurely. "No. You're meant to ride the gondola up the mountain—with all the supplies—and stay up there until you've created a winter park that will delight the guests' children. Top of the Heap." She points to the door. "Get to it."

"Aren't you going to share?" Luke asks Diggs, who is busy hoarding chocolate cupcakes for himself.

"Sharing?" Diggs says. "You're one to talk. Share some info, will you? Who'd you go off with last night?"

"I'll never say." Luke shrugs his friend off and gets back to the task at hand.

Melissa organizes her young recruits in the kitchen: Diggs in charge of icing the chocolate cupcakes—and not sharing the extra frosting—Luke in charge of the vanilla tops, and Jemma in charge of careful decorations on top.

"Everything's all set down there," Dove says. "Our plan is in action."

"Awesome," Melissa says.

With the day off cancelled, Melissa, Harley, and Dove have plotted their own day-into-night-off party. The earl and countess are on a long tour of the neighboring village of St. Anne's.

"Whoever thought I'd be glad the duke and duchess live so close," Jemma says. She uses a pastry bag to pipe designs on the cupcakes' tops. "They're, like, the most boring couple ever, but they have a castle in St. Anne's and notoriously long lunches and dinners, so there's no way Mum and Dad will interrupt the festivities."

"Good to know," Melissa says, admiring Jemma's work. "Too bad you're leaving tomorrow—I could use a sous chef in here!"

"Well, these are special cupcakes," Jemma says.

"Oh, yeah?" Luke says. "Got something in them I should know about?"

"No, loser," Jemma says. "They're pairing cakes. It's a Victorian thing I learned about at school."

"Um, useful," Diggs says. "Glad they're teaching you stuff."

Jemma rolls her eyes. Melissa nudges her to continue. "See? Here are two cupcakes with a snowflake. And another two with the letter *a*. And others with hearts or mountains or anything, really."

Melissa smiles. Dove leans in and smirks, remarking, "All in pairs. I get it."

Jemma goes on. "You split all the pairs up, okay, on two trays? And then everyone picks one and you see whom you're matched with."

"And then what?" Luke asks, suddenly interested.

"And then you . . . whatever," Jemma says. "We didn't get that far."

"Fine," Melissa says. "We'll say that pairs may talk in the bunkroom or excuse themselves to another locale."

Dove looks at the crumbs already littering the counter. "I'm going to have my work cut out for me."

Harley ducks in. "Damn it smells good in here." She reaches for a cupcake but Melissa swats her away. "I'm off to make snowmen—feeling like an ass."

"Oh, it's fun," Melissa says, wishing she could go.

"Maybe," Harley says. "I'll be back soon—in time for the party." She leaves and then comes tromping back. "Oh—and hey, Dove?"

Dove swivels, feeling again light and free from her princess hair, farther from her past, even if the future isn't as planned out. "Yes?"

"Your phone's been ringing for like an hour."

Dove's face changes and though part of her feels like bolting immediately from the kitchen, and rushing to her phone, she instead remains calm and looks at Melissa, Jemma, Diggs, and Luke. "Excuse me. I have to go check on something."

The peak least skied is only accessed by one long lift, the gondola. Shaped like a space pod, with yellow bottoms, silver sides, and black windows to dull the bright sunlight, there can be entire ski groups in them or just one or two people, depending on the time of day and the crowds.

Harley lugs a bag of long carrots, pieces of coal that started to blacken her fingers, oversized buttons collected from Matron's storage closet, and a variety of colored scarves, which Harley figures she can wrap around the snowpeople to make the group of them appear festive. Begrudgingly she leaves behind the beginnings of the cupcake festivities and walks past the Main House, past the ice pond with its hot-chocolate stand, past shops and other chalets, in front of the Mountain Inn, and up the winding path to the gondola loading area.

The fact that I'm in charge of making merry little snowmen is so ironic, Harley thinks, her scowl returning to her mouth. After last night with James, she thought for sure things were settled, but now he's been noticeably absent—and wouldn't even return her gaze in the Main House meeting. *Screw him,* Harley thinks. *No guy is worth the torture of feeling like this.* She's about to repeat this phrase in her head when she sees him—James—in his black and orange jacket—dashing from the front of the Mountain Inn, and straight to her. *I take that back,* Harley thinks. *It's worth feeling like this if the guy then makes up for his lameness by chasing after me.*

"Harley! Wait up!" James waves to her but Harley, convinced if she plays it cool, he'll warm up, keeps walking. He catches up to her, still lagging by a few paces as she gets closer to the gondolas.

The lift is running, picking up the few skiers and carrying them high up into the air and to the top of the peak.

"Are you going to talk to me or what?" James puts his hand on her shoulder.

Harley shrugs it off, even though she so wants it to be on her that she'd use Super Glue (which she brought to glue buttons on the scarves) to keep it there. She looks at James, hides her blush by turning around, and hefts the sack of snowman stuff over to the end of the line.

"So this is what you do? You play all cool so that a guy is forced to ask again and again for kindness or an actual conversation?" James shakes his head and pulls his gloves out of his pocket. He remembers losing one of the gloves, at the unnamed bar that night, waking up next to Mesilla, and how nothing happened physically, but how close he felt to her. "Look, Harley." James's voice is firm and serious. "We need to talk—"

"I don't need to . . . ," Harley says, the flirt rising in her voice just a little. She moves forward in line. *It's funny,* she thinks, *to be in line without skis.* Normally that was just a summer routine. For a great hike you could wait in line in shorts with a picnic, get taken to the top, and walk down. Now she'd have to ride up like this, then either deal with a very long walk back or convince the gondola controller at the top to pause the ride and let her snag a spot on the way down.

James steps in front of her as she tries to board the open gondola. "I need to talk, Harley. Me—the other person who was in your bed last night."

"This morning, you mean," she snaps, pushing him aside to ⸻ on. With the way their argument can be heard, no one else ⸻s to be near this gondola, so Harley spreads herself out over a ⸻ of the seats, placing the bag of goods on the floor.

"Fine—this *morning*. You win the time-telling prize. Well done!" James claps, looking at the gorgeous girl before him.

From the operations cabin, a trooper steps out. "Sir, are you on or off?"

James looks at Harley. "Off."

The lift then starts to move, grazing the snow with the door partway closed. Harley puts her hands to her mouth in megaphone position. "If you want to talk, climb aboard."

James gives it a two-second thought, figuring he'll ride up with her, talk, and circle back down, then head right over for the start of the cupcake party. He smiles for a second, picturing everyone eating frosting—the sweetness of it, maybe getting to share a cupcake with a certain person. The gondola is pulling away, up from the ground, so James books it, grabbing hold of the bottom, hoisting himself into the cavity, and slamming the door shut behind him as the whole thing tilts, starting the ascent up the peak.

"So." Harley looks out at the view behind her. The chalets seem tiny, people like bits of lint, the mountain swelling beneath them as the gondola rises. "It's a twenty minute ride—so get talking."

James, still by the door, holds on to one of the handrails and then turns to her. "How long have you known me?"

This is not the question Harley was expecting. In fact, what she's expecting is to have a face-to-face rehashing of what did—and didn't—happen last night at Fauxcean, in the bunkroom, outside in the snow. "Define *known*," Harley says, using her pageantry voice, skirting the obvious.

"Did you or did you not know about my boarding—and Olympic history—before we met?"

"I don't see what you're getting at," Harley says, feigning dis interest. "Haven't you been on magazine covers and been the subject of greater media interest?"

James crosses the small center of the gondola and sits across from Harley, resting his elbows on his thighs as he looks at her. "Yeah—that's true. But what I'm asking—and what you seem to be avoiding—is did you know me? Did you know who I am before you got here?"

Fear runs through Harley and she wishes she could just reach the top, make the damn snowmen, and be done with it—and get back in time for a chocolate cupcake. "Why does it matter?"

"Because it does," James says. "As you probably are aware, the rumor treadmill is at top speed here."

"Uh huh." Harley looks at the blue sky, the white slick of snow far below. Soon they'll reach the highest point of the ride and then mellow down. Thinking she has only ten minutes left of having to deal with him, she decides to get it all out in the open. "My question for you is, why all these queries now—why not last night, when you were getting into my pants?"

James looks as though he's been slapped—a combination of blushing and being caught well off guard. "I didn't . . . I . . ."

"Right." Harley stands up, steadying herself against the gondola's sway. "You're choosing to share all your questions now, when you had ample time last night. What happened, Mr. Olymdid you leave your note cards behind?"

James stands up, too, close to her, close enough that his breath, which smells of the morning's orange and pineapple juice, hits her. What she wants to do is drop the conversation and kiss him, let him kiss her—as if this will lock the deal that they are

but I was . . ."

"Dear god, don't even tell me you're going to play the old *I was drunk* card, are you? I expected so much more from you."

James licks his lips. "Why? You hardly know me—you haven't read about me, so you say—and I'm a seventeen-year-old single guy at a ski resort. What about that doesn't signal hookup and hook out to you?"

Harley looks him in the eyes. Then she touches his face, her palm on his cheek. He takes her hand, squeezing it in such a way that makes it difficult for Harley to know if he's holding her hand or asking her to back off. Then, without warning, the gondola stops.

"What the—"

James looks out the window. "Probably just something caught in the wire—a pause. One time a bird refused to move and they had to shut down for a full three minutes."

James and Harley take seats on opposite sides of the gondola to help even out the weight, to stop the swaying. Three minutes go by. Then five. Then ten. "You still think it's a bird?" Harley asks.

"It was just a thought," James says. He goes to the control speak and presses the red alarm button. After some scratchy noise, a voice comes though. "This is Dean at the base, how can I help?"

"Yes, this is James Benton-Marks. I'm in gondola..." He points to Harley to check the number on the side. She peers down out the closed window and shrugs, holding up a five. "We're in gondola five." Harley registers the *we* in his sentence and hopes it's the beginning of the usage. She decides when he finishes talking she'll say something, just come clean.

"We read you, five, and are aware of the situation."

James coughs. "What is the situation?" He looks at Harley, hoping she's not too worried.

"A malfunction on the lines at the top. We're going to try and get it working again, but sit tight."

"What else could we do?" Harley says quietly. James stops talking to the controller and turns back to Harley.

"Looks like we might be stuck for a while." James cups his hands to the tinted window and looks at the other gondolas, each swinging back and forth in the steady wind.

Harley leaves her side of the gondola and sits next to James. *If we have this much time up here,* she thinks, *I'm making the most of it.* James looks at her. "You have that look," she says.

"What look?" he asks, doing it again, head tilted, eyes up at an angle.

"That look guys get before they kiss you." Harley smiles, waiting.

James doesn't change his look, and stays in the same seat, but his voice comes out different than it was before, tender, quiet. "Harley—I get the feeling that you knew me—or thought you did—"

Harley nods. "Maybe that second part." She looks down at her jeans, feeling the cold, wishing she'd brought warmer clothing, not ever thinking she'd be stuck so many feet in the air for so long. "You're right. . . . I did read about you. All those *Sports Illustrated* articles, the coverage of the winter games. I mean, I'm from ski country for god's sake. Everyone knows everyone's rankings and tricks."

"You knew my tricks?" James gives her a half smile, putting his hand on her knee.

Harley leans forward, in one motion kissing him and sitting on his lap, moving his arms so they go around her back. James kisses her, hard, but then right in the middle of it, stops and he looks conflicted. Harley is annoyed. "Are you suspending action, too?" Harley asks, looking at James and then the gondola.

"Funny, funny." James picks her up, depositing her back on the bench. He goes to the door and looks out at the view. "Man, we're up high."

Harley lets a thin wire of panic run through her. *What if they can't fix the problem, and we're stuck? And what if this applies to me and James as well as the lift?*

"I thought if I admitted all that to you—you know, that I'd kind of worshipped you from afar—that you'd relax. I mean, I told you the truth."

"Well, first of all, it's a little overwhelming, Harley. Like, hi, I'm a pseudostalker and I like you. . . ."

"That's mean." Harley shakes her head. "I'm not like that. I just knew."

"Knew what?"

"That we'd click. Hit it off. Didn't you ever feel that way about someone, even if you'd never met them—or met them once?" She pauses, blushing and nearly in tears. "I mean, I did meet you, you know. You probably don't remember it, but two years ago when you were on some promotional tour—you came through Breck-enridge, okay?"

"Yeah . . ." James looks concerned and waits for her to go on.

"You and Gabe Schroeder had just won that cup and came into the International Burrito Shack—"

"Snuck in is more like it," James says, remembering. "We had to climb out three stories and walk all the way there—in the snow. But we had a . . ."

"Really fun time—with the piñatas, and the famous forty-ounce margarita."

James looks amazed. "How do you know that?"

Harley tucks her knees to her chin. "I was there. And I served you guys and I just thought—there's got to be more than this. My life with cheese and beans and drinks and—these awful pageants my mother made me get into to prove I wasn't trashy, even though I kind of was." Harley starts to cry. It's the first time she has since she can remember and it feels both jagged, ripping her apart, and good—a release.

James comes over to her and hugs her. She leans up to kiss him again but he pulls back. "No. Harley. No."

She pushes his chest. "Why? You know it's good. Last night . . ."

James tightens his mouth, breathing in through his nose. "Yeah. Last night. I don't want to say it was a mistake. . . ."

The word stings like a welt and Harley covers her face with her hands. *This can't be happening—everything I wanted, rippling away from me.*

"Last night—was great," James says. Harley looks up through her tears and smiles, using one finger to try and dry her eyes. "But—"

"Oh, shit—there's a but?"

"Just let me talk, okay? But what it did was tell me sort of what you just said."

"Wait, I'm confused," Harley says. "Was it great or not?"

"You know how we—that we didn't . . ."

"Yeah, I was there? So, I know we didn't go the entire ski route, if that's how you want to phrase it," Harley says.

"I prefer to complete the entire revolution—boarding terms," he says, smirking. Then he goes on. "I would've. Obviously—I mean, look at you. You're an inferno in terms of hotness; you're a kick in the pants to be with—witty, mellow. . . ."

"Please don't say I'm your buddy," Harley says.

"No," James says. "Not like that. Maybe if it were another time. Or another place. . . ." He looks away from her, out the window, his face glazing over with other images.

Harley stares. "You like someone. This isn't about me. This is about you liking someone else, isn't it?"

Without looking at her, James nods. "Yeah."

"So . . . what does that mean?"

He turns to her. "It means—last night goes down in the record books as a fun thing, Harley. A typical thing. But not what I'm looking for."

A typical thing? That sucks. Harley's breath catches in her throat. *Maybe this is what it feels like to be rejected, to lose.* Harley tries to accept this. That she woke up next to him, still partially clothed, and saw her new boyfriend, and he woke up next to her and wanted to leave. "And in the future?"

James shrugs. "I'm not a forecaster of futures. Coach taught me that. You can try and try and use up all your energy figuring out what might happen, but it doesn't change what will. Better to use the time to reassess what you want."

"Or who?"

He nods. "Yeah."

Harley's heart is heavy with the rejection—but the door isn't completely closed. He said another time, another place. *Maybe in the off-season. Maybe some other resort. Maybe not now doesn't mean not ever.* Harley braces herself for the long haul. *You want to play like that? Fine.* "So who is this lucky girl?"

James crosses his arms over his chest. "That is classified information." He stops, presses the button on the control panel, and waits for a response. Then he whispers to Harley, "Someone is going to catch your attention—and he's going to be one hell of a lucky guy."

Harley thanks him with her eyes, and feels herself sway back—back to when she'd never even seen a picture of James—and forward to now where they've been together and won't be again—and further forward, to what lies ahead. Maybe someone new, or maybe James, still, but somewhere else. Anywhere but here in Rejection Central.

"We still haven't fixed the problem," the commander says. "We're sending ski patrollers to rescue stranded passengers. They'll traverse the cable using rescue equipment."

"Like James Bond!" James says.

"I can't believe you're happy about this," Harley says.

"Well, we are missing cupcakes," James says. He takes her hand, squeezes it, and waits for further word from the ground. "They'll have to take us down by snowmobile."

"Yep," Harley says.

"See? Another point in your favor," James says. "So many girls would be freaking out up here about all this."

Harley shakes her head, shoving her hurt way inside. "Not me. I don't get flustered by sudden situations." She looks at James again, wondering if they'll meet some other place—or if they'll hook up again this season, and if it would mean anything. *Maybe I don't need to be his girlfriend,* Harley thinks, *as long as I'm able to be near him. I can work my way into his life, being his friend, and then—boom—suddenly we can be more.*

"Well, then I'll tell you something else," James says. "I'm taking off tomorrow."

"What?" Harley's voice goes high up with concern. "Why?"

"A race—more training. There's a place called Der Vannimore over the border—guess coach thinks it's best I go there for a while."

Harley doesn't know what to say or what to do. Her reason for being at Les Trois is trickling away.

"Hey," James says, trying for levity. "Don't look so sad." He reaches inside her bag. "Here—let's split a carrot."

They stay there, sharing the carrot, suspended from the ground, both of them waiting for their rides back to earth.

20

Even on your day off, you're still on.

"No," Dove says, cradling the phone as though it were actually attached to William. "We should have a day off, but we don't. Just call it another mark on the board of the unjust."

She says this, and then wonders if maybe she should also add herself—or her actions—to the same board. She and William are past the hellos, and despite starting the conversation filled with anger about the fact that William bagged the ritual call, Dove now finds herself so guilty about the stolen kiss with Max that she doesn't even bring it up.

"Have you forgotten what today is?" William says.

"Oh, you didn't mean my day off?"

"No, something else." William's voice sounds different now. Of course it's the same tone, the same person—maybe it's just going longer than one day without hearing him. Or maybe it's that tiny fraction of her that's broken away.

"Tell me then," Dove says. She sits on her bottom bunk, phone to her ear, her feet splayed onto the springs above her.

"Exactly twelve days until I see you." William's smile is audible—Dove can imagine it, how one side slopes up a little higher, how those quirks were the kinds of details that made someone hard to forget. She thinks of Max, how the hair that falls onto his forehead covers a scar way up into the hairline from when he'd jumped into a swimming hole as a kid and bashed himself on a rock. She feels guilty for knowing that, too, even though it's innocent when compared to a kiss.

"Twelve days—and then I'll be with you," Dove says. "It still seems unreal."

"Well, get real," William says. "You'll love it here—Nevis is like this untouched beauty. Except that it's been touched by a lot of wealthy vacationers." He laughs. "But that's not such a bad thing—I mean, it is affording me my life on the *Seventh Wave*."

"How is the boating life?" Dove looks at the snow outside, thinking William is looking at sea and sand and how that very dissimilarity makes her feel sad, like there's no way he can understand her world right now.

"It's . . ." William pauses, talking to someone else in the background. "I'll be there—just hang on. Sorry about that," he says, coming back to Dove. "That was Becca—she works on a schooner on the other side of the dock."

"A schooner?" Dove nods as though William can see her. "She's a friend?"

"Yeah," William says. "She's from Florida—a real beach girl—she's a kick."

"Sounds it," Dove says, her voice tight. All of a sudden she feels like crying.

"What's up, Dove? Don't be weirded out by Becca—she's just a friend."

Dove sits up, bumps her head on the wooden slats of the bunk, and holds her forehead. "Right, she's probably just a bikini-wearing buddy, of course." She hates herself for sounding so pissy and jealous—and all because she's the one who did something wrong.

"Dove, what is it?" William's voice sounds concerned. She's sure that if he were here, his brow would have the V-shaped crease in it, his mouth in a frown. "You've got to tell me what's going on—this isn't like you."

What is like me? She wonders. *Am I a princess with long hair waiting for my prince to fetch me on a boat that's not his? Am I a pixie-haired girl who can cook and stand on her own two feet? Or just a duplicitous girlfriend who doesn't deserve anyone's affection?* Then she remembers. "Why didn't you call me?"

William coughs. Dove hears water running and William sipping. "Um."

"Um? That's what you have to say? You who's usually a boundless talker?"

"I was going to—totally. I've never missed a day, right?"

"Right," Dove says. She looks outside the window to the pathway, sure she can see shadows of her make-out session with Max. But it wasn't just a kiss, was it? It was more—like a tying together of who she was, and who she is. Not superficial—is that better or worse? She tries not to think about it. "Which made it more confusing, like I had to interpret it even more—I was so upset, Will. . . ."

"I know. I'm sorry. I wish I had a good excuse, and I could try hard to make one up but I don't want to be that guy."

"What guy?"

"The guy who messes up and then covers it with some clever tale or some lame but heartfelt lie."

Dove sighs, feeling confused and tired, her nonday off catching up with her early morning and later nights. "So what is it?"

"It was nothing—a good thing, really. Honestly. But I can't tell you until you get here."

Dove chokes out a sound of disbelief. "So I have to wait with all this ambiguity and just have faith that you did something good? Something good that involved making it okay not to call me? To break your promise? And then not tell me about it?"

William's silence goes on for what feels like too long. "Can you do that?"

"Do you still want me to come to Nevis?" She thinks of the borrowed money, the ticket she purchased, the thin cardstock of it in her drawer.

"Oh course I do, Dove. And once you're here, everything will be exactly the same between us. Trust me."

Dove hears his words as though he's whispering them right into her ear, filling her up with surety. "Okay." She smiles. "Okay—I'll just wait then."

They get ready to hang up and then William asks, "One more thing."

"Yeah?"

"Was there something you wanted to tell me?"

Dove falters. "Ah, no. Why?"

"No reason—just something in your voice—you're the same, but different."

Dove gets chills, thinks that's exactly what she'd said to herself about him. Maybe both of them had incidents best left unsaid. "Soon, right?" Dove whispers.

"I'm counting the days—and nights," William says. "My berth on the boat is the perfect size for us. Good thing you're petite."

Dove laughs and they end with their usual *miss you,* but Dove is left wondering if everything will be the same when she sees him, if she should tell him about Max—although there's really not much to tell; it was a mistake, one dumb kiss that meant nothing—and if William is expecting to do more than just sleep in that berth. If going to Nevis means something else entirely in his mind than in hers.

Halfway through the cupcake party Harley and JMB are noticeably absent.

Determined not to have her hard work ruined by Harley's behavior, Melissa tries to let it go.

"Whatever," Melissa says. "I'm not going to think about it. He's too much of a crush for me—one of those feelings that'll never be returned, so I'm not even going there." But inside, she knows it's too late. *What the hell does she have that I don't?* She wonders but then remembers Harley's legs, her face, her good-enough-for-gold exterior that sometimes masks her interior motivations. *Never mind. If I were a vengeful person, Harley would bring it out. But I'm not. Right?*

Melissa looks around the crowded room, fountains of bubbling white and dark chocolate, the sliced fruit for dipping. Already people have rings of sweet frosting around their mouths.

"Man, are we all going to be on sugar overload after this," Dove says. She's about to swipe a cupcake from the tray when Jemma swats her had.

"These are the special ones—Melissa, is it time?"

Melissa looks at her watch. To wait any longer to put the matching cupcake trays out would be to admit fully that she was waiting for JMB to return—in the hopes they'd match. "Sounds like now is as good a time as any!"

Trays of beautifully decorated cupcakes—half done in white frosting, half in chocolate, but each with a design that has a twin lurking nearby—are set out on the top of the living room's long wet bar.

"Let the picking begin!" shouts Melissa. With everyone scrambling for a grab, the picking is frantic, with all the staff, nannies, skiers, troopers, and guests reaching for a baked good. Once they have one in hand, they hold it facing outward, speaking aloud.

"I have a diamond."

"I have a thing that looks like an anchor."

"Me, too!"

The splitting off of pairs is immediate. Random couples form, talking, laughing, eating their cupcakes; getting up to who knows what on the snow; trading stories inside the kitchen, or just sitting in awkward silence on the rug in front of the fireplace.

Outside on the balcony, Luke revels in matching with Celia Sinclair. A long-range lens has them together, and Luke makes sure to smile for the paparazzi, hoping their photo will grace the cover of some magazine back home. In the bunkroom, Diggs complains about being stuck with Jemma, but she's clearly thrilled, wanting to catch up on any and all gossip. Max shows Melissa his room upstairs. Dove, having witnessed Gabe's switching his cupcake choice to avoid the nanny Charlie, winds up in the wraparound hot tub with him.

"In we go," Gabe says, pulling off his shirt and sliding into the hot water with his boxers. "Don't tell me you're too queenly to get in something as banal as a hot tub?"

Dove shoots him a glare. "Do I look like a queen?" She eases herself in, thankful for her layered tank tops and boy-cut shorts.

"No." Gabe gives her a thoughtful once-over. Dove notes that, more interested in her face, he hardly looks at her body. "Actually, you look like a bird—not in a bad way, but a fluffy chick. The kind someone should take extra care with." He looks at the bubbling water"Sorry—that sounded weirder out of my head than in it."

Dove smiles and leans back onto the edge of the tub, enjoying the intense heat. "Well, thanks, I guess—it's not exactly what I pictured from a round of hot tubbing with the likes of you."

"Meaning what, exactly?"

"Well, your reputation does precede you. . . ."

Gabe bites into his cupcake, chewing and swallowing before replying. "I'm sure it does—and there was a time when I'd have been glad to have those misconceptions as part of my cosmic makeup."

"Cosmic makeup?" Dove shakes her head and nibbles the cupcake, trying to keep it from getting wet. "You sound like such a snowboarder."

"Well, I am," Gabe says. He looks at her from across the tub, stretching his legs out under the water. "But I'm not like that—the way I was, I mean."

"So you're a reformed lothario?"

"I don't know that I'd use that particular word. . . ."

"Okay—how about hookup artist?" Dove raises her eyebrows and licks the frosting.

Gabe shrugs. "I suppose. . . ." He finishes his cupcake, then submerges under water for a minute, then pops back up. "Those are some amazing cakes."

"I know," Dove says. "Melissa's definitely got a way with sweets."

Gabe's eyes flicker with the memory of something, the sweets

ing is the same color as his hair, and Melissa thinks about how funny it is, to be in some guy's bedroom—some beautiful guy's bedroom—and feel nothing for him. How half of her is still on that mountaintop with Gabe, eating jelly beans and naming stars, and the other half of her is still wishing for JMB, for the affection and crush to be requited. She wonders where he is—if the fact that both he and Harley are missing means anything—or if she should just let the coincidence go.

"Look," Max says, holding out a five-by-seven photograph. "This was a while ago—sorry about the scratches." Melissa wipes her hands on her pants and goes to look. "That's me—and Lily. Or, as you know her—Dove."

In the picture, Dove is radiant—in a fitted lilac dress, her long light hair coiled up in classic movie star position, revealing her collarbone, her graceful arms both linked around Max, who is clad in a dinner jacket—a smile wide as a crescent moon. "You look so happy," Melissa comments. "When was this?"

Max takes the photo back, slipping it into his chest pocket face in. "My eighteenth—thus the fancy dress. She was unbelievable that night—everything I'd ever wanted."

"So what happened?"

Max shakes his head and pulls at his hair. "A misunderstanding. Some girl—"

"Named?"

"Does it matter?"

"It does to me," Melissa says. "And it should to you—you're the writer, right?"

Max concedes. "Fine. There was this girl—someone at school with us last year—called Claire. She was Dove's good friend, and I vaguely knew her. Enough to know she might not be reliable—but . . ."

"But let me guess—she was gorgeous."

Max shrugs, regretting the memories. "It wasn't that Claire was bad—she wasn't part of the cruel set. And I knew—know— why Lily, I mean Dove, liked being with her. Claire was funny where Dove was shy; together they were a good pair. It was Claire who first told me Dove liked me—and I couldn't get my head around it."

"Let me guess—Claire was also the one who told you that Dove didn't feel the same anymore." Melissa wipes the crumbs from her lips.

"That night, at my eighteenth, Lily and I had this talk—and danced—and for me it was . . ." He stops and looks at Melissa. "I don't know why I'm telling you this."

"Maybe because I'm here—and I'm not just a piece of paper. . . ." She points to his books. "And maybe you need to see where the plot's going?"

"It just got screwed up," Max says, his voice full of frustration. "I wanted to be with Lily—Dove—whatever she is now. And then Claire told me it would never happen—and for some stupid reason, I believed her. When Dove found me next . . ."

"You were with Claire, attached at the mouth, and more than a little drunk." With a towel wrapped around her shivering body, Dove stands in Max's doorway, looking at both of them while water pools at her feet. "While I'd been off looking for Claire to tell her this was it—that I was finally ready to tell Max how I felt, to be with him—on every level . . ." She glances at his bed and then back to the two pairs of eyes looking at her. "By the time I got there, to Max's room at his parents' estate, it was pretty clear I wasn't first choice—or that I wasn't a choice at all."

"Lily . . ." Max reaches out for her.

Melissa pinches her own mouth shut and takes this moment as her cue to leave. Nodding good-bye, she walks past them and down the back stairs, out onto the deck for some air.

"Just who I've been looking for," Gabe shouts to her from the hot tub.

Melissa turns to him. "You can't have been looking that hard—what'd you think, I'd magically appear in there with you?"

Gabe raises his eyebrows, his cheeks ruddy from the cold air and hot water. "A guy can dream, can't he?"

Melissa shivers with the thought that Gabe Schroeder could use the word *dream* in reference to her.

"You coming in or what?" he asks. "I promise I won't bite."

Melissa looks at her clothing, wondering why she chose today to wear a thong. *I don't even like them. They're uncomfortable no matter what anyone says, they don't flatter my rather cushioned behind, and the thought of dropping my pants right now . . .* "I don't think so," Melissa says. "I should get back to work."

"Work, work, work," Gabe says. "What does a guy have to do to get you alone? Strand you on top of a mountain?"

Melissa leans onto the tub with her forearms, trailing her fingers in the water and finally breaking into a smile. "I get your point." She thinks about it and then just talks, figuring Gabe's seen her humiliated before; she may as well be honest. "I'm just self-conscious, I guess."

"About what?" Gabe is genuinely confused.

Melissa shrugs and looks down at herself. "I don't know—me?"

"Oh my god," Gabe says. "If you only knew . . ."

Melissa leans closer to him, watching him cup water in his hands and spill it out. He rubs his hands onto his face, giving his skin a sheen Melissa finds enticing. "You have everything worth

211

looking at, Melissa. And nothing that should make you think twice about getting in here right now."

She looks at him, realizing her feelings—is it a crush? A real like?—just got a little bit deeper. "And you're not just playing me?"

Gabe sighs. "Can't I ever lose that image?"

"Well, you were on the cover of *Ski Life* magazine as their number one international player...."

"But I'm not—really. Not anymore. James and I both did a lot of that stuff for publicity, anyway." Gabe thinks for a second. "Have you seen him, anyway?"

Melissa swallows, her mood bubble threatening to burst. "No. No, I haven't." She looks at Gabe and thinks about absent James, how he could be off anywhere with anyone, and even if he were here how he hasn't made the slightest overture toward liking her. And just like that, Melissa strips down, into the thong and her T-shirt, and jumps in.

"Now what?" she asks Gabe, who stares at her from across the tub.

"It's up to you," Gabe says. The night air settles in, bringing a chill, and later hours that will lead into the next day—to Change-over Day. "You have to decide."

In his room, Max hides the photo in his pocket, hoping Dove won't see it. But she's close to him, close enough that her wet hair drips onto his feet.

"Do you have something you want to tell me?" Max says. He sits on the edge of his bed.

Dove looks around, impressed with the state of his room. "Looks like you didn't need me in here, after all."

"I did—I do, but not to clean." Max pulls her in her towel

between his legs, not caring that she's wet and that the dampness is moving from her body to his.

"You do just fine without a maid, it seems."

"I don't want you to be my maid."

Dove drops her towel, angry. "What do you want, Max?"

"Don't yell at me—you're the one who kissed me, Dove. You. Outside on the snow, on my mouth."

Dove blushes at the truth, leans down to pick up her towel remembering William's words—*twelve days and we'll be together*. Always a countdown—backward to Max's eighteenth or forward to leaving her parents and her loaded trust behind, or forward again to Nevis, and seeing William. As she picks up the towel, Max grabs it from her, slips it behind her, and pulls her forward with it until she's pressed into him. He kisses her with so much intensity and tenderness she feels she could be back there, dancing at his party, in her lilac dress, her hair long, her future still steady.

"Stop." She pushes away. "I can't."

Max bites his lower lip and stares at her. "I know you, Lily. Dove. You could change your name a million times and it won't erase what we had."

"We had nothing—we had you carrying around the knowledge that I liked you and you did nothing with it. We have you running off at your party with my supposed best friend. We have me finding you both—in bed. Together."

Max stands up and walks away from her. "That night is filled with the most regrets I have. I never should have questioned you—I never should have believed Claire."

"Then why did you?" Dove asks, wondering if it's because Claire was *the* girl—that girl that every boy at school wanted in some way or form—that girl had behind her a mass of power and beauty, and a persuasiveness that never failed.

"Because I thought there wasn't any chance that you would feel the same about me." Max hides his blush with the photograph, taking it out to study it.

"So rather than wallow for two seconds in your perceived sorrow over me you went to bed with Claire?"

Max turns. "I never said I slept with her."

"Max, I did in fact find you in the bed with her—you're telling me nothing happened?"

"I can't tell you nothing happened, Dove. But I can tell you that I regret it. That making a quick decision—drunk or not—to be with someone who isn't your first choice—is a terrible thing. For all involved."

"And now?" asks Dove, wondering whether even she knows the answer.

Downstairs, the party filters out into the snow, with people retreating for their own chalets, or final dinners. Melissa looks at Gabe. "We should get out—I'm getting all pruny." She studies her wrinkled palms and fingers. "Plus . . . I have to make the final dinner. Weird. Our week here is almost all over."

Gabe looks at her, swimming to her so their arms are touching. "Is it? Don't we have all next week and so on?"

Melissa looks at him, unsure what to do. "What are you saying?"

"Just this." With a push of a button Gabe turns on the jet sprays and envelops Melissa in a kiss.

"Changeover Day's tomorrow—hectic haze that it is." Melissa kisses him back, enjoying it, enjoying the feeling of being free in her potentially unflattering thong but not caring, feeling glad to be with someone who likes her so much. Someone whom she liked first who liked her back.

"And what's the plan for tomorrow, then? And I know you have to go clean up the mess from this—I'll help." Gabe stares at her.

"Thanks—we'll need a crew to get it back in order. And in terms of tomorrow? I read what it says in the informational packet—cleaning, packing, organizing, making lists for shopping, that sort of thing—but it doesn't cover the realities of saying good-bye and dealing with the transition."

Gabe nods. "I guess you'll have to see."

Melissa nods back, wondering if she should kiss him, if they are together, if he wants to be, if she does or if he's only a second choice—or even if that's true, if it's okay. "I guess we'll see what happens in the light of day."

21

Changeover Day is more complicated than you think.

Melissa, Harley, and Dove finish their last shifts for the week—some guests will stay on, others will leave. A foot of fresh powder has fallen and the sun glints off the snow.

"Should we go for a quickie run?" Dove asks, peering up at Melissa on the top bunk.

Harley nods from her bed. "Count me in."

Dove slips out of her bed, her white flannel pajamas blowing in the air that seeps through the cracks. "What time is it, anyway?"

"Past breakfast. Almost eight!" Melissa hops down onto the floor. "Oh, it's so weird not to have to make breakfast for everyone this morning. I felt almost guilty setting out a buffet . . . but then it felt so good to get back in bed." Melissa thinks back to burning things, making croissants, learning to melt jam for sauces, learning just about everything all so fast she hardly had time to keep track of her newfound knowledge. She looks forward to her tip envelope. Maybe she'll do something extravagant—or save it—or travel somewhere. "I guess next week should be easier—now that I have a vague notion of how to cook." She remembers a recent attempt at a kung pao sauce and revises her words. "Make that *very* vague."

"I hope everything's easier," Dove says. "But . . . not to be the voice of pessimism—it *is* Holiday Week with capital H and W coming up. Cons for you are that people really expect gourmet cuisine that's holiday-oriented."

"And the upside of that?" Melissa asks.

Harley and Dove overlap. "Drinks and mistletoe."

Melissa thinks back to Gabe, to his drunk kiss, the session in the snow, and wonders what it means. She knows now she enjoyed it. A lot. But sleep with him? That seemed like a whole other level. She remembers walking by where they'd kissed. In the morning you could still see snow-prints.

Dove goes on. "Holiday Week is notorious for the overimbibing . . . so if you make something bad or something doesn't turn out just right, make sure you offer starters that have lots of brandy."

"Or nudge me—give me a wink and I'll delay the dinner with my charming hosting powers. And by that I mean I'll serve a round of sherry." Harley smirks.

All three laugh in the comfort of their room. "I'm used to this place now," Dove says. "Odd to think I've got only another week and then I'm off. . . ." She whisks herself right to a tropical image. "Just think—from this"—she does a *brrrr* with her arms wrapped around her small frame—"to lying on the beach."

"Sounds like a good time," Harley says. "But don't go anywhere just yet. We still need you—and your services."

"Thanks," Dove says. Harley's not all tough—and she's not all sweetness, either. A good mixture. Dove pauses. "Was that the doorbell?"

Melissa shrugs. "I don't know, but we better get going if we want a run before reporting to the Main House. Another cycle of people in here—another round of who knows what."

"Does another round mean anything for you with your romantic entanglements?" Dove asks Melissa while Harley's in the bathroom.

"I don't know," Melissa says. "It's all up in the air. Who ever thought that it would get this complicated? And it's not. Not really. But I . . ."

"You're just confused, that's all," Dove says.

"It's like my past self—the one that wanted Gabe Schroeder—still wants him. Not only because I couldn't have him before, though that's part of it, but also because he's great." Melissa, still in her pajamas, listens. "I swear that's the doorbell again."

"I'll get it!" Harley shouts from the bathroom. "Hey—I just shouted! And no one yelled at me! Cool!"

With the guests packing or gone, some grabbing a croissant for the road, the chalet staff can be dressed out of uniform, yell, and generally slob around until the next shift starts all over again. "But, Dove?" Melissa pulls on a sweater and thick socks, ready for a run down the mountain. "There's a part of me that likes JMB . . . sorry, James—more. He was the first person I met here who got my attention—and it had nothing to do with Gabe."

"So why not just pursue James, then?"

"You know why," Melissa whispers.

Dove looks out the door, checking to see if Harley's coming. "She doesn't know?"

Melissa shakes her head. "With all of the confusion and names and stress and . . . no. The point is, no I didn't tell Harley. Plus, I still don't know what he thinks—if he thinks anything. Probably all this confusion is over nothing. Gabe is terrific—and I should just be happy I finally got what I wanted."

"I know what you mean," Dove says, letting each word leak out slowly.

Melissa's eyes widen. "What's this? The tight-lipped Dovelet is going to speak?"

"Oh, come on," Dove says and chucks a ball of socks at Melissa. "I'm not that bad." She pulls Melissa over to the window and points to the pathway. "See him?"

"Who, Max?" They both stare out the window at him, their breath making condensation circles on the glass.

"Yes."

"But you . . . ," Melissa starts, then stops herself.

"But I . . . right. I have my ticket. And I'm sure—one hundred percent sure. Well, not that sure—nothing's that sure, right? Ninety-eight percent sure that going to the islands, following William there, is the best thing for me."

"So what about Max?"

"Same thing—there's nothing here now, really. Okay, maybe there's something. But I can't help but think life would just be limitless—people would just filter in and out if you didn't pick something and stick to it." She puts a finger to the window, pointing to Max, and at that moment he turns around and squints in their direction.

Dove ducks down, laughing. "Do you think he saw me?"

Melissa cracks up. "No—he's too far away."

"Anyway, he has nothing to do with my present—"

"Except that he's in it—which is more than William can

say. . . ." Melissa puts her hand on her mouth. "Oh, that came out wrong."

"William is completely in my present. . . ." Dove looks annoyed, then softens. "No—I get what you're saying. Max is nothing—just a memory. And he's leaving today, so it doesn't matter."

Melissa and Dove stare out the window again, this time without Max in view. Then, footsteps from behind them. At the doorway, Max stands with fresh snow still cloaking his coat. His eyes penetrate the distance to Dove.

"I'm just a memory?" he asks.

Dove opens her mouth to speak, but doesn't know what to say. Melissa excuses herself from the room. "I better see if Harley needs help."

"Don't leave on my account," Max says to Melissa. "I'm only here to ask Dove one thing."

Dove raises her eyebrows, looking dignified even though she's in her pajamas. "Fine—I should be able to tolerate one question."

Max takes two long steps into the room, close enough to Dove that he can see her hands shaking. She can see the flecks of yellow in his eyes and wonders if she'd noticed them before, way back when, in the past. "If I'm just a memory, then I'll let you close the door."

"What do you mean?" Dove leans on the bed frame to keep from swaying. He always made her feel like this—a mix of comfort and unsteadiness, whereas William was more exuberant; he made her excited.

"What I mean is," Max says, matter-of-factly, "is that you and I have this unfinished history. And sometimes that's just it—it's better left undone." He leans next to her, their legs touching, until Max moves away. "My parents are leaving today."

"I know—it's time for turnaround," Dove says.

"They've given me the choice of staying on another week. Classes don't start for ages—and I've finished my papers, anyway."

"You did always like to get your work done early," Dove says. She thinks how last-minute William is—the charm of his sudden ideas, his quick planning. Or his oversight in calling her and then fumbling for a reason.

"See? You refer to me as being in your past, yet you're the one who brings up the fact that we know each other now."

"I'm only being . . ."

"Polite? This . . ." Max sweeps his palm between his chest and Dove. "This is just part of your job description?"

"No." Dove's chest pounds. "It's not that. It's just not—being with you—having you here makes my life messy. Complicated. And it shouldn't be like that. It should just be . . ."

Max goes to the door. "Well, then I think you've answered my question."

Dove pauses, wiping her hands on her face. "What do you mean? What question?"

Max clears his throat. "My parents said I can stay. I've decided to turn that question over to you. Do you want me to stay another week? Here. At The Tops?"

Dove's mouth hangs open. Max goes on. "Whatever you decide, I'll do—no questions, no implications." Max leans his tall frame into the doorjamb. Dove watches him, tracing her eyes over his face, his arms, hands, then back to his eyes. Dove hears the words, lets them fall from Max's mouth around her like snow, like birds, knowing she'll have to come up with an answer.

In the corridor, Melissa looks for her boots.

"Hey!" Harley says, popping her head down the stairs for just a second. She's already in her jeans and skintight white turtleneck.

"Are we going or what?" Melissa asks. "I thought we were headed for the trails."

Harley takes a few steps on the staircase, her face serious, her voice breathy. "You need to come upstairs—quick!"

"Why? What's the big deal?" Melissa asks.

Harley peers at her again, hands flailing. "That doorbell?"

"Is it someone for me?" Melissa gives Harley a confused glance.

"It's more than one person for you," Harley says. "For us."

Gabe? JMB? Someone from home? "Who?" Melissa asks. "And why are you so serious?"

Harley huffs down to the same step where Melissa is. "I'm not trying to freak you out or anything, but I think you'll want to see what's upstairs."

"Of course—no one's hurt or anything, are they?" Melissa thinks about something happening to JMB, how she'd feel—or to Gabe. Then she thinks briefly about spilling her crush to Harley, that maybe they should get everything out in the open before Holiday Week starts. "Harl—can I tell you something?"

Harley holds her hand up. "Now's not the time."

Melissa blushes faster than ever before, her cheeks their own holiday decoration. "Right. Of course."

As Dove deals with her own forced decision downstairs, Harley drags Melissa into the living room.

"One thing—before we get in there," Harley says to Melissa. "You were always nice to me. Even on that first day when I was full of attitude." Melissa smiles. "But I just wanted to say—if I ever seemed bitchy—or something—it's only because I'm determined to get my way."

"With James, you mean?" Melissa says softly, feeling herself tense with the sound of his name. JMB. James. She pushes any traces of crush for him aside, or away, and brings back the feeling of being with Gabe on the mountaintop—the constellations.

Harley looks back at Melissa, pausing for long enough that Melissa wonders if Harley knows. If she's aware that James might have more than one fan. "He's leaving."

"What?" Melissa's stomach registers the blow.

"James told me yesterday—he's leaving. Some race somewhere." She shrugs, like now she'll have to follow him elsewhere, leaving Melissa to wallow in the news. "But part of me wonders if it's something else."

In the living room, the guests' cases are stacked by the door. Each trunk and leather duffel is worn-out enough so that it's clear they're well traveled, but clean enough to offer up the fact that they've been toted by bellhops and sherpas. Upon final signal, the bags will be sent down to the Main House, leaving the guests to check out and walk freely to their transportation.

"So, Harley?" asks the countess. She's dressed for the plane ride, elegant in her camelhair skirt and white blouse, as though there weren't three new feet of snow outside.

"Excuse me for one second," Melissa says to the countess and earl. When she has Harley off to the side, she asks, "What's the important thing—why'd you drag me up here? Aside from the fact that we had to vacate to give Dove and Max some room?"

Harley shrugs. "Nothing. I just wanted to show you that they liked me, in case you had any doubts. They like my hosting. 'Refreshing and honest,' the earl said. The countess said she liked my candor. Whatever."

"So?" Melissa asks. "They came back after checking out to tell you that? I mean, that's great and everything, but I thought you had something for me. . . ."

"That I do." Harley pulls three red envelopes from her back pocket, slyly showing them to Melissa. "They came back with this!" She thrusts the envelope marked *Melissa Forsythe* toward her. "Quick—open it—I'm so curious."

"Oh crap!" Melissa says too loudly, then coughs to cover it. "I can't wait to see . . . hey—mine's opened." Her mouth falls to a frown and she looks at Harley.

"Sorry—I rushed—I saw *The Tops* and just ripped it. I didn't count it or anything, I swear."

Melissa tilts her head, looking at Harley through her spirals of hair. "Okay. . . . I guess, but next time . . ." Melissa's voice trails off when she sees the money inside. "Jeez—I never thought . . . oh . . ." She smiles as she counts the bills. *They liked me, too. They liked my food. Or at least they liked my effort. And Dove's. I know there's no tip sharing, but Dove did cover me for that first breakfast, those croissants, the roast while I was stranded. . . .*

"Let's see what Dove got," Harley says, and before Melissa reaches out a hand to stop her, she opens the second envelope. "Man, looks like they dig clean rooms." She parades the wad of cash in front of Melissa.

"Guess I won't have to share after all," Melissa says, glad Dove did well. Dove needs money to pay Harley back, to get ready for the trip to see William, to get farther away from her parents' financial grasp. "Now what about you, if you're so nosy . . ." Melissa swipes Harley's sealed envelope and taunts her but doesn't open it.

If they got that much in tips, I can only imagine what I'm about to receive as host of it all. . . . Harley slips her pointer finger under the envelope flap, all smiles and haughty looks until she sees what's inside.

"What's wrong?" Melissa leans forward.

"There's nothing in it." Harley locks her jaw, angry and confused. "Just a note."

"Well, at least read it," Melissa says, and pats Harley's back to try and comfort her.

Harley sucks air in through her teeth. "You guys'll share, right?"

Melissa's eyes convey her conflict. "Sorry—Matron specifically said we can't . . . and you just repeated those very words to me when—"

"Never mind," Harley says. "Dove owes me—I'm sure she can think of a way to pay me back."

Melissa thinks back to all the teas, the meals, the desserts, the brownie swirls, and acidophilus cakes for the countess. *I earned my money.* She thinks about Dove's scrubbing and changed soiled sheets, the earl's request for new soap every day, Luke and Diggs and their scruffy ways. *Dove earned her money, too.* Not that Harley doesn't deserve it, but maybe the rewards of being a host were just getting to have more free time. "At least you got a good time out of it," Melissa says.

Harley takes the cream-colored note card out of the red envelope, reads it, and slides it back in without revealing its contents, her eyes flickering with news.

"What?" Melissa asks.

"Nothing—just a job well done is all," Harley says, but her lips curl up, hiding a huge smile. Just as Melissa is working up the courage to ask again what the note says, Harley adds another issue to the pile. "And—even though I said I could go skiing early today with you and Dove . . ." Harley pushes her hair behind her ears. "I might not be able to."

"Why not?" Melissa asks. "Hot date?"

Harley looks caught off guard. "Maybe. What's it to you?" she laughs, but there's a pointedness to the question. "You never did tell me about your big crush here."

Melissa's throat tightens. *I can't say anything—what is there to explain, anyway? That liking one guy who wants you as his buddy, then hooking up with his best friend as a replacement who turns out to be pretty great isn't an easy situation? That the first guy is the guy you like? Nope—definitely not saying anything now. Maybe I'll tell her during Holiday Week. Or not.*

The countess glides over to where Harley and Melissa are standing. "Girls—it's been lovely. A pleasure. We must go." She looks at Harley. "Have you made your decision, Harley?"

Melissa looks confused as Harley hems and haws.

"I know—it's sudden." The earl steps over. "But we think you'll love it."

Harley wrinkles her nose. "I'm not sure. . . . I came here to . . ." She looks at Melissa. "To take care of some things and I'm not sure I could . . ."

The countess brushes the earl aside. He sits in a plush chair in his dark jeans and flawless loafers, his button-down shirt complemented by his monogrammed cufflinks. Diggs and Luke yell from outside. Jemma stands by the doorway, waiting.

The countess looks at Melissa. "You'll find another hostess, won't you? Or—we can suggest that *you* be the hostess. And that other girl—she could be the cook, yes?"

"I'm sorry, I don't understand. . . ." Melissa looks at the countess and then at Harley, hoping for a clue.

The countess steps in, offering a small smile and the scent of mango from her pricey perfume. "We're headed to the islands for the sun part of our holiday and we'd like Harley to come with us."

"Sun?" Melissa asks, realizing she's parroting the countess and perhaps sounding foolish. Her mouth is agog. *That's Harley's tip? A ticket elsewhere?*

"Sun and fun," the earl says, puffing his chest out as though he created the sun and the islands. "All the rage at home—half ski holiday, half beach."

Harley drinks in the information. "And when are you headed there, exactly? And which island?" Harley hates that she's not well traveled, that she can't identify with the wealthy and wonderful—yet.

"It's a small island in the Lesser Antilles. We have a cottage there. You could use the cabana. But we're leaving now, of course. Flight's in four hours. Of course, we have to get to the airport and check our luggage."

"Cabana?" Harley says, taking a turn at imitating. The Lesser Antilles sounds familiar to her but she can't think why. *Four hours. I won't have time to say good-bye.* She checks her watch. *James said he was leaving this morning, anyway. And I've never been anywhere tropical. I might never have the chance to go ever again.*

"It's fully functional—with a small kitchen."

"And what would I be doing?" Harley stares at the wad of money in Melissa's back pocket, thinking how much easier it would be to have received a compliment in cash. But maybe that's one of life's lessons—you can't predict what will happen or why. And she should be grateful for the potential of going somewhere new. *If I can keep working with the earl and countess, maybe they'll double my tips—in two weeks I could have what I counted on making the entire season. Or maybe I'll just travel with them, sucking up new cultures and places.*

"What you do here," the countess says. "Host, relax with

the children, keep Diggs mildly entertained. . . ." She clasps her leather bag and adjusts her silk scarf. "Luke is going home; Diggs will be with us—before his stint in America."

The earl butts in. "The USA—right. To the Northeast."

"Oh, whereabouts?" asks Melissa, trying to be polite while Harley picks at her cuticles.

"One of the oldest prep schools in the country—Hadley Hall. Outside of Boston. They do a reciprocal with Diggs' school. He'll be there for a term."

"Sounds nice," Harley says, distracted by everything that's going on around her and in her mind. Harley pauses. *If I leave, I can't come back. Matron wouldn't allow it. And I haven't fulfilled my goal—yet.* She thinks about James, how he said he was leaving. How she hasn't gotten him—yet.

From the back staircase, two voices echo. "Hey? Anyone home?" Melissa and Harley turn.

Before they see who it is, Harley turns to the countess and earl. "Yes! I'll come. I'll go, I mean—with you. To Nevis."

From the front porch, Luke and Diggs give each other the high five. Luke pokes his face inside before trekking to the Main House. "Excellent decision, Harls. You won't regret it."

"You know at least we won't!" Diggs chimes in.

"Shut up!" Luke elbows Diggs.

Diggs explains, giving a conspiratorial look. "Luke's just happy you're not disappearing. Two in one week would be too much!"

"What's that supposed to mean?" Harley asks, her mouth still smiling over her decision.

Luke sighs. "Let's just say fame isn't all it's cracked up to be."

"What he means," Diggs offers, "is that Celia Sinclair is on her way to rehab. Too much of this, too much of that . . . her agent booked her into Sunny Palms."

"You win some, you lose some, I guess," Harley says as the boys leave. The reality of her choice hits again. "How psyched am I? I'm going to Nevis!"

Melissa, having paused for a minute of relief that Celia won't be a presence at Holiday Week, finds herself reeling from the shock of Harley's announcement. "Nevis?" she blurts out. "Nevis is . . ."

"In the West Indies, I know." Harley begins to throw herself into the decision. "I have to go pack. Actually, I might need to buy clothes—I didn't exactly plan for the beach."

"Oh, we'll give you money for that," the countess says. "Just say your farewells and we're off. We'll wait for you by the Main House. Max may or may not be joining us; we're waiting for his decision."

Dove's decision, Melissa thinks, suddenly realizing what may or may not be happening downstairs. "Harley—" Melissa's voice is firm.

"What?" Harley flits around, so excited about more travel— one more step ahead, away from where she's come. "Don't say anything. . . . Don't be the downer on my sudden festivities."

"I'm not. I'm all for spontaneity. Just—you do realize what Nevis is, right?" Melissa raises her eyebrows and puts her hand on her hips, hoping Harley will say something. When she doesn't, Melissa continues. "It's an island. . . ."

"Thanks for the geography lesson, Mel, but I'm kind of in a rush."

"Well, just so you know, I don't think Dove's going to take this well."

"Dove's fine—she can stand on her own. Besides, it's not as though she's totally present here. Don't you think she's a little distracted?" She pauses long enough to let Melissa know Harley's aware of Max. "I mean, half of her is off with William, anyway."

"Exactly," Melissa says, wondering if it's really one half, or just one fourth. Then she whispers, "Nevis—the small island where you're headed for sun and fun. That's where William is. That's supposed to be their special reunion spot."

Harley stops in her tracks. She's about to say something when the clomping footsteps from downstairs sound again and voices boom up with them. "Hello?"

Diggs, Luke, Jemma, and their parents have gone, but two other voices shout up, "Can we come in? Are the monies gone?"

Monies was a staff moniker for guests—those who pay. "Come on in," Melissa shouts.

"I'm going to Nevis!" Harley says, jumping up and down. She looks at Melissa, first apologetic, then just happy. "I'm sorry to leave you like this—in the lurch—but maybe you'll get to be host. And Dove . . . she'll get over it. It's not like I know William—or like I did this on purpose. It's just a weird coincidence."

"Maybe," Melissa says. "I did read a lot of articles about Nevis being a hot spot right now. . . ." Melissa sighs. *The truth is,* she thinks, *no one can protect you from the truth. Or from your past. Or from coincidence. Whatever happens, happens, and you just have to wade through to find what it is you're looking for. Who knew that I'd wind up liking Gabe again this year after everything that happened last year? And who knew that liking him would help me put to rest any feelings for the guy Harley likes—for James. Even though he's a dream catch.* "We'll miss you though." Suddenly with the thought that Harley won't be here, Melissa realizes she could have kept her crush on James, even if it wouldn't have led anywhere. But now there's Gabe—Gabe who wrapped her up on the mountaintop and who folded her laundry. In her mind, she melds the two of them together; wishing both of them liked her. *Oh well, they don't. And I'm happy to be starting something with Gabe. . . .*

"Seriously—maybe you'll be host." Harley grabs items of hers from around the room. *And maybe I'll find more than just another hosting gig on Nevis. I deserve love, don't I? If James were staying at Les Trois, that'd be a different story. But he's leaving. And he was my reason for coming here.*

"Host? That doesn't sound bad," Melissa says. *In fact, I could get used to free time, toting people around to parties, having nice dinners cooked for me. Sleeping past dawn.*

"Hey there campers." Gabe bursts into the room, filling it with blond light and his huge smile. Melissa feels that split—one half? One fourth? One third? Who can say—part of her lighting up in his presence. It's only when he's joined by JMB that she starts to compare and contrast. *But what's the point of doing that when JMB is so far out of reach? Or maybe I'm kidding myself and Gabe's not a sure bet, either—he hasn't exactly made a statement about what our mountaintop reunion meant.*

JMB follows, checking out the room. "I could so get used to this place," he says. "Remind me why Coach makes us stay at the hotel?"

"Because you'd trash the place," Harley says, sounding very familiar with them.

"They wouldn't trash it." Melissa steps in. "They'd just rather hang out in it than be on the slopes—that's the reason."

JMB nods. "You got it."

"Yeah," Gabe says. "You sure have us pegged."

"Well, too bad you're leaving—guess you won't have to feel like you're missing out on everything," Harley says to James.

James grabs a croissant from the breakfast buffet and rips off a piece. "No—that's cancelled."

"You're not going?" Melissa asks, hope rising in her voice. *Oh my god, I hope that didn't sound totally obvious.*

"But I thought . . ." Harley stammers.

"The race was changed. They've decided to have it here. Next week—during the holidays—the camera crews think it'll be better viewing, with the crowds and stuff."

Melissa stares at JMB. *James. I wish I could tell him how I feel.* She looks at Gabe. *But what about him? Not that he's a fallback guy. He's not. He's too good for that. And James is—how did Gabe phrase it? Smitten. Utterly, totally smitten.* The doorbell rings and standing there is Charlie, grinning and waving. *Of course,* Melissa thinks, so sure that she almost blurts it aloud. *He's in love with Charlie.*

"I have to go," Harley says, tears in her eyes for the first time. *What if I miss them? What if I miss James too much? What if . . .* There are too many what ifs. She can feel part of her firm interior start to crumble and she's determined not to let that weakness show. She pinches the skin between her thumb and pointer finger—an old pageantry trick to stop the tears.

Melissa turns. "Are you sure?"

Harley shakes her head. "I'm not sure—but I said yes. . . ."

Melissa bites her lip. "Maybe it's for the best?"

"Well, boys, if you feel like getting a real tan—or hitting the surf . . . look me up," Harley says. Melissa stares at her.

Harley and Melissa back away from Gabe, away from James, and away from Charlie, who comes in and hugs both guys. Downstairs, Dove and Max are still talking, and Melissa wonders what the outcome of their conversation will be. "You might be right. I mean, I probably should just go to Nevis. When will I ever get another chance to do that, anyway?"

Melissa nods. "They say Changeover Day is crazy—but this is . . ."

"I know," Harley says. "Probably I should go. Definitely, right? I mean, I found out that he likes someone, anyway."

Melissa looks back at the group in the living room. "Yeah? I heard that, too. Someone with a foreign name."

"French, maybe. Or Croatian." Harley tucks a curl behind Melissa's ear. "I'll go to Nevis . . . and you'll be here with Dove. Gabe'll just be . . . Gabe." She pauses, making Melissa wonder if there's more about Gabe she doesn't yet know. "And James? My James? The reason I came here?"

"He'll be off with . . . ," Melissa starts.

"With some girl." Harley grimaces.

"Charlie. I know. At least she's nice, though, right?" Melissa looks at Harley. Then she explains. "Her real name's Karlotta—you say it with a rolling *r*. Thus, the foreign thing. I've known—I just didn't want to say. . . ." Melissa feels badly for Harley, but maybe worse for herself—that her original feelings weren't met with matching tones.

"Charlie?" Harley shakes her head. "That's not the name—"

"What name?" asks Dove, coming up from behind on the stairwell.

"What happened?" Melissa asks Dove. Dove doesn't say. "And yeah, if it's not Charlie, who is it?"

Right then Melissa gets it. *Not Charlie. Not Karlotta. Not even Harley, which could sound foreign in its own way.* She smacks her head. "Celia Sinclair."

Harley rolls her eyes. Dove, Melissa, and Harley lean forward, the three whispering. Harley sighs. "You would think someone like Celia Sinclair would be the obvious choice." Melissa looks at Dove, who gives her an understanding look. "But Celia's not it, either." Harley stands up, breaking their triangle. *I have nothing to lose,* she thinks, *I'm leaving. Why not go out with a bit of a bam?* She raises her voice. "The one who claimed his heart?" She jumps over to James, pointing right to his chest. "The girl who got this guy hooked?"

Charlie waits, hoping her name will come out of Harley's mouth. Melissa stands with her hands in her pockets, swaying from nerves. Dove bubbles with her own decision. "This guy's hell-bent on getting his love to love him back."

Gabe interrupts. "What's with all the drama?"

"What's your deal, Harley?" James asks. But he can't hide a blooming blush.

"I'm saying—you might as well let it out, James. You like her." Gabe shuffles his feet, looking down as though he lost something.

"Who?" Melissa asks. She can't wait any longer. She pictures dodging James and his woman now and into Holiday Week, when everyone says the atmosphere just gets more intense.

"Why do you care?" Gabe sidles up to Melissa. He gives her a peck on the cheek, trying to claim some territory that's not been formally announced.

"I don't," Melissa says, lying and sure it shows.

"You don't?" James asks. "And here I thought this whole resort was partially powered on gossip." He shakes his head and starts to walk away.

"Hey—James," Harley shouts. Her mouth twists to the side, betraying any innocence. She knows perfectly well who James is after but refuses to cough it up. "I'm leaving for Nevis." To everyone she waves as she moves toward the stairs. "See you around!" Then, just when the air has started to settle, she darts back up. "And James? Good luck . . ."

"Thanks," he says from the doorway. He shoots her a look, solidifying that he knows what she knows. He stammers. "Right. Good luck for us, for the race. The big race—Holiday Week . . ."

He looks at Gabe—his teammate—and Melissa, and Dove, and Charlie—and gives a weak smile.

"Good luck with Mesilla, I mean!" Harley shouts from downstairs. Pleased with herself, she smirks and rushes off, leaving everyone else to deal with the fallout.

Melissa feels her pulse race, like an engine in one of those car ads—zero to sixty in mere seconds. James stands in the open door—all of the resort and its possibilities behind him. *He likes me? He likes Mesilla. I'm Mesilla.* Melissa tries to sort it all out in her head. *And Harley doesn't know I'm Mesilla. But she's leaving.* Dove comes to Melissa's side, the only one in the room who understands what's happening.

Gabe steps toward the door to follow James, his expression slightly pained, as though dealing with his best friend's romantic overtures is too much. He sighs. James flicks him a look to keep him quiet. Gabe starts to open his mouth in protest but then bites his tongue. "We have practice—and then the insanity of Holiday Week sets in—New Year's and all that." He looks at Melissa, then hands her something. "Here's your ID—in case you were looking for it."

"You found it?" Melissa takes it, remembering when she dropped it outside, talking with Dove.

"I found it—and I kept it. . . ." Gabe looks at the floor, then to Melissa's mouth, then to James in the doorway. "He said he liked a *Mesilla*—I didn't know it was you. Until just now. I mean, how could I?"

Melissa is so tongue-tied she doesn't know what to do. "Gabe!" He turns back to her but she doesn't go on. "I . . ."

She pauses long enough for both guys to walk—not together—but out the door into the bright white snow.

"Oh. My. God," Melissa whispers to Dove. "I have to do something!"

Dove squeezes her hand. "I know . . . you do. We all do. I have all of five minutes to decide if Max stays the week—and if he does, if it means he's with me—or not."

"Well, what do you think?"

Dove puts her hands on her face. "Max is more than a memory, but I'm so caught. If only William were here . . . it'd be so much easier." She looks through her fingers at Melissa. "But I won't be anywhere near Will until I land in the West Indies."

"But Harley will be—you could have her report back . . . ," Melissa suggests.

Dove sighs, and smiles. "This is so crazy—this day is so incredibly crazy. . . . If only there were a scale for love. You could plunk your heart down and have some accurate measurement of how you feel."

Melissa looks at The Tops—the big room—where Gabe, James, and Charlie, Max, she, and Dove are all splintering from. She can hear Harley slamming doors and packing downstairs. "Isn't that better known as figuring out your feelings?" She sighs, chewing on her lower lip. "This is crazy, though," Melissa says. "Any future I have with Gabe and James is totally up in the air—or on the slopes—we don't have a host, and the new guests arrive tomorrow. It's all a bit more than I can handle."

"Well, we'll have to," Dove says. "Together." She looks around at the forgotten gloves, stray books, and empty coffee mugs on the sideboard—the detritus of the past session. "Bonkers, ridiculous week," she says again.

Melissa nods. "And it's only morning. We have the whole day to get through. And there's another whole week ahead."

Turn the page for a peek at Holiday Week:

With brazen Harley cast-off to the island of Nevis and working for a wealthy family while supposedly spying on William, her friend Dove's adorable, scruffy surfer boy, the rest of the crew is back for session two at Les Trois.

Holiday Week at Les Trois is notorious for its champagne toasts, ice-skating parties, and the winter ball—not to mention the buildup to New Year's. Will Dove stick it out, slogging through the treacherous world of cleaning toilets and pining for two guys? Will Max, her blast from the past, remain at Les Trois or head to Nevis? How will Dove resolve her feelings for William before she sets foot in paradise?

Meanwhile, Melissa has news of her own—a job promotion brings with it new responsibilities and lots of possibilities, both in and out of the chalet. What's the story with JMB? And how will he take the tryst Melissa had with Gabe? She's not sure what to do about those guys—or if maybe neither one is right for her. All she does know is that perky, strawberry-haired Charlie, nanny to the stars, is her new bunkmate—who brings with her a whole new set of fun, games, and issues.

Love, flirting, snow, and skiing all lie ahead—not to mention a brush with disaster that could change everything—and all of this during

Chalet Girls:
Slippery Slopes

Book Two in the Chalet Girls Series

Coming in December 2007.
Check out www.emilyfranklin.com.

Chills run their course from Dove's neck, down her back, all the way to her toes, when she's finally close enough to Max to tell him. *How do I say it? "Stay with me." Or, no, that sounds like a command. How about, "I made my decision." Or, "You're right, Max: There is something between us."*

"Max." Dove says his name and breathes deeply. He leans one hand on the wall, towering over small Dove and staring at her intently.

"Lily." He corrects himself right away. "Dove."

Tension fills the few feet of space that separate them. Dove wonders whether she should leave words behind and just reach for him, but then figures he needs to know. "I made my decision."

Max takes a step closer to her. Close enough that she thinks she can smell wine on his breath. Close enough that she can see the spot on his face that he missed shaving. Close enough that if he wanted to, he could kiss her without much effort. "And?" His tongue traces the outline of his mouth, and Dove wishes she weren't so nervous saying all this.

If only I didn't feel as though asking him to stay meant losing Wil-

liam forever. *But that's what a choice is, I suppose: letting one thing go so you can reach for the next.* She decides to just say it, simply and easily. "Max, I feel that you and I had . . ." She starts to say that they had something back in London but that what they could have now is even better. But before she can get it out, before Dove can reconnect with Max, someone beats her to the punch.

"You did have something—past tense being the crucial part of that statement." Claire smirks as she says this. Shaking her long, dark hair so that it swishes onto her back, she walks past Dove and stands right next to Max. "See? I told you, Max. She's just using you. Just like before."

"Claire, what right do you have to even . . ." Dove gets out only a few words before Claire tramples her.

"I'm a paying guest. Not like you these days." She raises one dark eyebrow at Dove, her lips perfectly gleaming with gloss, her cheeks pink. "Same as Max."

Max sticks his hands in his pockets and looks first at Claire, then at Dove. "Look, Dove, just so you know . . ."

Dove looks at Claire's hand, how close it is to Max's, and wonders just how long Claire's been at Les Trois. How long she's planning on staying. If Max had invited her all along. "You don't have to explain. I understand completely." She points to Max, feeling her plans crushed. "I don't care what you two do—just leave me out of it." Tears sting her eyes, but Dove refuses to show the emotion. Instead, her voice is steady, reasonable, the same voice she used to tell her parents that she didn't want their money, didn't need their support. "Stay, go, do whatever you want, Max." She starts to walks away.

"Don't you have anything to say to me?" Claire asks after Dove. "After all this time?"

"Claire, don't." Max's voice houses concern.

All three of them immediately flash back to Max's eighteenth birthday, the black-tie party, the night everything changed. Dove whips around. "No, Claire, I have nothing to say to you. In my mind, you don't exist." *Except she does,* Dove thinks. *She does, and yet again, she's ruined everything.*

The morning light brings a refreshed sense of power to Melissa.

"Just because I'm not supersuave doesn't mean I can't handle being a host, right?" She pulls her hair into a ponytail, slides into her black pants and red shirt, and does a last look in the mirror before heading upstairs to wait for the guests.

From her top bunk, Charlie groans. "It's too early for all this. I want a vacation."

"Look at it this way," Melissa says. "Last week you dealt with crap from toddlers as the nanny. This week you'll only have to deal with real crap. . . ."

"That's disgusting." Charlie sits up and rubs her eyes. "While you guys were out having fun last night, I was here polishing the brass by the fireplace."

Melissa wrinkles her nose. "I wouldn't say we were having fun, exactly. . . ."

Charlie jumps out of bed, landing with a thud on the cold floor. "I thought everything was supposed to be festive this time of year. Stockings, menorahs, trees, lights."

"Festive, yes. Fun no." Melissa recalls Gabe and his mouth-to-mouth, and the way James gave her nothing but silence. "It's not like we get to have a holiday of our own, you know."

"Holidays are what you make them." Charlie smiles, making her freckled cheeks wide. "Did I hear rumors of you and a certain ski guy?" Charlie runs her fingers through her tousled strawberry blond hair and instantly looks put together. Melissa wishes she had those kinds of looks. Not movie-star gorgeous, just honestly lovely.

"What rumors were those?" Melissa blushes. "I'm not usually the kind of person who has rumors spread about them."

Charlie shrugs and slithers into straight-legged pants and a turtleneck. "Maybe you're not the kind of girl you think you are." She pulls her socks on. "I'd love to stand here and gossip all day, but I have two mudrooms to clean and you—Miss Host—have to go entertain the masses. After all, people want their Christmas days jam-packed with fun and food."

Melissa nods. "Hey—I was so crazed last night I didn't even think to check the guest log. Who do we have the pleasure of hosting?"

Charlie's face shows a massive grin as she gestures with her broom. "Correction—*you* have the pleasure of hosting. Apparently some didn't like their luxury hotel rooms and wanted to check out life in the chalets." Charlie bows as though the guests are entering the room.

Melissa starts out and then turns back. "But who are they? Aside from disgruntled ex-hotel guests?"

Charlie taps Melissa on the shoulder like she's a fairy godmother and her broom is the wand. "That dubious honor goes to the ski team. That's why I was asking about any unsubstantiated rumors." She pauses and grabs the dustpan. "All those guys are staying here."

I won't freak out; I won't freak out; I won't trip over the bearskin rug and fall on my ass. I will not offer the guests champagne and spill it on myself. I will not humiliate myself like I usually do. Melissa surveys the large living room, knowing that, though it's empty right now, in two minutes it will be filled with this week's guests. Her guests.

Including one guy she kissed, Gabe, and the guy she wishes she did, James. *I won't mess up, even if I have to pretend I know what I'm doing.* She puts her face to the window, looking out at the path that leads to the chalet.

"Anyone there?" Dove calls from the kitchen.

"Not yet." Melissa checks that the doorbell works, and then goes to find Dove. "Could I be more nervous?"

"Yes, in that you could actively be fainting or vomiting." Dove slides a sheet of croissants into the oven and checks her watch. "Five minutes, and the breakfast buffet will be served. I'm making a traditional Christmas pudding for later—it's de rigueur for Les Trois." She pauses, remembering holiday meals at the resort as a child. "They always serve it warm with brandy butter."

"Sounds incredible." Melissa shakes her head in awe. "How'd you get all this done so fast?" She opens and closes the pantry doors, taking in all of the newly purchased goods, the organized way that Dove has prepared a gourmet spread. *It took me ages to find my way around the kitchen. Let's hope hosting comes more easily.* "Was that the doorbell?"

Dove rolls her eyes. "No, that's your imagination playing tricks on you."

"Well, it wasn't my imagination last night when Gabe and some girl were going at it under the mistletoe." Melissa reaches for a cranberry scone but then stops herself, knowing that if she eats it now, she'll just get crumbs everywhere and look less presentable.

"Are you jealous?" Dove spreads out layers of crumble cake onto sterling silver trays, readying the food for the guests, wishing that her own night had gone differently.

"I'm not jealous. It's not like I want Gabe. . . ." She shrugs and doesn't mention whom she does want. "Except we did have fun.

There was this whole other side to him, like when he and I were on the mountaintop. . . . He was sweet, romantic."

Dove shakes her head and wipes her floury hands on her apron. "I'm beginning to think that guys just don't change. No matter what." She considers something. "Girls, too. Look at Claire. Evil then, same thing now. Only with better hair."

Melissa winces. Bad enough to have unresolved feelings for someone—worse when they clearly like someone else. "I can't believe they're all going to be here." Melissa shows her hands to Dove so she can view them shaking.

Dove hands Melissa a double-sized bottle of champagne. "By 'them' I'm guessing you mean him, right?" Dove gestures with her chin to the living room.

Melissa turns, gripping the champagne bottle as James unzips his coat, drops a heavy duffel on the ground, and looks right at her.

About the Author

Emily Franklin is the author of the *Principles of Love* series as well as the novel *The Other Half of Me*. Her two novels for adults are *The Girls' Almanac* and *Liner Notes*. She has edited several anthologies, including *It's a Wonderful Lie: 26 Truths about Life in Your Twenties*. She lives in Massachusetts with her family.